REVENGE

REVENGE

NOEL HYND

NEW ENGLISH LIBRARY

TIMES MIRROR

First published in Great Britain by W. H. Allen & Co Ltd, in 1976
© 1976 by Noel Hynd

*

FIRST NEL PAPERBACK EDITION SEPTEMBER 1977

*

NEL Books are published by
New English Library Limited from Barnard's Inn, Holborn, London EC1N 2JR.
Made and printed in Great Britain by Hunt Barnard Printing Ltd., Aylesbury, Bucks

45003255 8

For E.D.H. – and, in Memory, A.H.

PROLOGUE

On October 14, 1970, the pilot, co-pilot and six crew members of a United States Air Force bomber buckled themselves into position in their aircraft. They reviewed their assigned mission in the undeclared war waged by the United States against the Democratic Republic of Vietnam. The bomber's engines roared to life. Moments later, flying with a fighter escort, the jet was airborne.

The airplane thundered eastward above the Pacific Ocean where Americans have warred with Orientals for the better part of a century. It flew in its proper formation northwards from Guam, its home base, towards its intended targets forty miles south of the North Vietnamese capital, Hanoi.

Soviet ships, cruising in the international waters around Guam – the island itself a dubious trophy of previous American adventures in the area – spotted the formation of American aircraft. The ships radioed to their ideological allies. The peasants and militiamen in North Vietnam, rushing to their battle stations, knew when the sky above them would be heavy with enemy bombers.

The airplanes neared Hanoi at ten minutes past nine, Hanoi time. Ground anti-aircraft crews in the jungles and towns south of the North Vietnamese capital fired in well-disciplined patterns at the airborne invaders above them. Forty miles south of Hanoi, just above the hamlet of Den Bing, the giant bomber was racked with the hot exploding lead shot skyward from the defending guns below. The giant plane convulsed with the hit and began to lurch at an altitude of 45,000 feet. It became quickly and deathly apparent to the pilot and crew that their plane would crash within seconds.

7

Four of the eight-man crew were, for reasons that will eternally remain a mystery, unable to eject. They died when the plane exploded into a thick forest.

Major Ronald Mecili, the pilot and a veteran of forty-one previous missions, parachuted into a watery rice field where he immediately disentangled himself from his parachute. A hundred metres away, Airman First Class Leonard Lewis, a black man from Memphis, landed within sight of Mecili.

The men, seeing each other's chutes, crawled and scrambled towards each other, keeping their heads and bodies low so as not to make an alluring target.

Captain William DeMeo landed bruised and battered but not seriously injured two miles away. Captain DeMeo was disengaging himself from his chute's confining cords when Lieutenant Richard Silva, at twenty-two the youngest member of the ill fated mission, hit the ground.

Silva winced in pain as soon as his body, dropping sixteen feet per second, crashed into the branches of a tree. But he did not know the extent of the injury until he had slashed himself loose from the tree and cracked down on the flat rocks below.

The left side of his uniform was soaking with blood. His hipbone and upper left leg had been splintered. The broken bones protruded through the torn flesh of his hip. He attempted to move. But the pain tormented him with an agonising throbbing that made him wish he had ridden his aircraft to its fiery destruction miles away.

He gasped for life and tried a second time to move. When he knew he'd be unable to stand, he attempted to crawl. He managed to pull himself along the ground with his hands, desperately seeking to reach a clump of bushes that might conceal him. Surely enemy soldiers would come looking for him. Richard was too obsessed with pain and fear to consider that the remains of his parachute, hanging splendidly from that tree, served as an excellent marker. The enemy would know just where to find him.

A dozen local soldiers came upon Richard less than two hours later. They beat him with heavy sticks. It wasn't until they saw his leg that they knew he was already disabled. Richard thought he would be killed.

A local nurse was eventually called and Richard was given bandages. Then two black-clad women made a splint out of a bamboo tree. His leg was placed in the splint, and they were beginning to carry off their captive when the sky was again rumbling with the roar of airplanes.

The loss of the bomber and its crew had set off a noisy rescue attempt. Richard's leg, hip, and groin were torturing him. His mouth was bone dry, and he pleaded for water. But because of the rescue planes above, his captors gagged him and temporarily abandoned him in a forest.

He lay there for five hours. He had no way of knowing that as he lay in agony under a tropical tree at the side of a dirt road, a U.S. air rescue team was pulling to safety two of the other three survivors of the crash.

Major Ronald Mecili and Airman First Class Leonard Lewis were plucked from the jungle. Mecili had a broken arm. Lewis, wearing around his neck a *figa* given to him by his sister in Tennessee, had escaped with nothing more than bad bruises and a few cuts. Lieutenant Richard Silva and Captain William DeMeo were, after an arduous five-hour search, declared missing in action.

Once the rescue planes had departed, Richard was taken from the forest by the soldiers and placed in an old Citroën truck that was a relic of the French campaigns of the 1950s. He was driven north on rocky rough roads. He was given enough water to preserve his sanity.

As the truck travelled through villages towards Hanoi, he was pelted by bottles, sticks, and rocks. In three days, during which his wound remained untreated and his torment intensified, he was delivered to the Hoa Lo prison camp in Hanoi. Richard Silva was then asked to sign an admission of war crimes against the people of North Vietnam.

He refused.

Since prisoners were to be broken immediately if possible Richard was beaten by guards and denied medical attention for several days. He was allowed a subsistence level of food and water and was not allowed to sleep for more than two hours at a time. His captors kept him isolated and continued to demand a confession. After ten days, delirious and beginning to come down with fever, Richard scribbled a few words onto a paper pushed in front of him.

'The United States,' he scribbled with a trembling feeble hand, 'must end the killing.'

For his 'confession', Richard was permitted to see a doctor.

His hip and leg were placed in old wooden braces and he was given shots of antibiotics. He was then locked in a cell with a second

9

prisoner. Richard thought he was hallucinating when he recognised Captain William DeMeo. But it was DeMeo. Alive and, considering the circumstances, unharmed.

Eventually the brace was removed. The wound, however, had not properly healed. The infected leg swelled relentlessly until Captain DeMeo, trying to keep his comrade alive, pierced the wound and tried to drain it.

Richard lay motionless by day and then shivered through the freezing nights at Hoa Lo, the camp that the prisoners – with the grim sense of humour that was critical to survival – had renamed the 'Hanoi Hilton'. During those shivering nights DeMeo and Silva slept together and shared a single torn linen sheet. It was DeMeo's care as well as Richard's own intense will to resist that kept him alive.

Richard gradually neared death over that winter of 1970, his body in endless agony. His strength ebbed. His wounds remained open and badly infected. Captain DeMeo frequently fashioned makeshift bandages from odd bits of cloth found around the prison. It was only his minimal medical attention that separated Richard from death by blood poisoning.

That following spring, in April of 1971, Richard's pain began to subside. For no apparent reason he was taken to another cell where he was held alone. Then he was called before a lean, sad-eyed Vietnamese interrogator whom the prisoners nicknamed Grumpy, an understated and ironic comment on the man's vicious disposition.

Grumpy spoke a smattering of cracked and occasionally incomprehensible English, but his command of the lanaguage – or lack of it – did not prevent him from being understood.

Grumpy began by speaking politely to Richard. He told Richard that if Richard would cooperate his name would be placed on the list of prisoners of war. Richard had parents and a sister back in Massachusetts. They had no idea, six months after his plane had crashed, whether Richard was dead or alive.

'What am I supposed to do?' Richard asked.

'We pick an American to tell facts about the war,' said Grumpy in fractured English. 'Tell facts about Vietnamese people struggle against Yankee imperialism.'

'Shove it,' muttered Richard.

'You must cooperate,' said Grumpy.

Richard, lowering his gaze to avoid the piercing slanted Oriental eyes in that mean sunken face, muttered a further word that was barely audible to Grumpy.

'Never,' he said.

Grumpy boxed Richard on the skull. Then Grumpy summoned two assistants from the next room. Richard's arms were held behind his back and iron manacles were placed on his wrists. There were screws on the manacles. The screws were tightened right down to the bone. Then a rope was looped around Richard's arms and his arms were pulled tight. The procedure continued until Richard passed out. Then when he was revived the process was repeated on his swollen ankles.

'You must surrender and sign a statement,' Grumpy insisted as he stood like a vulture above Richard's tortured body.

'Never,' Richard panted again in agony. He repeated over and over in his mind the words to songs, hymns, or prayers. Anything he could think of. He was made to kneel for two days. He refused to break. He felt it his duty to resist.

Then on the following morning Richard was first faced with the Imp.

Grumpy returned with a small man with an olive complexion and dark almost catlike gleaming eyes. He was European and spoke French with an odd accent. Some of the prisoners called him Jacques out of deference to the language that he spoke with the Vietnamese. Other prisoners called him the Imp, a name that was more appropriate for the fiendish excesses of the short dark man.

Others had even less flattering names. But although none of the prisoners knew the Imp's precise name, identity, or origin, they knew what he was. A torture expert.

Richard was left alone in a cell with the Imp.

'No one cares you not talking,' said the Imp in readily understandable English.

'*I* care,' muttered Richard.

'You are a prisoner,' said the Imp. 'We can let you live or let you die.'

Richard remained silent. He began to think that this would be the final stage of his captivity. He was too stubborn to give in, too duty-bound not to resist. He would never allow himself, he thought, to be turned into a propaganda tool by his enemy half a world away from the peaceful beaches of Cape Cod where he had been raised.

'You will have to cooperate,' said the Imp. 'It will be so much less painful for you. So much easier for everyone.'

'What do you want?' Richard muttered.

'You will sign and read a statement,' said the Imp. 'Sign and read in front of film cameras.'

Richard looked up at the Imp. Then he spat into the Imp's face.

The Imp pounded Richard across the head with a fist. Richard was made to kneel again on that torturously painful side that supported the broken hip. As he crawled to a kneeling position the Imp smashed him again across the face. Teeth were loosened. Blood ran down his cheeks. Richard thought he would be beaten to death. He wasn't far wrong.

The Imp placed Richard's hands in those manacles behind his back. The Imp tightened the screws until the flesh was broken and the screws stabbed through to the bone. Then a rope was strung between Richard's wrists. The Imp, holding Richard down with a foot on his shoulder, pulled the rope upward until Richard would scream in agony, thinking the Imp was going to pull his arms right out of their sockets. Eventually the Imp kicked Richard over onto the floor again.

'Now you surrender?' asked the Imp.

'Never,' said Richard between loosened teeth. 'Never.'

The Imp continued the torture through that day, enjoying it. The next day consisted of hourly sessions of the same. Then the Imp substituted a hot wire for the rope. Richard continued to resist, even though he was nearly senseless.

For the four days that followed, Richard was beaten with a wooden club every hour around the clock. He was not allowed to sleep. By this time his body was a red and white sea of welts, scars, and cuts.

Then on the morning of the fifth day, Richard began to break. He agreed to do whatever the Imp wanted.

For two days he was left alone and a doctor was even sent to see him. The visible bruises and scars on his face were attended to so that they would not be conspicuous for a camera. He began to think. He knew that he had agreed to surrender and do what was asked of him. But he had not done it yet. Richard began again to resist.

He refused to discuss a statement when the Imp brought him a pencil and paper. In a rage, the Imp kicked him in the face. Then the Imp ordered him transferred.

Richard was dragged by that agonised leg to another cell, which consisted of concrete on three sides and iron bars on the fourth.

He was beaten inside that cell for several more days. Then one morning the Imp told him he was being given a last chance.

Another American soldier was placed on his knees outside the iron bars of Richard's cell. The soldier was handcuffed and bound at the ankles. He too had been beaten mercilessly.

Richard looked at the soldier. Had Richard been capable of tears at that point he would have shed them. He recognised William DeMeo as that other soldier. One of the guards was standing over DeMeo, holding a pistol to his head.

'You want to save your friend's life?' asked the Imp.

Richard looked up with imploring eyes that were crazed with fear and pain.

'You write a statement,' said the Imp. 'Now.'

DeMeo managed to raise his head and look at Richard from the other side of the bars. DeMeo shook his head slowly and resolutely at Richard, indicating that Richard should not cooperate.

Richard's gaunt searching eyes stared at the man who had saved his life. Then he looked back up at the Imp. The Imp gave a signal to the guard. Richard heard a short cracking pop. Then another. DeMeo had been executed. His body slumped to the dirt, his head ripped obscenely open by two bullets. Richard stared at his friend's body.

'We leave his body here,' said the Imp. 'You can look at it until you decide to make statement.'

Richard felt his sanity escaping him. The Imp was winning. Richard began to curse himself for not talking. He began to wish he, too, would be executed. The Imp was right. No one cared he was resisting.

Beatings began again the next day. Then the Imp promised to bring another American soldier to the same spot where DeMeo had been executed.

'We shoot one man a day until you make statement,' said the Imp. The next morning when a battered young blond soldier was dragged into the same spot, Richard cracked. He said he'd talk before a camera.

'You keep word this time,' said the Imp. 'If not, we kill ten more soldiers.'

Richard then wrote a statement that he was eventually forced to read and sign before a camera. The sequence was then released by the North Vietnamese to the world press. In many places around the world it was carried on television. In Massachusetts it was the first indication to those who knew Richard that he was still alive. The date was June 10, 1971.

Richard was kept in solitary confinement even after writing an obviously contrived confession, reading it, and signing it. He was given better food, however, but his leg was still painful. And even though the spectre of the executed William DeMeo haunted him incessantly and almost destroyed his own will to live, Richard finally brought himself to beg for what he really wanted.

A doctor.

In August of 1971 he was placed in a hospital near the prison. X-rays were taken of his leg. The doctors discussed amputation but decided against it. The shattered hip-bone and battered upper leg then received its first real medical treatment by the North Vietnamese doctors. It was ten months after the wound was first inflicted.

As his leg healed over the course of months Richard gradually regained the ability to walk. First he could struggle on two legs with a cane. Then as more time went by he was able to walk with a limp. The doctors told him the limp would last. Perhaps forever. It would be his lasting punishment for bombing civilians, they suggested.

Able to reason rationally again, Richard became aware of a new room in the Hanoi Hilton prison camp known to the prisoners as Disneyland.

It was in this room where certain prisoners were now placed in chains. They were unable to move their hands or feet for days at a time. It was in this room, Richard knew, that the Imp was continuing his own brand of warfare.

The rumour around the prison asserted that the Imp had tortured to death a dozen men in Disneyland. The sudden absence of those soldiers after sessions with the Imp confirmed the rumours in a circumstantial way. All twelve names would remain forever missing in action.

Eventually Richard acquired a cellmate, an army lieutenant from Mount Vernon, New York. The man had been captured the preceding month, September of 1972. He was silent and in shock much of the time he was imprisoned. Richard struggled to help the man retain his sanity, just as DeMeo had struggled to help Richard. The lieutenant, a gaunt, intense young soldier named Howard McKiernan, talked sometimes coherently about the rumours that the war was almost over. There was an election coming in the United States. Surely, said McKiernan in one of his more lucid moments, the war would end before the election and the prisoners would be home by Christmas.

Yet there were certain prisoners who were not destined to go home.

On one October day, as rumours of the war's conclusion buoyed the spirits of the POWs, the Imp attempted to break their will a final time.

The Imp singled out four men. They were placed in cells visible to the others. Then, in what was to serve as an example, the four were subjected to wires, ropes, razor blades, shards of glass, floggings, and starvation. Their anguished screams and groans were audible throughout the camp.

Then, after eight days, the four men were marched, pushed, or dragged to the centre of the camp. In full view of their compatriots, each of the four men took a rifle bullet through the brain. All four times, at close range, the Imp pulled the trigger. The last of the four to have his brains blown out was Lieutenant Howard McKiernan.

Then, with a spirit of demoralised hopelessness again prevalent at the camp, the Imp disappeared. Slowly, a few new prisoners arrived. And gradually the talk of the war's conclusion returned. The torture sessions lessened with the Imp gone. Then they stopped completely.

The men knew. Something political was happening. Less than six months later, the men were going home. For almost all of them the agony was finally over.

But not for Richard Silva. Throughout his torture, throughout his imprisonment, and throughout those executions, one thought alone had been growing with maniacal obsession.

Richard would find the Imp. And kill him.

Part One

1

For Richard, the freedom that followed his release from prison was tempered by his obsessive and methodical desire to begin his mission of revenge. There was much for which Richard held the Imp accountable.

There was the personal torture. There was the execution of William DeMeo. There were the sixteen other murdered soldiers. And there were two other related deaths. Those of Mr and Mrs Raymond Silva. Richard's parents.

In April of 1971 Raymond Silva, a carpenter who had lived his entire life on Cape Cod, had died quietly and painlessly in his sleep. Richard's father died an unhappy man. Richard's name had never appeared on any prisoner of war list until July of 1971. Raymond Silva died thinking his only son was dead. Then four months later a woman with her mind on a grocery list failed to notice or obey a red stop sign at the access to Route Six in Massachusetts.

The woman hurtled through the stop sign with her tanklike Ford station wagon and fully sideswiped the car driven by Mrs Raymond Silva, fifty-four, of Hyannis, recent widow and mother of a prisoner of war. Mrs Silva was laid to rest beside her husband in a peaceful and sunny old cemetery in Provincetown, just yards away from some of the country's first settlers. It fell to Richard's only sister, Maureen, to inform her brother of the dual tragedy.

Richard learned of his parents' deaths by long distance telephone upon returning to Collins Air Force base in March of 1973. The cheering children and the enthusiastic flag-waving adults who greeted the returning prisoners were hollow echoes to Richard. Richard knew that much of what he had loved as a child was gone. He didn't want it to be. He would like to have seen his parents again for five more minutes.

It wasn't fair. For this, too, the Imp would pay.

'I guess we just have to pick things up and continue as best we can,' Maureen said when she saw her brother for the first time. 'What else can we do?'

Richard was silent to that question. After his return he was silent to many questions. Silent, but not unresponsive.

Richard came home again to Cape Cod, although coming home again, in the fullest sense of the words, was something that Richard would never be able to do. Home was where his parents were. Yet the house he had grown up in had been sold. There was a stranger sleeping in the upstairs bedroom where his mother had once hung white curtains and where his father used to discuss the Red Sox with him. Richard went back once to see the house. He swore he'd never do it again.

His sister, three years his junior, had married a man one year his senior, a bland, inoffensive, and occasionally likeable fellow who hadn't served in the army for reasons about which Richard had never cared to ask. Maureen Silva, who was now Mrs Frederick Downes, had prepared a room in her new home for her older brother to stay in 'for as long as it takes to get resettled'. Whatever that meant.

Frederick Downes, who did something involving numbers in a Hyannis bank, had no objections to the brother-in-law he'd never met moving in indefinitely. Downes, faceless and boring, was a generous man, except with the bank's money.

In the first days and weeks back in Massachusetts, Richard would borrow his sister's car and drive to a deserted section of the Provincetown shore line. Then he would walk. Alone. And with that limp that was his lasting memento of the war. He would also think. He would determine elaborate schemes for tracking down the Imp.

As the days went by, fantasy turned to practicality. Richard would ponder ways in which he could identify and then find the Imp. Each time he devised a method he would examine it a second time. With his methodical, calculating, and obsessive mind he would pick apart each plan until it became impractical.

One conclusion was clear. He would never find the Imp without help. Whose help? Anyone's. What Richard needed was a place to begin. And it was that which he found on an evening in late April of 1973.

'You're quiet again,' said Maureen. She, her husband, and her brother sat in the living room of the modest grey-shingled Hyannis house. On the television Walter Cronkite explained the instruments to be used on an impending space mission.

Waste of money, Richard thought, looking at the screen. Then he turned to answer his sister.

'I've been thinking,' he said. 'That's all.'

'You really shouldn't dwell on what it was like over there,' she said, alluding to his imprisonment.

'That's not what I was thinking about,' he said calmly. 'I was thinking about the future. Just the future.'

'Oh,' she said. She turned her attention back to the television. Downes's attention had never swerved from it. Richard reached beside him and picked up a newspaper. It was his habit to read everything he could find. He wanted to know what had happened in all the time he was gone. And he wanted to know why it had happened.

On the seventh page of the Boston *Globe* a drawing caught his eye. It was the type of line drawing that police artists sketch from descriptions given to them by the living victims, if any, of crimes. The drawing was the likeness of a man who was subsequently arrested for a series of thirteen rapes in the greater Boston area. Beside the drawing was the man's actual photograph.

'Boston hasn't changed a bit,' Richard noted wryly. 'Still has the best sex crimes in the United States.'

But instead of dismissing the article as he might often have, Richard continued to read.

The article was a featured news story about a police artist named Kermit Kelly. Kelly, in the Boston police headquarters building on Berkeley Street, sketched six to ten faces per day, compiling them from descriptions given by witnesses or victims. Often the drawings proved valuable in solving crimes. Often they did not. But always, said the article, Kelly provided the police somewhere to begin.

Somewhere to begin. A drawing.

Richard read the one column on page seven and then turned on to page thirty-four where the article continued. He read that Kelly had once aspired to be a commercial artist, but had taken a job with the police force out of financial necessity in the early fifties. And although a new televiewing device was imperiling the jobs of police artists like Kelly, there continued to be a need for men who could transform a witness's words into a picture.

Richard turned back to page seven. He looked at the drawing Kelly had made. He looked at the photograph of the arrested man.

The drawing made the man look slightly heavier than he was. The eyes were narrower. But the nose approached perfection and the hair style was the same. In all, the likeness was remarkably accurate.

Richard folded down the paper and laid it alongside his chair.

'What are you reading?' his sister asked.

'Do me a favour,' he answered.

'What?' she replied.

'Lend me the car again tomorrow,' he said.

Downes turned and looked at Richard.

'Where are you going?' she asked.

'Boston.'

'Should I ask why?'

'No,' he said. 'It's not important.'

He looked at his sister. His answer hadn't been quite good enough. It wasn't that he was obligated to tell her anything, it was simply that an incomplete answer left her suspicious. And for what Richard was embarking upon, he would want no suspicions.

'I might have a job lined up,' he lied. 'I don't know yet. I have to go into Boston to see a few people.'

'Why didn't you say so?' she asked.

He shrugged. 'There's nothing definite yet.'

'Take the car in the morning,' she said. 'I'll have someone else drive me to work.'

'I knew I could count on you.'

2

Richard drove from Hyannis to Boston in less than two hours. Then, upon arrival in Boston, he bought a city map. He found his own location and the location of the main police station on Berkeley Street, the building in which Sergeant Kelly could be found. It took another half hour to inch through the traffic to Berkeley Street. Then there was a matter of parking.

'A lousy place to park illegally,' muttered Richard to himself. Every empty parking place was flanked with either a yellow line on the kerb, a driveway, a hydrant, or a bus stop sign. Richard finally left the car in a metered space on Berkeley Street, a block and a half from the police station. He was pleased to have avoided a parking lot. One of the hardest things for a returnee from 1970 to comprehend was how expensive it had become to breathe, drink clean water, and park cars.

Richard walked to the police headquarters. It was a quarter past twelve. Lunch for some.

In the main lobby of the police headquarters there was a blue-shirted uniformed officer in a glass booth. It was impossible to pass him without being seen. No doubt, Richard thought sceptically, the Black Panthers would announce themselves before calling on the commissioner.

The uniformed cop in the booth was already watching Richard from behind a plate of apparently bulletproof glass. Richard noted that the police in American cities, like infantrymen, had to secure themselves against guerrilla attacks.

'Can I help you, sir?' asked the cop, diverted from the cross-word puzzle he'd been working on.

Richard had aged in prison. Before he was captured few people had called him 'sir'.

'I'm looking for Sergeant Kelly,' said Richard. 'Sergeant Kermit Kelly.'

'Do you have an appointment?'

'No,' said Richard. 'But it's important.'

The officer eyed him and then picked up a black telephone. He dialled three numbers.

'Name?' asked the cop.

'McKiernan,' said Richard, choosing a name to match the occasion. 'Howard McKiernan.' The young prisoner from Mount Vernon, Richard's final cellmate, would never know that his name had been temporarily borrowed.

The officer in the glass booth mumbled something to Kelly. Then he looked up.

'What's it about?' the cop asked.

'Sorry,' said Richard. 'I'm only talking to Sergeant Kelly.'

'He's on his lunch hour,' said the cop. 'Can you come back at one thirty?'

'No,' said Richard. His response caught the guard and Kelly, who was on the other end of the line, by surprise.

'He says he can't come back,' said the guard. Richard complimented himself on a good show of strength. The guard continued to speak on the telephone to Kelly. Then he put down the phone and looked up at Richard.

'Go on back,' said the cop. 'Room oh-five-seven, ground floor. Take the corridor down there,' he added with an indication of his hand. 'Take it all the way to the back. Kelly'll talk to you now.'

'Good,' said Richard. 'Thanks.' The guard made no reply. He went back to the crossword puzzle with which he'd been wrestling. He needed a three-letter word with a clue of 'Stamp or Mann'. The answer he couldn't think of was 'act'.

Richard crossed the concrete lobby and passed through the door that led to the east-wing corridor. Richard followed the grey sterile hallway on the other side of the door and passed several small rooms, all numbered. Some doors were open. Others were not.

Through a few of the open doors Richard saw cops in blue shirt-sleeves sitting in rooms littered with papers, files, and battered cardboard coffee cups. Other uniformed police bent over files or mug-shot books. Richard followed the descending numbers on the doors until he came to one marked 057.

At a desk cluttered with pens, pencils, cirgarette butts, ashes, coffee cups, papers, and a half-eaten sandwich, was a red-haired, red-faced Irishman with a scowl on his face that bespoke the two decades he'd spent on the Boston police force. Kelly was reading a newspaper as Richard entered the room. Kelly's eyes were glued angrily to the coverage of the Bruins' loss to the New York Rangers. There's no such thing as a Boston Irishman who doesn't take his hockey religiously.

'Yes?' asked Kelly looking up suddenly.

'I'm looking for Sergeant Kelly,' said Richard.

'No one here by that name,' replied Kelly.

Richard looked at the name plate on the desk.

'Isn't this Sergeant Kelly's desk?' he asked.

'Nope,' said the man.

Richard linked the name and the face of the man he saw before him and knew something was wrong somewhere. He also knew that this was the room he had been sent to.

'Then who the hell are you?' Richard asked.

'I'm *Detective* Sergeant Kelly,' muttered Kelly with a mouthful of his sandwich. He slammed his newspaper onto the side of his desk. 'And I'm also on my lunch hour.'

'This may come as a surprise to you,' said Richard calmly, 'but I don't really give a shit whether you're on your lunch hour or not.'

Kelly looked at Richard through squinting eyes. 'What's your problem, kid?' Kelly finally said. 'My day was complete before you came in.'

'I want you to do something for me,' said Richard, speaking in the regional Massachusetts accent that they shared.

'What?' asked Kelly.

'Draw a picture.'

'What are you, smart-assed or something?' snapped the cop. 'I sit here all day and draw pictures.'

'Then I came to the right place.'

'You think I haven't got enough to do?' Kelly asked. A patrolman looked into the room, saw Kelly occupied, and left again. Kelly was about to call after him. But Richard spoke first just as Kelly was opening his mouth.

'If we cut the comedy,' Richard said soberly, 'I'll tell you who I want a picture of.'

Kelly turned his attention back to Richard. 'Just a minute,' he said with a resigned tone. 'Before you waste your breath, have you reported the crime yet?'

'It didn't happen in Boston,' said Richard.

'Jesus H. Christ!' snapped Kelly. 'What are you bothering me for if it didn't happen in Boston?'

'I'm bothering you because I need your help.'

'I can't do anything until I get your case referred to me by Precinct Command. Even if some black bastard raped and killed your paraplegic grandmother ten minutes ago, I can't listen to you till Precinct Command tells me about it first.'

'That may be so,' said Richard calmly, 'but I'm not leaving until I tell you about it.'

Kelly looked harshly at Richard, then shook his head slightly. 'Shit,' he snapped with resignation. 'I get all the nuts. What the hell's your problem?'

'I'm twenty-five years old,' said Richard, 'and I just spent the last two and a half years of my life in a North Vietnamese dung-hole called Hoa Lo. You know it by the name of the Hanoi Hilton. I was there since my jet crashed in 1970.'

There was a pause as Kelly's eyes drew a bead on Richard. 'Are you levelling?' asked Kelly.

Richard nodded.

'What did you say your name was?' asked Kelly.

'Howard McKiernan,' said Richard.

'You know,' said Kelly suspiciously, 'I make my living studying faces. And your face is not one that matches the name McKiernan. Do you get my message?'

Richard did. 'There's a black football player named Kelly,' he replied. 'Plays for the Cleveland Browns. He doesn't look like any brother of yours.'

'Keep talking,' said Kelly. 'I'm almost starting to like you.'

The hard Irish eyes were softening. And as Richard began to tell the veteran cop about the Imp, about imprisonment, about torture, and about Captain William DeMeo, he was acutely aware that Kelly was listening.

Richard, sensing now a fully sympathetic audience, dwelt on how the manacles screwed into the wrists and ankles and how twelve Americans were assumed to have been tortured to death by the Imp.

'The little gook bastard,' Kelly finally muttered when the story was concluded.

'He wasn't a gook,' said Richard flatly. 'He was Caucasian.'

The cop wrinkled his face in a gesture of both distaste and confusion. 'White?' he asked.

'Most Caucasians are,' said Richard. 'White and probably French. Some sort of European Communist. He really pulled rank over those slopes. They'd obviously imported him from somewhere else to break people. As soon as peace was in sight he cleared out. I figured that out chronologically after I got back to the States.'

Kelly was nodding. Richard knew he'd hooked him.

'But you don't know who he was?' asked Kelly. 'A name? A definite country?'

'Nothing,' said Richard. 'Not even a picture. That's why I'm here.'

There was an uneasy silence as Kelly looked at the young man seated before him. 'Oh, I get it,' he said. 'You want me to draw him.'

Richard nodded.

'What for?' Kelly snapped.

'I'm going after the guy,' said Richard. The words leaped out of his mouth. He would have preferred not to have given that answer so enthusiastically.

'What do you mean by "go after"?' asked Kelly.

'What do you think it means?' said Richard. 'I have a score to settle. I want to find him.'

'Are you sure you came back from that place with all your screws nice and tight?' asked Kelly.

'The air force psychiatrists thought so,' said Richard, 'even if you don't. Look, are you willing to draw a picture of the guy or not? There must be other men who – '

'Now hold it, just hold it,' snapped Kelly as he held up a beefy left hand. 'I'll let you have your picture. You just have to tell me one thing.'

'What's that?'

'Are you planning to kill the bastard?'

Kelly managed a sly and vaguely sympathetic smile as he waited for Richard to respond. It was as if he wanted to share a secret, a secret that he liked being a party to.

'You can think what you like,' answered Richard. 'But I'll settle my score with him outside the city limits of Boston. It won't concern you at all.'

Kelly's face broke into an admiring, beaming grin.

'You're serious, aren't you,' mused Kelly in softer tones. 'You're out to kill the punk.' Kelly paused thoughtfully.

'How are you going to find him?' he asked.

'I'm starting in Washington,' said Richard. 'If I have my basic information and a picture, I might be able to find out who he is. From there I might be able to find out where he is.'

'Son of a bitch,' muttered Kelly in open admiration. 'The bastard deserves to have you hounding him. He'll deserve whatever he gets from you.'

Richard restrained a smile. He now knew he'd get what he wanted from Kelly.

'There's just one more thing,' said the cop as he leaned over his cluttered desk and lowered his voice. He spoke again in low tones.

'What's that?' asked Richard.

'If anyone ever asks, you never told me you were going to zap the little bastard. Okay?'

Richard nodded. He and Kelly broke into grins of mutual understanding.

'Start telling me about him,' said Kelly. 'What about the shape of his head? A point? Any horns?'

Kelly picked up his pad and a pencil. He listened to Richard and began to draw.

3

Richard had a drawing. And it looked like the Imp.

He crossed Berkeley Street from the police headquarters and walked a block and a half to his car. With a touch of paranoia he glanced around, wondering if anyone by chance might have been watching him. Then he glanced at the windshield of his car.

A parking ticket.

'Damn,' he snorted when he saw it. The ticket was less than five minutes old. The time in the meter had expired less than ten minutes earlier. Richard disgustedly crumpled the ticket in his hand and stuffed it into his jacket pocket. He had no intention of paying.

He beat the late afternoon traffic out of Boston, arriving home in Hyannis between five and six. Less than an hour later he found himself at the dinner table, seated with his brother-in-law and sister across from him.

'What kind of job was it that you were looking for?' asked Downes.

'It has something to do with the government,' said Richard, replying with a prepared answer to an inevitable question. 'I can't tell you much about it.'

'Really? Why not?'

'It's something that might be arranged through the air force,' said Richard. 'I shouldn't even be telling you that much.'

Downes was now intrigued. Richard, amused, had no intention of elaborating.

'Some sort of secret thing?' pressed Downes as he looked up thoughtfully.

'You might call it that,' said Richard.

'How did you get involved with this?' his sister asked. She wasn't pleased. Her brother had just returned from one episode that had been secret enough.

'Through my old air force unit,' said Richard. He found it easy, even enjoyable, to lie. 'I was suggested for it.'

'Sort of an outgrowth of the armed forces work?' Downes asked.

'You can think that if you like,' said Richard. 'I really can't tell you anything else.'

There was a pause. His sister ate. Downes ate too. Richard could see Downes's nine-to-five mind working overtime. Richard wished that he were in front of the banker asking for a mortgage. He could picture him squirming at the prospect of a mortage application from a man who couldn't even disclose his precise line of work. Before Downes could speak, Richard spoke again.

'I can only tell you one thing.'

Downes and his wife in unison looked up from their plates.

'I have to go to Washington,' said Richard.

'Washington?' answered two voices at once.

'The sooner the better,' Richard said. 'Monday of next week perhaps.'

'And you want the car?' asked his sister.

'That would make it easier,' Richard said.

Downes was obviously displeased. That in itself pleased Richard.

'For how long?' asked Maureen. It was her car, not Downes's. At the time of their marriage, Downes had come equipped with his own Volkswagen fastback.

'It might take a week,' Richard said. 'Maybe two.'

'You *are* planning to come back, aren't you?' she asked.

'I've come back from everything else, haven't I?'

She smiled grudgingly. Downes slashed at a piece of meat loaf so firmly that the knife clanked against the plate.

'All right,' said Maureen. 'The car's yours. And you're leaving Monday?'

'If that's all right with everyone here,' said Richard.

Maureen nodded. Downes looked up. 'Fine with me,' he said. 'Stay in Washington as long as you like. Two weeks. A month. I don't care.'

'I didn't think you would,' said Richard.

Maureen looked at her brother with her best that-wasn't-necessary expression. Richard gave her a gleeful smile and then lapsed into his newly characteristic silence for the rest of the evening.

4

The children of Ambassador Kenneth W. Thatcher appeared as normal as any other American children in Paris. They attended the English-language lycée Américain on the avenue Bosquet, a tree-lined boulevard in a fashionable Left Bank residential section. They had picked up a smattering of French. And their classmates were the children of other American diplomats, businessmen, and casually wealthy expatriates from within the American community in Paris.

But unlike most children, and unknown by any Thatcher of any age, these particular children were different in one important respect.

They were targets.

Anne, eight, and her younger sister, Cynthia, six, were the products of a reasonably happy marriage between Kenneth Thatcher, the fifty-three-year-old heir to the Thatcher department store chain, and his thirty-year-old wife. His second marriage. Her first. His second family. Her first. But judging by their disparity in ages, Barbara Huntington Thatcher would eventually catch up and overtake her husband at least in marriages and possibly even in affairs.

The only child of socially prominent Long Island parents, Barbara was said to have made the proverbial 'good catch' with the multimillionaire department store board chairman from Chicago. It was for her, so the gossips proclaimed, an excellent first marriage.

And it was. Kenneth Thatcher had divorced his first wife of sixteen years in order to replenish his marital bed with a younger woman, Barbara Huntington, age twenty when she married the forty-three-year-old Thatcher in 1963.

A radiantly beautiful young woman with dark hair and dark laughing eyes, Barbara excelled at being both the centre of attraction and admiration in any gathering, either within the ballrooms of New York City or on the lawns of the far and fashionable reaches of Long Island. She had, from time to time, attended college. College bored her. So she finally quit to pursue a modestly successful modelling career.

It was at the outset of this career that she met Kenneth Thatcher. She was shooting a layout for a series of Thatcher ads at the time. Kenneth Thatcher, then married, liked what he saw wearing his stores' clothes. Instincts told him that he would like what he saw even more once those Thatcher clothes were removed. Thus the reigning chairman of Thatcher Stores, Incorporated, was diverted from the wife and family he already had.

Always ready for an adventure with a man – age didn't matter as long as he was attractive – Barbara Huntington was soon sharing more with Ken Thatcher than simple dinners at The Colony or lunches at Orsini's. And the first Mrs Thatcher, Loretta, two years younger than her husband and the mother of a boy and girl, was not slow to realise that her husband was doing more than indulging his frequent bad habit of casually grazing in another pasture.

This time Kenneth showed every indication of wanting to stay in that other pasture. A strong woman who had tired of her husband's frequent affairs and who frankly longed for her own independence, Loretta asked her husband if he wanted a divorce.

'Now that you ask, yes,' he replied. And it was almost that simple. Loretta managed to put a liberal tap on the keg of the Thatcher fortune. No bitter divorce, but lots of lovely alimony money for Loretta and the teenage children. Loretta had her children, a comfortable supply of money indefinitely, and her independence. The one thing she did not want any longer, Kenneth, she did not have. In return Kenneth soon had a new young wife. Two daughters, Anne and Cynthia, followed at biologically and fashionably sound intervals.

Successful in love, business, and procreation, Kenneth Thatcher was seeking new worlds to conquer by the mid-1960s. He found them. Long a generous contributor to Republican causes, Thatcher sought first to pay his way into a senatorial nomination in Illinois, New York, or any other viable state where he might be able to establish temporarily a quick permanent residence. Eventually Thatcher found himself running for the Senate from Delaware. Unfortunately, the local Republicans, their toes smarting from the trampling they had received, resented the glamorous divorced Chicagoan and his beautiful young wife. Barbara looked as much at home in the Delaware farmlands as the average factory worker would have looked in the du Ponts' living room. Thus the local Republicans resorted to a primary, running a loyal state party nonentity named Everett Bigley, a man who had paid his dues through years in the state House of Representatives.

Despite the impressive presence of a Thatcher department store in downtown Wilmington, Thatcher came out with only 47 per cent of the primary vote. Bigley got the other 53 per cent. Thatcher let the lease expire on the fashionable Rehoboth Beach waterfront home he'd rented for the occasion and returned with his wife in tow to Chicago, licking his political wounds. He had never liked Delaware anyway. Eventually, in the 1964 Johnson landslide, a Democrat won the contested Senate seat. Then in 1965, Thatcher closed his Wilmington store.

The Republicans, however, were not about to let a man of Thatcher's resources go to waste or, worse, to the Democrats. A place could always be found within the party if a man were as wealthy as Thatcher. So Thatcher began to receive the appropriate election year messages and he responded appropriately, by rolling out his inexhaustible bank balance.

Over the years Thatcher's contributions to Republican congressional, senatorial, gubernatorial, and presidential war chests swelled to six figures. Thus it was not surprising that the millionaire who could not be elected to an office was eventually appointed to one. Ambassador to France.

There were mild rumblings of discontent among Senate Democrats about such a blatantly political and financial appointment. But upon Senate examination it was discovered that Thatcher had done nothing more sinful than write large cheques for Republican candidates. Further, Franco–American relations were quite likely to survive a well-mannered department store mogul from the Midwest, even if he did speak French with a Chicago accent. Thus Thatcher was confirmed to the ambassadorship that had originated with an ageing but still rather lecherous Benjamin Franklin. Off went Thatcher to Paris in 1971, his wife and two young daughters with him.

Anne and Cynthia were met each afternoon after school by a long black Citroën limousine, which had been provided for the personal use of the American ambassador's family.

On a particular day in April of 1973 the Citroën was waiting patiently in its usual parking place on avenue Bosquet just outside the huge brick wall and black iron gate that surrounded the lycée Américain.

At thirty-two minutes past two in the afternoon the large and formidable iron gate swung open. The first to walk through were two supervising members of the school's faculty. Then several children followed. They walked off together, singly, in pairs, and in groups, spreading in all directions like a bag of spilled marbles. They walked home like school children all over the world.

Other children were met by parents. The front doors of the Thatcher Citroën opened.

Barbara Thatcher stepped out of the car on the kerb side. A man, a hired driver in civilian clothes, stepped out the other side. He was Lieutenant William Simmons of Sumter, South Carolina, the unofficial armed bodyguard for embassy wives and their children. He stood by the car door on the driver's side and watched as Barbara Thatcher walked chicly, in a red plaid skirt and dark round sunglasses, toward the iron gate.

'*Vous avez complété vos leçons pour aujourd'hui?*' she asked her two daughters when she saw them. Late in life, and for obvious reasons, Barbara Thatcher had come to grips with the French language, a tongue she spoke with a heavy accent at best. But she was trying, even if French had not yet come to grips with her. And she spoke to her daughters in French, too, to encourage them to learn. Occasionally they could correct her.

'*Oui, maman!*' they replied. She kissed them both. She then turned and walked back to the Citroën with one little girl on each side of her. The conversation immediately changed to English.

Lieutenant Simmons, the marine attaché called Bill by everyone who knew him, smiled at Barbara Thatcher and waited until she and her children had returned safely to the car.

Yet everything Simmons, Barbara Thatcher, and the two girls had done had been observed. Even now, as they drove to the ambassador's home, a car was following.

From another car parked thirty metres down the avenue and on the opposite side from where the Thatcher Citroën had waited, three men had sat patiently waiting for that schoolyard gate to open. When it had opened, the three men had watched every movement, from the soft gracefully feminine stroll of Barbara Thatcher to the standing, guarded position of Lieutenant Bill Simmons. And now that same car, an inconspicuous brown Renault, followed the Thatcher Citroën through the main boulevards of the Seventh and Eighth Arrondissements until the Citroën led the other car around the Arc de Triomphe and down the avenue Foch to the Thatcher residence.

Every turn the Citroën took was duly noted by the three men in the following car. It was a procedure that would be repeated day after day until the daily pattern of the Thatcher wife and children was clear. Once it was established that the black Citroën travelled virtually the same route every day, it would be that much easier for the men in the Renault to execute their intended plan.

The kidnapping of the ambassador's daughters.

5

There remained some paper work to be done before the long drive from Hyannis to Washington. And it was to be completed just as it had begun, in the late hours of the night before Richard would sleep.

Since returning home from Indo-China, Richard had voraciously absorbed every news publication he could find. Newspapers from Boston or New York. Issues of *Time* and *Newsweek*. He had made notes from some and had cut clippings from others. His notes and his clippings were kept in a large manuscript-sized envelope that had been tucked among the other magazines on the bottom of a bookcase. On his final night home before his journey to Washington, he removed that oversized envelope from the bottom of his bookcase. Then, seated at a desk behind the closed door of his bedroom, he spread the contents before him.

He leafed through the clippings, turning them all face up. Every clipping concerned a specific congressman or senator, men who had been in the government during Richard's imprisonment. From the more than five hundred men and women who were elected to Congress, Richard had distilled a list of ten names of the legislators who might be most sympathetic to his cause. There were no women on the list. There were no senators. Richard believed that a member of the House of Representatives would be easier to meet than a senator. Richard took out a lined index card and removed the cap from a black felt-tipped pen. He began to write.

Congressman Fowler of Alabama. Ciccia of Illinois. Phillips

of Michigan. Davis and Hunter of Mississippi. Potvin of Louisiana. Haley and McAllister of California. Hickock of Wyoming. That made nine.

For the sake of an arbitrary number of ten, Richard went through the clippings a final time. Then he added the tenth name, like the others a man far to the right on the political spectrum.

Johnny Ray Logan, a congressman from Texas. The tenth name. Richard completed his list, which was formed not necessarily in order of preference, and carefully returned the neat folded clippings and notes to that large envelope. Then he folded in half the list of names and placed it in his wallet. The envelope was placed on the bottom of a suitcase that lay on his bed.

Then Richard removed a second envelope from the bottom of that bookcase. He opened it to check its contents. There inside the envelope were twenty-five photostatic copies of the drawing made by Kermit Kelly.

'It won't be long now, you bastard,' Richard whispered to the line drawing. 'I'm coming after you. Wherever you are.'

Richard put the photostats back in the envelope and placed it with the other envelope on the bottom of the suitcase. The original drawing had already been placed in a white business envelope that Richard had tucked into his inside jacket pocket. With these details attended to, Richard packed.

The name of one particular congressman had not appeared on Richard's list. That was the name of Irwin R. Coffin, the elected representative from Richard's own district. It would be Coffin's office where Richard would begin, despite the fact that Coffin was on the wrong side of political ideology. Coffin would not be comfortable with Richard. Richard knew it and expected it.

But Coffin would represent the token courtesy that Richard planned to pay to legality and legitimate political channels. It would be through Coffin that Richard would ascertain the legal possibilities of finding the Imp. Richard already knew that the legal chances were nil. But being of the conviction that even the impossible should be attempted once, Richard had already decided that Coffin would be the first legislator upon whom he would call. And that act, the prospect of walking into an office and asking to be announced, brought Richard squarely up against one of his trickier problems.

His name.

He would have to use his real name. There was no choice about it. A simple check of the official POW lists would reveal it. Even the use of Howard McKiernan's name again involved risks. To establish the credibility of his story and his proposed mission he would have to stand or fall with his real name, except when regisering in a hotel.

On a clear Monday morning in April, Richard left Hyannis for Washington. It was nine o'clock. Within minutes he was driving through the long stretches of Route Six that cut through the scrub pines and sand dunes of Cape Cod. He passed through New Bedford and then crossed the giant span of bridge at Fall River. Beneath the bridge the retired U.S.S. *Massachusetts* sat in its grey glory as a tourist attraction.

Then Richard drove at seventy miles an hour through the tedious stretch of Route 95 that led through Rhode Island and eastern Connecticut. Then down through the New Haven area and Fairfield County where the twenty-five-cent tolls began. There were seven such tolls between there and New York City.

At a few minutes before three o'clock that afternoon Richard crossed the George Washington Bridge for the first time in four years. Through the meadows of New Jersey he drove, letting the speedometer flirt with but never exceed eighty. You could go seventy-nine on the New Jersey Turnpike and not be stopped. Eighty-one and you were in trouble.

Richard passed by Exit Four which led to Philadelphia, his college town for four years before going into the air force, at four thirty. He was in Delaware soon after. He stopped for a tasteless Howard Johnson's meal and then continued through Maryland.

In Maryland there was an Oriole game on the car radio. The Orioles made him think of the 1969 World Series, which they had lost to the upstart New York Mets. It was the last World Series Richard had witnessed before going into the service. Thoughts of baseball made him think of his father who had died while Richard was being tortured by the Imp.

He leaned on the gas pedal, saying to hell with the speed limit. He arrived in Washington by seven thirty. By eight he had registered under his rightful name at the Key Bridge Marriott Motor Inn, just on the Virginia side of the Potomac.

Richard dined, unpacked, and slept soundly after leafing through a few pages of a book he had already studied thoroughly. It was *The Criminals Among Us* by Simon Wiesenthal, the Austrian Nazi hunter.

At ten o'clock the next morning Richard telephoned the office of Congressman Irwin R. Coffin, a Boston lawyer who had been propelled through the Irish and Italian jungle of Massachusetts politics to become the cautiously liberal congressman who represented the Cape region.

Richard spoke to a secretary. He sought an appointment.

'Congressman Coffin's schedule is extremely crowded this week,' the female voice replied with apology and appeasement. 'What would this be in reference to?'

'I'm a returning prisoner of war,' said Richard after giving his name. 'I'm from Mr Coffin's district in Massachusetts.'

'Could we return the call?' she asked. 'An appointment next week may be poss – '

'I'm very sorry,' interrupted Richard. 'This is a pressing matter. Next week won't do.'

'Surely, sir, the congressman wou – '

'What about this afternoon?' Richard asked. It was phrased as a question and posed as a demand.

'Impossible, Mr Silva,' she said. 'The sched – '

'Why don't you ask him?' Richard asked. 'Or shall I go back to Massachusetts and tell all the VFWs and American Legion posts that Congressman Coffin refused me five minutes of his time?'

There was a pause. 'What number may I call you back on?' she asked.

'None,' he said. 'I'll hold.'

There was an exasperated sigh. Then a click. Coffin was in his office reading a newspaper when the secretary, Sally Wendel, buzzed on the intercom.

She explained the problem. Coffin listened. A decision was made. Returning POWs were to be treated with the softest of kid gloves and never antagonised.

'If he wants five minutes give it to him,' said Coffin. 'Maybe I can get him to pose for a picture with me. Brownie points.'

Sally Wendel, with a bachelor's degree in art and good secretarial skills, clicked back onto the line with Richard.

'Mr Silva?'

'Yes?'

'Congressman Coffin will see you today. Would three o'clock be acceptable?'

Richard said it would be. And thus at a few minutes before the appointed time that afternoon, Richard Silva, carrying Kelly's drawing in his inside jacket pocket, arrived by taxi outside the massive Sam Rayburn Office Building.

6

The man with the slight wiry build eyes, and dark Breton complexion stood at the head of the rue Rastignac.

The street, in an eastern section of the Fifth Arrondissement, was dead. Permanently barricaded. No traffic. No one walking. Only rodents living there. The old plaster buildings had been condemned for years. They were boarded, shuttered, and awaited demolition. They dated back to the last century.

The Breton walked slowly down the street. There was a public square behind him. The square was populated by older people in the mornings and afternoons, but rarely anyone past dusk. Halfway down the block, at the boarded door to number 11, the Breton turned. He looked back at the square.

No one was watching. The cul-de-sac at the other end of rue Rastignac protected him from being observed from that direction, too.

Quickly the Breton pushed the boarded door to number 11. With a creak it gave way, opening slowly into a rubble-strewn interior. It occasionally amazed the Breton that the house hadn't fallen down by itself. He pushed the door closed behind him, wedging a board against it.

Then he stepped nimbly through the rubble, moving to his left. There was a passageway, beginning with what was more a hole in the wall than a door.

The Breton followed the passageway and descended to the basement of the old house. Then he followed a corridor through crumbling basement walls. He continued further downward, now beneath the other old houses of the dead street.

The light was dim. He carried a flashlight but knew his way. He could smell the sewer. He didn't care. No one else came down here. Ever. It was perfect.

The corridor led eventually to a long-forgotten underground chamber. Built in the latter days of the nineteenth century – back when the street was first named for Eugène de Rastignac, a Balzacian character widely discussed in the salons of the day – the chamber was like so many of the other hidden underground nooks and grottos beneath Paris. It was completely unknown to the people of the city.

In that chamber the Breton lit a small battery-powered lamp. He looked down, then went to his knees. There, just where he had left it and leaning farther downward, was a trap door, double the size of an average manhole cover.

The Breton pulled back the trap door and shined his light downward.

There was a pit below, ten feet deep. Lined by red clay and rocks, the pit had once hidden God-knows-what for some eccentric or fearful Parisian.

But now, in the middle of that pit was a brand-new trunk, placed there by the Breton. It would, he considered, take years before anything would be discovered down there. Not even his two collaborators, Klemeur, the former railroad foreman, and Savard, the former teacher, knew of this pot. *No one* knew. Just him.

The Breton looked at the trunk and smiled. He replaced the trap door. Right there, in the centre of Paris, he had found the perfect untraceable spot to dispose of two small female bodies.

7

Congressman Coffin came to the door of his inner office to greet
Richard. He offered his hand and pumped Richard's in the most
traditional and political way. Then he led Richard into that inner
office. The two men sat down after the door had been closed.

'Richard Silva,' said Coffin. 'That was the name, wasn't it?'

'That was it,' answered Richard. 'In fact it still is.'

Coffin was a thick, dark-haired man with an open inquisitive
face. Glasses. A suit that was stylish among the other New Fron-
tier liberals of the 1960s.

'And you're from the Cape?' Coffin continued.

'From Hyannis,' said Richard. 'Grew up in Provincetown, then
Hyannis. Then off to Hanoi and back again.'

'That's right,' said Coffin, glancing down at a paper on his desk.
'You're the POW.'

'Not *the* POW,' said Richard. 'Just one of them. One who
came back.'

'Yes, yes. Just a manner of speaking. What I meant was that
you're the one whom I made an appointment with this afternoon.'

'That's right,' said Richard. 'Should I get down to business?'

'By all means. What can I do for you?'

Coffin was obviously wary and would retreat from committing
himself to anything. Aside from that, he would do everything
possible to appear helpful.

'I have something for you to look at,' said Richard. He reached
to his inside jacket pocket and pulled from it the envelope containing the drawing of the Imp. He handed it to Coffin. 'Open it,'
he said.

Coffin opened the envelope as if he half expected it to explode. He looked at the drawing and then looked back at Richard.

'Who is it?' asked Coffin. The question asked more than merely who. It asked for an explanation.

Richard told the story of his imprisonment, concentrating on the part that concerned the Imp. At first Coffin listened intently. But Richard, looking him in the eye as he spoke, caught the congressman's eyes occasionally wanting to wander. Coffin was bored, but wasn't about to admit it or interrupt. Richard concluded the story.

'Well,' said Coffin, trying to fill the silence that followed Richard's conclusion. 'You certainly suffered intolerable tortures in that prison camp. There's no way around that.'

Coffin paused. He knew there was more and he wanted to get to it. He knew that Richard hadn't brought him a picture just to sit in his office and tell war stories.

'I hope you realise,' continued Coffin, 'that the entire country is proud of you men. You resisted and were strong in time of trial and crisis. You – '

'I've heard all that before,' said Richard curtly. 'Forgive me, but I didn't come here to hear it all again.'

'Why did you come here?'

'That man,' said Richard. 'The one in the picture. I want to know how he can be found.'

Coffin looked at Richard with a slight frown developing on his forehead. He asked another question before committing himself to a response.

'I'm not sure what you're asking,' Coffin said.

'This man,' said Richard, his voice betraying emotion for the first time as he gestured to the drawing. 'This man is a war criminal as much as the Germans or Japanese whom we tried after World War Two. I want to know how he can be found.'

'And put on trial? For war crimes?'

'Perhaps,' answered Richard. 'If we can try one of our own army lieutenants, we must be able to try this bastard.'

Coffin, searching for the proper words, leaned back in his chair. He looked at the sunny Washington day on the other side of his window. Then he looked back to Richard.

'I suppose you're right,' said Coffin. 'But you're not being very realistic.'

'You can do better than that, congressman,' said Richard. 'I want to know what the chances are of finding this man.'

'Slim,' said Coffin. 'So slim that they're non-existent.' He paused and leaned forward with his elbows on his desk. 'I don't think you realise what you're asking,' he said.

'Don't I?'

'Evidently not. First of all, this man wasn't Vietnamese. We have no idea who he was or where he is. Second, let's face it, there aren't going to be any trials after this war.'

'That I understand,' said Richard. 'But there has to be some intelligence information on a man like this. This couldn't have been the first place he appeared. Someone somewhere knows where he is and who he is.'

'Sure,' said Coffin plaintively. 'Someone somewhere must know. But I don't.'

'Of course you don't,' said Richard. 'But you must know who might. You must know the channels.'

'You're wasting your time,' said Coffin. 'It may be hard for you to accept, but our government is trying to get out of that whole mess over there. We're not doing it fast enough to suit me, but that's merely my own opinion.'

'I didn't come here for a political science seminar,' said Richard tersely. 'I came here for help. One way or another I'm going to find this man.'

'What good will it do?'

'What? Finding him?'

'Yes.'

'I'm sure it sounds like a cliché to you, but the war doesn't end for me until I find him,' said Richard. 'One way or another, I'll do it. I've got a picture of him, ain't I? That's a start.'

Coffin looked down at the picture again and then looked back up into the shrewd tough eyes that were set firmly and intensely in Richard's head. Coffin shied away from an argumentative confrontation with his visitor.

Coffin tried to be sympathetic. 'Mr Silva,' he said, 'your picture may be a start, but it's a start in what I think is a noble but misguided direction. I understand your feelings about this man and if I were in your place I'd probably feel the same.'

'I can feel a "however" coming,' said Richard.

'You're very right,' said Coffin. 'However, I think you're asking the impossible. I have no way of knowing what sort of intelligence information might exist on this man. But I doubt whether a civilian, which is what you are at this moment, would ever be allowed access to such a file.'

'That's right,' said Richard. 'I'm a civilian. But you're a congressman.'

The atmosphere in the room was thick. Coffin knew what Richard was asking. And he knew a hedge wouldn't work. Coffin would have to make a flat refusal.

'You're asking me to see if there is such a file?' asked Coffin.

'I'm asking you more than that,' said Richard. 'I want you to find out if there's a file and then I want to know what's in it.'

'Preposterous,' said Coffin quickly. 'It can't be done.'

'Can't?' asked Richard. 'What you mean is *won't*.'

Coffin was stuck with his position. There was no way in which it would be wise to entrust a virtually unknown civilian with an official document. In theory at least, confidential intelligence reports were intended to remain confidential.

'Call it whatever you like, Mr Silva,' Coffin said, his voice rising slightly. 'But it would be a violation of ethics to give you what you want.'

'I've never known the House of Representatives to be so laden with ethics,' Richard replied. His words found their intended mark. Coffin bristled, but remained outwardly calm.

'Look,' replied Coffin, 'I take it that you want to go on some personal vendetta or Red hunt against this sadist you ran into in a prison camp. I'll tell you quite truthfully: I don't give a good goddamn what you do. But don't involve me in your personal crusade. If you want to go off into right field with a project like this, go talk to one of the nuts in the House like Drew of Alabama or LeBlanc of Louisiana or Logan of Texas. Maybe you can find your audience there.'

'Maybe I'll do just that,' said Richard. He spoke the words calmly but coldly. He reached to Coffin's desk and took back Kelly's drawing. He returned it to its envelope and tucked it back into his pocket.

'You want to know what I think?' asked Coffin as he leaned back in his leather swivel chair, folded his fingers into a steeple, and looked at Richard with thoughtful analytic eyes that were again trying to be sympathetic.

'What?' asked Richard, rising to leave.

'I don't think anyone in the whole House will want anything to do with something like this. I understand how you must feel about this Imp, but sooner or later you'll come to the only possible conclusion. You're wasting your time. You might as well put him and the whole war out of your mind.'

'You're entitled to your opinion,' said Richard. 'And I guess that makes us even.'

'How?'

'I asked you to do something you couldn't – or wouldn't – do. Now you're asking me to do the same. You're as unconvincing as I might have been. I'm not dropping this until I've accomplished what I set out do to.'

'What exactly *is* that?' asked Coffin. 'You're not interested in any trial.'

'We've been through all this, Mr Coffin,' said Richard. 'And you're not planning to help me. Thanks for nothing.'

Richard turned and walked to the door as Coffin's gaze followed him all the way. As Richard walked past the two silent typing secretaries in the outer office, he had one thought – one name – set firmly in his mind.

Congressman Johnny Ray Logan.

Coffin had mentioned Logan. And Logan's name was neither better nor worse than any of the other nine on Richard's list.

8

Six thirty in the evening. Paris. Françoise Durand walked through Montmartre down the long steep hill-side along rue Ravignon. Ravignon led from the busy and colourful place du Tertre where she had spent her usual working day as a painter. At age twenty-three, trim with fair skin, casually dishevelled brown hair and coquettish lips, she had spent the years since the 1968 student uprising living on whatever brushes, an easel, canvas, imagination, and oil paints could bring a young woman.

By day she would paint and display in the place du Tertre. On a good day she might sell a painting to a German, American, or Japanese tourist who would inevitably try to barter down her price. It had thus been her habit, since the day she departed the Université de Dijon and took up the unpredictable bohemian life of a painter, to place on each of her paintings twice the price that she wished to receive. It continued to amaze her how often she would get 50 per cent more than she would have settled for. Bartering with tourists had also earned her a good command of English and German.

She walked down the long hill until she passed through the green iron railings of the Abbesses métro stop. She took a red rattling old train in the direction of Mairie d'Issy, transferred at Sèvres-Babylone, and then rode three more stops until she arrived at Maubert-Mutualité in the Quartier Latin. She was almost home.

Her trim legs in paint-spattered blue jeans climbed the dark stone steps of the métro station. She carried her canvases and paint box in both hands. She walked two blocks and used the key for the outer door of her building on the rue de Pontoise. She climbed the stairs two flights. She pushed another key into the door of her two-room apartment.

And immediately she knew that something was not the way she left it. The door. The double lock on the door had been fully turned that morning when she left. Now it was singly locked. One turn of the key instead of two opened the door.

There was only one explanation. Yves was back. Again.

'*C'est toi?*' she asked as she came through the door, knowing the answer before she even asked. It was always this way. She never quite knew when he would appear. Or leave. Or take up with another woman. Or spend two weeks with his anarchist comrades who centred around the university but never went near class-rooms.

'*C'est moi même,*' he replied.

Against better judgement she smiled. She laid her easel and box of paints and canvases by the wall inside the door. He rose from the bed where he had been sitting. They approached each other and embraced.

'You'll take me back again?' he asked. 'Into your arms and into your bed?'

'I never said I was taking you back,' she said, half angry and half playfully. 'You jump to conclusions.'

'But you thought you'd seen the last of me?'

'I did,' she said. She drew away from him, making him release her as she thought back. 'And maybe it would have been better for me if I had seen the last of you.'

She looked at him with almost a pouting expression on her face. He was her one bad habit, the one that was hardest to break. She loved him both deeply and blindly, and for that reason she found it lamentably easy to forgive him.

'You should know by now that I keep coming back to you,' he said. 'I'm trained. In the end it's Françoise whom I want.'

She turned away from him again, repressing the desire to fall into bed with him. She knew how easy she was for this man. He walked quietly behind her and wrapped his arms around her, kissing her on the back of her warm neck and holding her arms, breasts, and shoulders within his two arms. It took every bit of strength that she had to ask him the next question.

'And Claudette?' she asked. 'How is she?'

'*C'est fini entre nous,*' he said. 'I don't see her anymore.'

'And that's why you've come back to me?' she asked. 'She no longer wants you so you come back to your Françoise? Is that it?'

'I came back to my Françoise because I love her and miss her,' he said. His arms had loosened around her as she asked her questions. Now he held her more firmly again.

'And each time you tell me that, I believe it,' she said.

'Each time I tell you that, it's true,' he said.

Again he kissed her and his hands lowered until they began to unbutton her blue denim work shirt, the shirt that like the jeans was spattered with colours that had missed her canvas. The shirt was open and he explored within. His warm hands searched for her bare breasts. She made no attempt to stop him. She hadn't had a man since she had forced Yves to leave three weeks ago.

'You're a beast,' she said, knowing she couldn't resist him. Not now. Had there been another man, one who would treat her more fairly, with more respect and with less deception, she might have easily said no to Yves.

But there was no other such man. So she allowed him to remove her work shirt as she opened the belt to her jeans. Seconds later they were naked together, he out of need for a woman, and she out of the habit that she had with him. She enjoyed their nakedness and the satisfying firmness of his body. For that evening they were lovers again, despite the animosity that she still felt for him and despite the casual assuredness with which he treated her.

They made love warmly and affectionately. When it was over they talked. He smoked, which annoyed her, as they lay naked side by side in bed.

'Do you still sell paintings to the American tourists?' he asked. He knew the answer. She had been waiting for the question.

'Yes,' she said.

In silent disapproval he blew a long stream of smoke towards the yellowed ceiling of the bedroom.

'I have to eat, you know,' she said.

'We have food in the communes. You could eat there, live there, and paint there.'

'I'm not interested,' she said. 'So I sell paintings to Americans for money. Is there anything so sinful about that?'

'Money!' he said. 'Capitalism. You fancy yourself an artist and actually you become more bourgeois each day.'

'Must you start on me already?' she asked. 'Can't we spend one evening together without your politics?'

'Politics is part of life,' he said. 'If you're accepting American money, you're accepting money from the system that burns babies in Vietnam. You know that.'

'I'm not concerned with it anymore. If I didn't sell to American tourists, I'd starve. Who am I supposed to sell to? Only Germans? They gassed the Jews. Only the French? They've given us de Gaulle and Pompidou.'

'So you've proven that painting is a bourgeois act,' he said. 'By your own admission it is bourgeois to sell your canvases.'

'What am I supposed to do?' she asked, turning her head towards him.

'I told you,' he said. 'Paint for the revolution. Live in a commune and paint for the revolution.'

'You and your filthy communes,' she said. 'You throw acid into the face of a gendarme and you think you've committed a political act. In fact, all you've done is blind a man and increase the suffering in the world.'

'People like you are part of the political problem,' he said. 'Not part of the solution.'

'If I'm so awful,' she snapped, 'why did you come back here? I've heard your polemics before. They bore me.'

'You're akin to some of the mine workers in Zola's *Germinal*,' he said. 'Too timid to act on the politics you believe in.'

'Oh, be quiet,' she said. She moved away from him. She sat on the side of the bed with her feet hanging to the floor. Her naked body faced away from him. Her back faced him. She tried to stand but he reached for her, grasping her bare hips with his strong hands.

'Hey!' he said, pulling her back down. Losing balance, she fell backwards to him on the bed. He wrestled with her, forgetting politics and pulling her soft naked form to him. He wrapped his hands around her breasts, hugged her, and pulled her to him. His hand reached around her and they kissed.

'No more politics,' she whispered. 'I can't stand it anymore.'

'Bourgeois pig,' he chided, half in earnest, half in jest.

'I mean it,' she said.

'I know you do. I want to make love again.'

'I want dinner,' she said. The movement of his hands told her that he wasn't going to let her have dinner. Not immediately.

'Can't it wait?' he asked.

'Can't you wait?' she replied.

'No,' he said.

'Someday I'm going to rid myself of you,' she said. 'Then I'll be able to paint and sell to whomever I please. And you can go live with your Maoist cell and make love to an anarchist Chinese girl.'

'I'd like that,' he said. 'But for now I have only you.'

'Pig!' she said. She still wanted dinner. But this man never failed to win any physical confrontation between them. She recognised exploitation and had so far accepted it.

It was true enough that they had known each other since the May 1968 student-worker uprising. They had manned barricades together and had torn up cobblestones from the ancient Latin Quarter streets. Those same cobblestones had eventually been hurled into the air against shielded, helmeted, club-wielding riot squads of the Compagnies Républicaines de Sécurité. It was part of the uprising which eventually retired President de Gaulle a year later.

But in the years that had followed, Yves Ramereau had nurtured his dedication to a Marxist guerrilla overthrow of the government of France. At age twenty-six, he spent his time and energy in Maoist cells, discussing ideology, printing leaflets that were universally ignored by everyone in France except the police and other Maoist cells, and aiding any sort of disruption in the established order in France.

There were, for example, occasional bombings of specified government offices. There were also bombings of specified companies that either did business with the United States, employed Americans abroad, or were in fact American owned. If Ramereau's great love in life was a Maoist brand of anarchism, then his great hatred was anything that was even vaguely associated or linked with the United States.

There had been a time in Ramereau's life, a relatively recent time in fact, when his activism had been limited to a reasonably active pursuit of a doctorate in French literature. But like countless thousands of others of his generation. Ramereau deeply felt the rumblings of social upheaval which marked the late 1960s. While not tiring of literature itself, Ramereau was bitterly disdainful of the passivity of his studies. Thus when the cobblestones were to be torn up from boulevard Saint-Michel and hurled at the charging steel-helmeted heads of the CRS squadrons, Ramereau found himself a sudden veteran of the pitched police-student battles.

Political activism, once in his blood, was soon to infect his entire system. His studies of Diderot, Beaumarchais, and Verlaine were now augmented by studies of Frantz Fanon, Ché Guevara, and Regis Debray.

For Ramereau, words were meaningless without the willingness to physically turn those words into revolutionary reality. What could not be obtained by intellectual argument, Ramereau had now concluded, had to be obtained by brute force. His former heroes were men of words. His present heroes were men of action.

There was, for example, a man newly arrived in Paris with whom Ramereau was understandably impressed.

Ramereau had seen the man at several Left Bank union organising and cell meetings. He had talked to the man at length, discussing ideology and practical political theory. Ramereau had spent hours – days, in fact – with the man towards the end of 1972 and during the first two months of 1973. Ramereau's new acquaintance had been all over the world for revolutionary causes – Africa, South America, and most recently Vietnam. In most places he had observed. In other places, he had assumed more active roles. Now he had drifted back to France to fight – in whatever guerilla way he found possible – for the cause to which he was most dedicated: Breton independence.

Ramereau had wanted to work with him in whatever way possible. But more recently, over the past weeks, this older revolutionary had made himself increasingly scarce. He was obviously involved in plans of a more secretive nature. Ramereau asked if he, too, could take part. The man replied in no uncertain terms: Ramereau was to mind his own business.

Yet Ramereau bled over being that close to the action and not being able to participate. He'd keep an eye open for the other man. The Breton.

André Guisseny.

9

The offices of Congressman Johnny Ray Logan were larger than those of Congressman Coffin. They were larger and more lavish, reflecting perhaps the styles of the two men who inhabited and occasionally worked in them.

While Coffin's office in the Sam Rayburn Building was comfortable yet sparsely decorated, Logan's was resplendent with thick carpeting, Frederick Remington prints, and all the souvenirs that serving a tiny number of people from Texas could buy.

Logan was elected ostensibly by the people of a small section of the Texas Panhandle, a constituency of field workers, migrant farmers, and rural drifters. Yet Logan's actual constituency lived outside his congressional district and inhabited some of the most expensive apartments and ranches in the Houston and Dallas – Forth Worth regions. Every other year the good people of this constituency – as faceless and nameless as they were wealthy – would finance and otherwise assist Logan's re-election efforts. One did not need to be an astute political observer to see that Logan's real constituents were not the simple folk of the Panhandle but rather the more complex and ultra-conservative folks of Texas's mighty gas and oil industries. Logan represented these people ably and profitably. And as if by magic, he was overwhelmingly re-elected each time he ran.

He had run virtually unopposed for his last two decades in Congress. Logan's voting constituency turned out for him so enthusiastically every other November that his winning margin in several towns was greater than the number of voters carried on the municipal voting registers. No matter. If people get the government they deserve, as many people believe they do, Logan confirmed the belief that the people deserve very little. In most such cases the opposition would have lodged vehement complaints of vote fraud. But most of the time Logan encountered nothing even vaguely resembling an effective opposition. And on those few occasions when complaints were lodged, things had a way of getting lost in friendly courts.

By the sheerest of coincidences, the day that Richard chose to pass by Logan's office happened to be one of those rare days when Logan was in his office. Logan made a quiet point of being away from both his district and his office as much as possible. That way he could better attend to the business that he was elected to conduct.

'I'd like to see Mr Logan whenever it's convenient with him,' Richard announced to a Texas-accented receptionist when he entered Logan's office.

'What's the nature of your business?' asked the young woman with a cool but civil tone of voice.

Sensing a would-be run-around, Richard opened his mouth to reply. At that time a door opened from the inner office and out stepped Logan, tanned, greying at the temples and angularly handsome with cold blue eyes that could have cut through steel.

'Congressman Logan I assume?' asked Richard, offering his hand and stepping past the receptionist's desk.

'Yes?' answered Logan. The man offered his hand in return to Richard. But his cold calculating gaze looked through Richard as if to assume the most and suspect the worst.

'It's always a pleasure to shake the hand of a patriot,' said Richard.

The flesh of their palms pressed hard together. Logan, going into one of his infrequent campaign acts, pumped Richard's palm.

'Good to meet a good solid American,' said Logan, already noticing that Richard's accent placed him just to the south of Maine. Richard sounded too much like a Kennedy for Logan to be immediately at ease with him.

Logan looked to his receptionist with inquiring eyes asking the identity of this man. Richard turned Logan's gaze away from his receptionist. He released Logan's hand.

'It's good to meet a right-thinking American,' said Richard. 'I just came to tell you how much I appreciate what you've done.'

'Done?' asked Logan.

'Your job,' said Richard. 'Standing up for our nation. Standing up for the flag and the armed forces.'

'It's my duty,' said Logan reverently. He looked past Richard and saw his secretary shrug to indicate that she knew nothing about the visitor.

'I've just come back from a hell hole in North Vietnam,' Richard said, uttering a sentence that would stop any conversation in Washington at the time. 'I just want you to know that I appreciate your being one of the men who took a hard line against the Reds while I was locked up.'

'You were a POW?' asked Logan, his voice softening not so much out of sympathy or admiration as out of interest.

'For two and a half years,' said Richard.

'In that case,' said Logan, pushing his hand back to Richard's, 'it's a pleasure to shake *your* hand. You're the one whom I'm proud of, Mr – ?'

'Silva. Richard Silva. Lieutenant, United States Air Force. From Hyannis, Massachusetts.'

'What can I do for you?' asked Logan. The congressman was clearly at ease now, having a better idea whom he was dealing with.

'I'd like to take ten minutes of your time,' said Richard. 'It's a matter of urgency. Concerning the war. And the prisoners.'

The receptionist tried to interrupt.

'Congressman Logan was on his way to a luncheon engagement, Mr Silva,' she said. 'If you'd – '

'Nonsense!' roared Logan with his booming Texas drawl. 'I've got all day for a man who was locked up by the Communists.' Logan looked back at Richard and the receptionist busied herself by shuffling papers on her desk.

'Talk,' said Logan to his visitor.

'In private perhaps?' asked Richard, indicating Logan's inner office.

Carefully Logan studied Richard for another few seconds. 'In private,' he agreed. Then Logan turned and led Richard into his office. He closed the door behind him. Richard installed himself in a large green leather chair.

'What's on your mind, son?' Logan asked. Richard reached inside his jacket and withdrew the long white envelope that contained Kelly's drawing of the Imp.

Logan watched Richard unfold the picture. Richard looked at the drawing for a moment and then handed it to Logan.

'This is what I want help with,' said Richard.

56

Logan took the paper with his right hand and looked at the picture. Then, after several seconds of scrutiny, he looked back at Richard.

'Nice drawing,' said Logan. 'Did you do it?'

'A friend composed it for me.'

'Should I recognise the face?'

'No,' said Richard. 'I doubt if you would.'

'Suppose we end the mystery,' said Logan as he set the paper down on his desk, stretched his fingers by folding one hand into the other, and sat back in his chair. 'What's the significance of the picture? I don't recognise the face but it's obviously what brought you here.'

'We're talking off the record?' asked Richard.

'Son,' said Logan with a devilish and conspiratorial tone of voice, 'if you'd been in politics as long as I have you'd know that that's the *only* way to talk. What's on your mind?'

Richard explained. He told the story of his final bombing run, his plane being hit and his capture. He told of imprisonment and torture. He told the attentive Logan about the Imp.

Richard spoke succinctly and methodically as if he were addressing an intelligence officer at a debriefing. Logan sat behind his long paperless desk with his hands to his lips and the fingers of his hands folded pensively against his angular chin. The hard blue eyes gazed intently out from the deeply tanned face. For one of the few times in recent memory, Logan was interested in what somebody else was saying.

Richard finished his story. There was a long cold silence. Finally, Logan spoke.

'And this is the man?' he asked. He motioned to the picture, the black and white face staring menacingly upwards towards the ceiling.

'That's him.'

'It's a nice drawing and a hell of a good story son,' said Logan. 'Why did you bring it to me?'

'I want your help,' said Richard.

'How?'

'I want to find the bastard.'

'I see,' said Logan, pausing thoughtfully for a moment. 'Suppose we take a walk.'

'What?' Richard asked.

'Suppose we take a little stroll,' suggested Logan a second

time. 'Out in the open air. Just the two of us. Where we can talk freely.'

Richard looked blankly at Logan for a few moments but then understood. Outside in the sunlight where the walls won't have hidden ears.

'Excellent idea,' said Richard. 'It's such a nice day.'

Leading Richard past his curious but discreet receptionist, Congressman Johnny Ray Logan led Richard down the elevators and out of the congressional office building. Logan was conscious of the limp that Richard walked with. It was slight, but Logan was shrewd and rarely missed such details. The two men didn't speak. Logan made no verbal acknowledgement of Richard's limp.

Richard was satisfied with the sudden knowledge that he had at last found someone interested in his project. Logan busied himself turning on smiles to people he passed in the corridors and the elevator. Richard recognised none of them.

On the ground floor they passed a battery of uniformed guards. Logan gave a wide smile to a mid-western senator whom Richard recognised from news magazines and television. The senator, politically sympathetic to Logan's conservatism, was a champion of the constitutional and unconstitutional rights of the grain industry. Logan and the senator exchanged greetings on a first-name basis.

'A damned bore,' said Logan to Richard as soon as the senator was out of earshot. 'But he's right on the issues. And if you ever tell him I said he was a bore I'll deny it.'

'You should know by now,' said Richard as the two men walked into the sunlight outside the building, 'that it takes a hell of a lot of pressure before I open my mouth about anything.'

'So it does, son,' said Logan with admiration. 'So it does. Don't ever let anyone tell you that silence isn't a virtue.'

They walked through lunch-hour traffic and continued to walk until they were in an uncrowded section of park a few blocks from the Rayburn building. The warmth of the sun suggested the advent of summer. Logan led Richard to an isolated bench where the two men could talk.

'Tell me the truth and I may be able to help you,' said Logan. 'You said your name was Richard Silva.'

'That's right.'

'Is that your real name?'

'It's the one I was born with,' said Richard. 'But of course that's what I'd tell you even if it weren't.'

'I know that,' Logan answered, grinning slightly in admiration for Richard's cleverness. 'It was almost a silly question for me to ask.'

They were silent as a black woman with a baby carriage ambled slowly by.

'Where are you staying?' asked Logan. 'Do you have a Washington address?'

'The Marriott Motor Inn near the Key Bridge,' said Richard. 'Know it?'

Logan nodded. 'You're registered under your own name?'

'Room 812,' said Richard. 'Why?'

'I want to know where I can contact you,' said Logan. 'Or where any interested third party could contact you.'

'Can you tell me what you're talking about?' asked Richard.

'No,' said Logan, 'but I'm going to ask you one more thing.'

'What's that?'

Logan looked his younger adversary squarely in the eye.

'You're all ready to go all over the world to track down this Commie runt who tortured you in a POW camp. Well, hell. You're not planning to do it just to kiss him on the buttocks.'

'That's right,' said Richard.

'What are you going to do when you find him?'

'I've got my plans,' said Richard.

'Don't play me for a fool, boy,' snapped Logan ferociously. 'You're planning to kill him, aren't you?'

'What if I am?' asked Richard defiantly.

Logan eased backward on the bench. His question had been answered. 'That's all I wanted to know,' he said, his voice mild again. 'You can cut off his balls first and it wouldn't bother me.'

'Are you going to help me or are you going to ask questions?' asked Richard after a few more seconds of anxious silence.

'Help has a way of finding those who need it, son,' advised Logan in his most avuncular voice. 'You go back to that hotel room of yours and you sit tight by the phone. Hear?'

'I hear,' said Richard slowly. 'How long?'

Logan hunched his shoulders in a shrug of would-be innocence. 'I wouldn't know, son,' he said. 'I don't know anything. I'd just advise you to go to your room and sit tight. That's the last time I'm going to tell you that.'

'You win,' said Richard. 'But if nothing happens, I'll – '

'If nothing happens you can forget about me. I won't be able to help you.'

Richard nodded. Again Logan's tone of voice had changed. Now it was forceful and definite. Then it softened again.

'I guess I better be getting back to work, son,' said Logan as he stood up. 'That's about all I can tell you about your ... problem.'

Richard stood and prepared to leave in the opposite direction. Then Logan spoke again.

'You've got to tell me one other thing, too, son,' he said.

'What's that?'

'Why me?'

'What?'

'Why me? Why did you come to me with this?'

Richard told him about the list of ten names. And he related the incident in Coffin's office, the point when Coffin dismissed Richard's request by involving three names including Logan's.

'Coffin used my name, did he?' mused Logan thoughtfully. 'How did he use it?'

'What do you mean by "how"?'

'Tone of voice, boy. Tone of voice. Did he act like he meant it or – '

'He acted like he was tossing your name out in contempt,' said Richard. 'You and LeBlanc and Drew.'

'Did he sound like he knew something?' asked Logan.

'Knew something?' asked Richard. 'It sounded like a flippant offhand remark to me.'

'I see,' said Logan, his thoughtful lips breaking into a grin again. 'That would be more likely. The people of the great and sovereign Commonwealth of Massachusetts ought to elect a more right-thinking American. That Coffin never knows what he's talking about.'

10

There were people in New York State who did not recognise Clifford Craig's face or name, but they were difficult to find. There were not many of them.

Clifford Craig was fifty-one well-preserved years old in 1973. He was also on the brink of what promised to be a new career. For Clifford Craig, if things went well, the move would be from reporting the news to making the news. There had been one temporary stop along the way, but it had done nothing to lessen Craig's visibility.

For several years Clifford Craig had been a creature of habit. The habit was reporting the news to an American television audience that ranged well into eight figures. As the anchorman on a national seven o'clock news show, it had been Craig's job to bring the city current each weekday evening. There was an odd irony that the man with the urbane voice had grown up in Missouri with hayseed in his light brown hair.

Clifford Craig had begun his career in news reporting by covering the local police stations for a paper in Joplin, Missouri. From the first day that Craig filed a report to the city editor, it was gloriously apparent to him that he would last longer than the newspaper. He was right.

The paper folded in 1942, partially at least a casualty of World War II. But Craig moved quickly onto the Kansas City *Star* where he became the paper's best young reporter. Yet eventually the war – and the U.S. Navy – caught up with Craig.

He returned from the war in 1946 and made short work of

Kansas City. He had passed through New York on his way to and from the ocean fighting front. What he'd seen on New York had clicked with Craig. Somehow the grain elevators and stockyards of Tom Pendergast's old home town had lost their big-city aura. Listening to the grass grow was fine for cows, cowboys, and corn huskers. It was not fine, however for Clifford Craig, a man whose passions for such finer things as the New York Philharmonic now ran high.

So Craig moved to New York. And he picked up a reporter's job with the New York *Mirror*.

Like most else in the Craig career, the job at the *Mirror* was simply a stepping stone to something better. The something better was broadcast journalism, a wide-open field in the late 1940s, and a field that – with the help of the powerful press unions – would deal a deathblow to five of the eight dailies that existed after the war.

Craig moved into a radio broadcast spot in 1949 and remained there until 1953. Then he moved to the television side, his handsome angular Anglo-Saxon face appearing on the screen for the first time in 1954.

His lean, almost stern face with its sharp nose and high hard cheekbones should have been loathed on sight by the ethnic minorities that form New York's ethnic majority. But it wasn't. There was enough midwestern candour in his voice and enough straightforward sincerity on that face to put across the Craig message. To the viewing audience, even bad news was palatable from a likeable source.

Craig's likeableness, though immense, began and ended on the home screen. To work with or for Clifford Craig was every bit as pleasant as being a marine recruit. 'Will Rogers never met Clifford Craig,' was a gleeful yet in many ways accurate assessment of being close to Craig in a newsroom. And similarly, station staffers had a little jingle that they'd sing to each other on their own time and far out of earshot of anyone loyal to Craig. It went, 'Everybody doesn't like somebody, but nobody doesn't not like Clifford Craig.'

It was true enough in the studio. But the public at large *did* like Clifford Craig. They liked him and they trusted him.

In 1966, Craig's network, trailing the other two networks badly in the national news ratings, needed a new face – 'a fresh personality,' they called it – as anchorman on the national news show. They asked Craig if he'd be interested. Craig gave a one-word answer and began the following September. Within two months, Craig had again crippled the opposition. Half the televisions on in his time slot were turned to *The National Evening News* with Clifford Craig.

There he remained for five years. No newsman in America was better known and few were as well trusted by the public. Craig had everything he'd ever wanted. Yet within three years he was unhappy. Having conquered everything in sight, there was little challenge left in his $225,000-a-year job. So he resigned. His goals were now higher.

A movie producer had for years been tempting Craig with offers to put that face to another kind of use. Now Craig was ready to accept. In supporting roles he made two movies in 1971 and 1972. But more important he began to move around within Hollywood's liberal community. Craig knew what he wanted next. Power.

Craig found movie people – their political liberalism and their seemingly inexhaustible access to money – to his liking. They in turn accepted him. So Craig began to present himself as a potential political candidate, one who could use financing when the proper time came. In his own humble opinion – the humble opinion of a latent egomaniac – Craig's brand of personality and liberalism could be unbeatable under certain circumstances.

And those circumstances began to present themselves in New York as early as 1972.

Since 1962 New York State had been represented by Senator Robert Armellin. Armellin had initially been elected as a moderate Republican but had gradually drifted rightward to a position that made him somewhat akin to a latter-day monarchist. Once he had run for re-election. A distinct underdog with the vaguely liberal voters of his state, Armellin had profited from a classic split among two habitually self-destructive factions in the Democratic party. An insurgent Democrat ran as a Liberal. An organisation Democrat ran as a Democrat. Armellin ran as a Conservative, as a Republican, and as the champion of every right-of-centre citizen in the state. He garnered 41 per cent of the vote. It was enough to win.

Buoyed by an almost incredible re-election in a liberal state, Armellin was all the more a nationwide hero for conservatives. There was a certain titillation to a conservative winning twice in the backyard of American liberalism. Other conservatives around the country savoured Armellin's Senate seat almost as much as he did. Would it ever be possible, they mused for Armellin to pull it off a third time, to be re-elected again in 1974? The answer was a qualified yes until an exceptionally strong Democratic candidate began to appear on the political horizon.

The candidate was Clifford Craig.

Personally Craig and Armellin had always disliked each other. Politically they had always despised each other. Now, in 1973, they were getting ready to go for each other's jugular.

Backed by moneyed friends in New York and California and sensing a vast moderate and liberal constituency that knew him and liked him, Craig did not keep his Senate aspirations a secret.

Those years in the newsroom had put Craig on a familiar basis with every important party leader in the state. The party pros were interested in a Craig candidacy immediately. First and most important, there was no one else who might be owed the nomination. And second, in Craig the party professionals saw at last a man with the money, the public recognition, the respect, the presentability, and the political instinct to retire Armellin on election day in 1974. So by May of 1973, with other aspirants sufficiently discouraged, it was all but settled that Craig would have the Senate nomination on a platter and could easily rout Armellin that following year. All that remained was for the votes to be counted.

But as always in politics, the most predictable end is never what happens. And so in May of 1973, Clifford Craig's path was crossed in the most distant sort of way by an ordinary New York City police patrolman named Tony Vecchio.

11

Logan did not return directly to his offices. Instead he watched Richard until Richard was almost out of sight. Then Logan walked to a telephone booth just off Constitution Avenue.

He dialled a number in Washington, a local number that could be called from the first unvandalised telephone booth Logan could find. It was a government number he dialled.

'Extension one-four-five,' Logan requested when a female voice answered at a switchboard. Logan waited patiently, occasionally scanning those who passed by to reassure himself that no one who knew him could see him.

'Rogers speaking,' said a male voice suddenly on the other end of the line.

'Johnny Ray here,' said Logan.

'What's doing?' came the response. The question was asked more out of a specific interest than out of politeness.

'Can I see you in a few minutes?' Logan asked.

'Sounds important,' noted Rogers.

'It is.'

'Something interesting?'

'Maybe,' said Logan. 'Usual place?'

'Good enough,' said Rogers. 'Twenty minutes.'

There was no need for further discussion. Logan hung up the telephone. He telephoned his own office and asked that his secretary cancel his previous luncheon date. He asked her to reschedule it for later that week. His secretary obeyed with neither hesitation nor question. A few minutes later Logan arrived at a park bench not far from where Fourteenth Street meets Independence Avenue, just across the Potomac from the Jefferson Memorial.

To a casual observer, Logan would have been just another civil servant passing a leisurely lunch hour. Actually, behind a pair of dark glasses, Logan was now scanning passers-by waiting for a slightly stooped man named Rogers who wore his fifty-odd years with considerably less grace than Logan did.

Rogers, who wore the uniform of a Sergeant Major in the U.S. Army, appeared less than thirty minutes after being telephoned. His hair was crew cut and grey. The jowly scowl that he also wore befitted a man who'd made a career out of taking orders, orders from within the U.S. Army command and from within the command of one other highly nationalistic organisation.

'What's up?' asked Rogers. It was his favourite and most characteristic expression. And it was, after all, what he was usually wondering.

'I want you to get me a complete file on a man named Richard Silva,' said Logan carefully as he maintained a frozen, unemotional expression.

'What branch?' asked Sergeant Major Rogers.

'Air force,' said Logan. 'A lieutenant. Returning POW, just released from the service.'

'What's the full name?' asked Rogers.

'Richard Silva,' said Logan. 'He says he's from Hyannis, Massachusetts.' Rogers wrote with a pencil on a piece of scrap paper as Logan spoke. 'If there's no one on file by that name,' Logan continued, 'I want to know right away. You can call me on that if the name's a fake.'

Rogers nodded. 'Who is he?'

'If he gave me his real name he may be just the man we can use,' said Logan. 'In any event, just copy that file and make sure we get a clear reproduction of the picture. I want to make sure I'm dealing with the man who really owns that name. There are so many clever fakes running around these days that you just can't trust anyone.'

'When do you want it?' asked Rogers.

'Tonight,' said Logan. 'Six o'clock. Here.'

'That's going to be difficult,' Rogers began. But Logan cut him off.

'I don't care,' Logan snapped. 'This guy could be perfect for what we want. You know how long it's taken to find someone.

I don't want this guy slipping out of Washington without checking him out first.'

'I'll have the file here at six o'clock,' said Rogers. A good sergeant, he was anxious to take an order and fulfil his task. 'Unless the name's a fake. In that case – '

'In that case, you'll call me.'

Rogers nodded and almost saluted Logan. Then he folded the paper he wrote on and carefully placed it in his uniform pocket.

At six o'clock that evening the same men met for one minute at the same bench. Logan received a large manilla envelope and tucked it into his briefcase.

'Richard Peter Silva,' said Rogers. 'Born in Provincetown, Massachusetts, later moved to Hyannis. College educated. POW while in the air force. Sounds like your man. I made a perfect copy of the entire file.'

'You're a patriot,' said Logan. 'Now do what you always do so well.'

'What's that?' asked Rogers.

'Forget about the whole thing,' said Logan.

'I already have,' said Rogers through a grin of sturdy yellow teeth. 'I don't even know what you're talking about.'

That night Logan spent an hour at the desk of his Washington apartment. He drew down the shades as usual and wouldn't have answered the telephone or doorbell if either had rung. He studied the contents of the envelope, the complete military records of Richard Peter Silva, illegally Xeroxed so clearly by Sergeant Major Rogers. It took only one glance at the reproduced photograph contained within the file for Logan to know that Richard was exactly who he said he was. That in itself brought a cunning smile to Logan's lips.

At nine o'clock that night Logan went to the bottom drawer of his dresser, removed two sweaters and then withdrew a small black .38-calibre pistol, one that he had never used and hoped never to use. But fearing physical crime in the District of Columbia streets, Logan loaded the pistol and tucked it under his jacket. Then he picked up four quarters and three dimes from the top of that dresser. He pocketed the change, carefully holding in his hand the file that Rogers had photocopied from air force records. Then Logan went down to his car.

Logan drove a few blocks, remaining in a safe white district of Washington. He stopped at a telephone booth. He left his car by the kerb next to the booth. He pushed two quarters and a dime into the pay telephone. He listened for the chimes and dialled a Viriginia number.

'Hello?' came a distant-sounding response.

'I may have the man we need,' said Logan.

'Background?'

'Almost perfect. I have it all for you.'

'Where is he?'

'Washington. A hotel. You'll have to get him before he leaves town.'

'Have you approached him about it yet?'

'He doesn't know a thing,' said Logan. 'He's in a position where he needs help on a project of his own. You might be able to work out a deal. Get the idea?'

'When can we see what you have?' the voice asked.

'Right away,' said Logan. 'Usual place in the car.'

'I'll come for it,' said the voice. 'Tonight.'

The man in Virginia hung up. So did Logan. Logan returned to his apartment, leaving the complete file on Richard Silva under the driver's seat of his car. He parked the blue 1972 Oldsmobile near its usual spot on the block where he lived. Then he went back to his apartment. His involvement was over.

Three hours later a brown Dodge with Virginia licence plates circled the block on which Logan lived. The car slowed as it passed Logan's blue Oldsmobile and continued to the end of the block. There it double-parked. The driver remained in the car. A passenger got out.

Slowly, as if to assess a foreign terrain, the man walked down the shadowy night-time sidewalk until he came to Logan's car. Then he pulled a key from his pocket and opened the front left door. He opened the door wide and remained unobserved except through the rear-view mirror of the Dodge.

The man reached into Logan's car and pulled the thick manilla envelope out from under the seat. He tucked it under his arm, closed the car door, and locked it. Then he walked to his partner in the Dodge.

Cautiously, observing all traffic rules and stopping even at yellow lights, the Dodge and the file on Richard Silva were driven to Virginia.

12

Logan had whetted Richard's appetite.

From the meeting with Congressman Coffin, Richard had concluded that it would be a waste of time and effort to try to get at
the Imp through legal channels. Those channels would be closed
to him. Permanently. He knew he would have to go outside them.

The conversation with Logan, and Logan's evident sympathy
for Richard's cause, had whetted Richard's appetite for a full-
scale manhunt. Yes, it would be Richard's personal vendetta
against an unknown European. And yes, Richard would need
outside help.

Financially Richard was ready to spend what he had to find the
Imp. He had the money the government had given him on sever-
ance from the air force. It was an ample sum, several thousand
dollars. If Richard were careful it would finance his expedition
until he either found the Imp or discovered that no trace of the
man existed.

It was difficult for Richard to imagine, however, that any man
could vanish from the face of the earth without leaving any trace
or trail. Somewhere Richard knew that the Imp would have had
to leave tracks behind him. Richard assumed that if enough relentless and meticulous work were done on his part those tracks
would be uncovered. And then there was the possible help that
Logan had mentioned. It made Richard itch with impatience.

He stayed near or in his hotel room for all of the following day.
He ventured out only for a brief walk by the Potomac, lunch, and
the newspapers. In the evening he sat in the lobby and watched

people for three-quarters of an hour. He was particularly intrigued by a young woman, perhaps twenty-two, who sat in the lobby across from him. Ostensibly she was waiting for someone.

Richard admired her pert face and her light brown hair. She was soft to his eye and nicely tanned. She wore a light blue dress that revealed enough of her two perfectly shaped legs to send Richard's thoughts into areas where they hadn't dwelt for many weeks and months.

He had had his casual friends and two more serious affairs in college. But he'd lost touch with every one of them since his capture in 1970. It seemed so long ago when he'd been involved with women. It was on the other side of his imprisonment, part of the section of his life that was gone. Closed. Back when his parents were alive and back when he was in school. It practically seemed like childhood. It wasn't that he was that much older, it was simply that he had aged so quickly.

Thoughts of women were secondary to his obsessive thoughts of the Imp. The Imp had to die before Richard could truly be free again to examine his future. Everything was secondary to Richard's current project, his manhunt, if that's what it was going to have to be.

But for these brief moments in the lobby of the Marriott Motor Inn Richard allowed his homicidal instincts to abate. He allowed himself to ponder the distant future, the days after the Imp had been disposed of. Richard allowed himself to think of the young woman across the lobby. He thought of the pleasure it might someday give him to love a woman with the same intense desire with which he now hated a man. It would be a day when he would no longer have to think of killing.

Damn, he thought. He wished that particular day were here. But he was painfully unable to remove this business of the Imp from his mind. The young woman across the lobby rose and met an athletic-looking man in a dark suit.

They embraced. She kissed him. He took her arm and Richard watched as the couple slowly meandered out of the lobby. Unhappily, Richard rose from his own seat and returned to his solitary room upstairs. He was still waiting. He would wait till hell froze over.

No message the next day. Or the next. Richard reviewed his list of congressmen. He was about to give up on Logan as so much hot air and false expectations. He selected another name and planned to visit that man's office the following Monday. He had put his list away again and was leafing through a paperback novel when the telephone rang. It was the first time since he'd been in Washington that the instrument had uttered the slightest buzz.

'Yes?' he answered.

'Mr Silva?' came a voice, an unidentified voice that was actually emanating from a pay telephone a few blocks away.

'Yes?'

'Mr Silva, you don't know me,' said the voice. 'But I know a bit about you.'

'Talk,' said Richard. He was ready to listen.

'You've been recommended by a friend of ours,' continued the voice. 'A good American whom you spoke to a few days ago.'

'Keep talking,' said Richard.

'He said that you were a good patriotic American and you had a project you wanted to undertake. A project that we might be able to help you with.' There was a pause. 'We might be able to help you,' the voice added, 'if you were willing to help us with a pair of similar projects.'

'Similar?' Richard asked.

'Similar,' said the caller. 'But nothing that a good American would have any objection to doing. Interested?'

'I'm interested,' said Richard.

'Be at New York Avenue and K Street Sunday night at ten thirty,' said the voice. 'If you're interested a car will meet you. You'll have to be blindfolded while you're driven to us. But then we'll be able to talk freely.'

'I'll be there,' Richard said. Richard heard a click and then a dial tone. When he replaced the telephone on the hook he rubbed his palms together and smiled.

13

The block of New York's East Sixty-seventh Street between Park and Madison Avenues is not unlike many of the other crosstown streets in the East Sixties. It is usually quiet and the property values thereon are high, even by New York standards. The block is clean, devoid of any litter, and the well-scrubbed brick and sandstone buildings reflect the quiet and anonymous affluence of the inhabitants.

This is a block which is, in short, unafflicted by most urban ills. Specifically, street crime here is virtually non-existent. That is why, to a casual observer, it might seem odd to see a police car continually stationed halfway between Park and Madison on Sixty-seventh.

But in the spring of 1973 a new blue and white New York City police car was stationed around the clock at precisely this location. The political tensions a third of the world away were to blame.

On the south side of the street, nestled among the doctors' offices, the quietly elegant townhouses, and the solid old apartment buildings is a solid brick and concrete edifice that might otherwise have been turned into the dream home of an urban multi-millionaire. But instead, this quarter-of-a-million-dollar chunk of real estate became the home of the United Nations mission from the Arab Republic of Egypt. There, in baronial splendour on East Sixty-seventh Street, the socialist republic of Egypt houses its diplomatic mission.

A white flagpole protrudes over the sidewalk, but an Egyptian flag does not fly. The building is noticeable in only two ways.

First, a small bronze plaque, engraved in English and Arabic, adorns one of the double doors in front. The plaque identifies the building. And second, when the political situation so demands, a New York police car is present in the No Parking area in front of the mission.

In a city such as New York where there are in fact about as many Jews as there are in Israel, Egyptians are not at peak popularity The reasons date back to biblical time and take almost as long to understand. It suffices to say that New York City, to discourage acts of violence at unpopular missions, takes regular New York City police off normal duty and assigns them to embassies as guards.

The police officers are to remain at these positions under almost all circumstances. Only in the event of a flagrant felony within their sight are they permitted to leave their posts.

These assignments are unpopular with the police, the people of the city, and with the city government. The police dislike being removed from their regular duty, which is, in theory at least, the deterrence and detection of crime. The people of the city dislike this drainage of police protection for precisely the same reason. And the city government dislikes it because the city receives not one penny from the federal government to pay for this loss in salaried police manpower.

Nor, ironically, is the protection even popular with those who are protected. Many foreign diplomats maintain that the police are spies. Others claim them inadequate as protection. Still others alternate back and forth between the two theories.

For a police officer drawing such an assignment, however, none of these is the paramount problem. The worst aspect of such an assignment is the sheer unadulterated boredom of being assigned for eight hours to a stationary post where nothing happens. Such was the case with Officer Anthony Vecchio when he and his partner, Ike Lamont, drew guard duty for the night shift at the Egyptian mission.

Vecchio, after just one night on quiet Sixty-seventh Street, inwardly wished that someone would lob a can of paint at the Egyptians' tightly sealed front door. First, Vecchio disliked the pro-Russian Egyptians on principle. Second, a can of paint would provide a modicum of excitement and might allow Vecchio to make an arrest. For the same reasons that little boys think they want to grow up to be policemen, Tony Vecchio still got a kick out of making an arrest.

Vecchio, twenty-six and the son of a Brooklyn cobbler, had been on the police force for three years. Previously he'd served in the U.S. Navy, based in Boston for most of his stint. He'd been assigned to the relatively peaceful Nineteenth Precinct in Manhattan for the last two years. He had a good record as a patrolman. Only three times had he ever drawn his gun on duty; only one time had he fired it. He'd broken up a liquor store holdup in progress and he'd collared a knife-wielding fifteen-year-old who'd held up a stationery store in Yorkville. He'd written a lot of parking tickets and he had no major screw-ups since joining the force.

But Vecchio aspired to trade in his silver badge for a detective's gold shield. That could take years, he figured, and it would take breaks, breaks that would distinguish him from every other cop on the beat who aspired to be a plainclothes man. If only, Vecchio mused constantly to himself, he could somehow join an important case.

And Vecchio, a bull-necked, dark-browed kid who might have passed for one of Caesar's legionnaires, knew that would take some doing. Tony Vecchio did not impress immediately. He impressed slowly. Friends in the police academy kidded him about being as strong as an ox and almost as smart. The first part was accurate; the second part was a vast underestimation. Beneath that thick skull and among those muscles lurked – surprisingly to some – a brain. A good brain, one that was always in use. Vecchio was always thinking, even about things he should have been ignoring.

Vecchio was rough, coarse, often crude, and slyly funny. His education was not the best. But he was intuitively intelligent and instinctively curious. And the boredom of working through the night on the eight-hour graveyard shift in front of a quiet Egyptian mission was excruciating.

Tony Vecchio, always thinking, invented ways to pass the time. He would observe people on the street and would wonder about them. He would train himself to observe the tiniest details and then would try to imagine what those details told him. It was half good detective work and half idle reverie. But it passed the time.

Vecchio found that on this ungodly shift through the dark hours, a shift he'd drawn for three weeks with Ike Lamont, he would see many of the same people each night at the same time. Each night followed a pattern and anything that veered from that pattern was memorable. It was not surprising then that as Vecchio began to observe the same people each night, he began to observe details and wonder about each of them.

The police car was parked between the canopies of two large apartment buildings, numbers 26 and 34. An occupant of number 34 caught Vecchio's attention almost immediately.

She was a thin blonde in her early twenties, who would return home each night around twelve thirty and leave again the next morning before eight. Who exactly she was and what exactly she was doing was a matter of intense speculation – and no importance – to Vecchio. Intense enough was his curiosity that Vecchio would watch the face of her building carefully each night after she returned home. Vecchio watched to see which light would go on.

By pure chance, the girl lived in the front of the building rather than the side. One night Vecchio noticed that a light on the eleventh floor went on two minutes and thirty-eight seconds after the girl had disappeared into the building. On the next night Vecchio timed her again after watching her walk into the doorway.

The same light after three minutes and ten seconds. Had to wait for the elevator, Vecchio reasoned. Either that or she couldn't find her keys.

The game grew even more complex a few shifts later. Vecchio saw the girl leaving one morning, carrying a bag monogrammed with the letters TFH. Tony Vecchio couldn't resist a game like this.

TFH, he repeated in his mind. Then he made up a man's name. Theodore Frederick Hamilton. No, he thought, it's New York. Make it Theodore Frederick Hartzman. Then Vecchio left his car one morning and walked to the Puerto Rican doorman he knew at 34 East Sixty-seventh Street.

'Hey, Chico,' he said, 'this doesn't have anything to do with the Egyptians, but do you have someone on the eleventh floor named Hartzman?'

'Hartzman?' The doorman shook his head.

'It might be a name similar to that,' Vecchio suggested.

Again the doorman shook his head. 'No name even close,' he said.

Vecchio appeared nonplussed yet undaunted. 'Tell me then,' he said. 'I'm sure there's a man on that floor with the same initials. Let me know if a name matches those letters.'

The doorman went to a Rolodex file and flipped through to the H's. 'Theresia F. Hauser. Eleven J,' said the doorman. 'That's it. No man on the floor by that name.'

'Are you sure that's a woman's name?' asked Vecchio, holding a perfectly straight face. The doorman looked at the cop as if the latter had just left his brains on the back seat of the patrol car.

'Are you putting me on?' replied Chico. 'Ever seen her?'

Vecchio shrugged. 'How would I know?'

'She's a German model,' said Chico. 'Really fine.'

'Oh, yeah?' said Vecchio. 'You're sure?'

'Sure, I'm sure.'

Vecchio placed his hands on his hips and shook his head slowly. 'Guess I got a bum lead,' he said. 'Son of a bitch. I won't bother you again today.'

'Don't worry about it, Tony,' said the doorman with an air of superiority and with obvious amusement.

Vecchio returned to his car. 'My girlfriend's name is Theresia,' he said proudly to Lamont. 'She's a kraut model and lives in eleven J.'

'Did you leave a silver bullet so she knows who you are?' asked Lamont.

'Very funny,' said Vecchio. And the matter ended there. Except now each morning and evening when Vecchio saw the girl he said in his mind, 'Good morning, Theresia, you luscious kraut, you,' or simply, 'Good night, Theresia,' depending on the hour. He did this, that is, until one night when Theresia returned to her apartment arm in arm with a man six inches shorter and several inches wider than she. She then emerged with him at a later hour the next morning. On that occasion Vecchio, whose moral code dated from the 1930s, had a much earthier silent greeting than a simple 'good morning' or 'good night.' And after that Vecchio turned his interest to others who casually wandered across his path.

For example, during his second week on that assignment Vecchio peered up from his parked patrol car and saw a man with a familiar face rounding the corner from Madison Avenue.

'Hey Christ, Ike,' said Vecchio. 'Isn't that the guy who used to do the news?'

Lamont looked up, recognising Clifford Craig. 'Sure is,' he said.

The two cops watched as Craig, returning home from a meeting of local Democrats, nodded to his doorman and disappeared into 26 East Sixty-seventh Street. 'Wonder what the hell he's doing there?' mused Vecchio.

'Did you ever consider that he might live there?' asked Lamont.

'Son of a bitch,' muttered Vecchio. 'I suppose he could.'

14

Richard spent Sunday reading in his hotel room, looking calmly out the window at his view of Washington, sitting in the lobby and glancing at his watch. The day seemed interminable. When another step in this incipient manhunt seemed so close at hand he was anxious to get on with it. The sooner it began the sooner it could all end.

At seven that evening Richard went to the hotel dining room and had a satisfying dinner. It was past eight when he ascended to his room. He stayed there until a quarter to ten. Then he dressed in dark clothes and left the hotel, being careful to slip one drawing of the Imp into his inside jacket pocket again. Then he set out on foot to the corner of New York Avenue and K Street.

He arrived on the specified corner at ten fifteen. He waited. He waited almost twenty minutes, standing and watching occasional passers-by. The corner was usually deserted but he saw why his caller had picked that particular block. There was a bus stop there. He could stand at that block as if waiting for a bus and arouse no suspicion. For a few minutes there were other people on that corner waiting for a bus that came and went. Richard was alone there, however, watching the illuminated Washington Monument in the distant background, when a brown Dodge without a front licence plate pulled alongside him.

'Mr Silva?' asked a subdued voice from the car.

'Yes,' he replied.

Richard squinted. The car had one man in front and one in the back. The car was dark. It was impossible to see a face clearly.

'Get in,' said a voice. 'We're going to where we can talk,'

Richard approached the car. He was instructed to get into the back seat. The door was opened for him and he slid in.

He turned toward the man he was seated next to. The man moved a white handkerchief up to where it hid his face. Richard glanced towards the driver. The driver faced away from him.

'You do understand that we have to blindfold you?' asked the man next to him.

Richard nodded.

'It would be better for now if you did not know where you are going,' added the man. 'I think you're enough of a patriot to know that some secrets are better left unknown.'

Richard, propelled both by curiosity and his desire to find what if anything this might have to do with his catching the Imp, agreed to look away. A heavy dark cloth was wrapped around his head at eye level. The blindfold was tied securely and tightly by hands that knew what they were doing. Richard was then instructed to lie down on the seat. He obeyed.

The car began to move. Eventually the paving beneath the car changed. Richard was conscious of crossing a bridge. Then, after driving through what felt like city blocks with their stop lights, Richard was aware that the car was moving steadily without stopping. He estimated that the car was moving at fifty miles an hour. He asked how long he'd be required to lie in that crouched position in the back seat.

'Are you uncomfortable?' he was asked.

'It's not my idea of relaxation,' he answered.

Richard was allowed to remain sitting up for the rest of the drive, except for times when other cars passed and might see his blindfold. Richard assumed he was on one of the parkways around or leading out of Washington. When told to put his head down, he obeyed. After what seemed close to an hour, Richard felt the car leave the expressway and travel on back roads. Eventually the car turned onto what felt and sounded like a gravel driveway. Soon afterward the car came to a halt. Richard, still blindfolded, was led out of the car, into a house, and through a room.

'We're going down a flight of stairs now,' said the voice of the man who had blindfolded him. 'Be ready. You'll be able to take your blindfold off in a few minutes.'

Richard, with the other man holding his arm, allowed himself to be led to a chair. He sat down.

'Welcome, Mr Silva,' he heard a voice in front of him say. 'You may remove your mask if you wish.'

Richard reached to that cloth which had been bound so securely around his head. He struggled with it. Then a pair of hands reached to the knot behind his head and loosened the cloth. The blindfold came off. Richard blinked. He was in a strange place and was blinded by the light, just like a man who has been sleeping in a room where the light is suddenly thrown on.

'Welcome,' the voice repeated. Richard looked across from him. The man speaking, seated at a desk flanked by two American flags, was addressing Richard from behind a Halloween mask.

'I hope you don't resent our method of bringing you here,' said the speaker. 'But as I'm sure you noticed, we place a high priority on secrecy.'

Richard was still blinking. The Halloween mask he was looking at had the face of a canine, a dog or a wolf perhaps. It was the type of mask that children buy for a dollar or so. But it was being worn here by no child, nor was amusement its purpose. Its purpose was to conceal the speaker's face. And it did its job perfectly. The man behind it coughed for a moment, a cough which sounded chronic.

Richard looked around the room. There were more people. Men of indeterminate age. Perhaps a dozen. All with one sort of mask or another. Some with Halloween masks, others with ski masks or gauze nets. There was not a face visible, nor any face that could in any way be discerned. It reminded Richard of films he'd once seen about the French Resistance or the Irish Republican Army.

'You've gone to a lot of trouble for me,' Richard said, looking around the room and then returning his gaze to the absurd canine mask that faced him. 'You must have a reason.'

'Of course we do,' replied the voice behind the mask. 'We think you may be the man we've been looking for.'

'How so?' asked Richard.

'You need help with a project that you wish to undertake,' explained the speaker,' 'Something about an Imp.'

'That's right,' said Richard.

'Well,' said the voice behind the canine mask, 'this is simply a business proposition of sorts. You do some work for us. We do some work for you. In the bargain you get paid.'

Richard searched that mask for a sign of an expression. He saw none. He couldn't even spot a flicker behind the eye slits.

'Keep talking,' Richard said. 'I'm listening.'

'This Imp,' said the voice, playing on the shortness of the second word. 'We know your story and we know what you went through at this man's hands. We understand how he is believed to have murdered several American soldiers.'

'Tortured them to death,' said Richard, unable to keep his thoughts to himself. Mere mention of the Imp impassioned him and keyed him for revenge.

'We understand,' said the voice, well spoken and with a vaguely southern inflection. 'That's why you're planning to kill him.'

The bluntness of the statement took Richard by surprise. But he found his response rolling freely through his lips.

'That's correct,' he said.

'Excellent,' said the speaker. 'You obviously have no compunction about killing for a just cause.'

'Look,' said Richard, trying to move onto the offensive for the first time in that meeting. 'Let's not play games. You know who I am and you know what I want to do. You've brought me here to make me an offer of some kind. What is it?'

'Our proposition is very simple, Mr Silva,' said the masked man at the table across from Richard. 'There is a man you want dead. We know two whom *we* want dead. Our proposal is something of a package deal.'

'Go on,' said Richard. He felt all eyes in the room on him.

'Three people are to be killed. Your Imp and two people of our selection. I hasten to add that, considering your patriotic thinking, the two people we want killed will not offend your sensibilities any more than your proposed victim offends ours. Our organization,' said the masked man as he glanced at the flags on each side of him, 'has a certain point of view. We think that those traitors who try to sabotage our nation have no right to live within it. Do you understand what I'm saying, Mr Silva?'

Richard nodded, though not necessarily in agreement. He would hear them out since he was in no position to start an argument. He already disliked them. Masks were for cowards, he felt. And sneaks. 'Can I assume that you're inclined to agree?' the speaker asked.

'You can assume whatever you like,' Richard replied slowly as he played the question as best he could. 'Someone in my position who has been in a prison camp and who has seen friends murdered and tortured might be at least moderately sympathetic to your cause.'

Richard thought he sensed a smile from behind that mask. He saw a few other heads nod around the room.

'I'm pleased to hear that, Mr Silva,' said the masked speaker. 'We're *all* happy to hear that.'

Richard glanced around quickly and deduced that he was most probably in the elaborately converted basement of a house in Maryland or Virginia. The drive had been too long for him still to be in the District of Columbia, unless he had intentionally been driven around in circles. He looked at his watch. Past midnight. It had been an hour and a half since he was picked up.

'Why don't we get to specifics,' said Richard. 'How do I know you can help me? I like your flags, I like your spirit, and your masks are the cutest things I've ever seen. But how do I know what you can do for me?'

'Do you have your picture of your Imp?' the speaker asked.

Richard handed him the envelope from the inside of his jacket.

'May I keep this? Temporarily at least?' the speaker asked as he looked at Kelly's drawing.

Richard nodded.

'We all know about you, Mr Silva, but you know nothing about us. That's a little unfair. So to answer your question, I'll bring you up to date at the same time. We're patriotic Americans, Mr Silva, just like yourself and millions of other men. And just as you probably are, we're appalled at the way this republic is creeping leftward. We are simple Americans who wish to save our republic from her enemies. Internal and external. We have common enemies, Mr Silva.'

'Fine,' said Richard. 'But how are you going to find me my man?'

'I'm coming to that,' said the speaker. 'Perhaps you've wondered about our masks.'

'Wondered? No,' said Richard. 'I understand.'

The man hacked a cough, then continued. 'Many of us do not even know who the rest of us are. But within our membership are people of, shall we say, authority. Within the government.'

'Uh-huh,' said Richard.

'People with access to government resources.'

'Like intelligence files,' said Richard.

The man nodded slowly. 'Very quietly we are very strong. Mr Silva. Our country has many loyal Americans who still believe in her. We have many friends in many places. People who might not want to help us out in the open but who are enthusiastic about helping us in secret. Am I beginning to make sense?'

'You are,' said Richard. 'But I'm still waiting to hear how you're going to find the Imp for me.'

'I'll be honest,' were the words from behind the child's Halloween mask. 'There is a possibility that nothing exists on your Imp. If that's the case, we won't be able to help you. But what we will be able to do is scour the entire intelligence files of the United States armed forces. If we can't find anything that way, Mr Silva, then there's no way you'll ever find your man.'

Richard nodded. It was making sense. To Richard's monomaniac point of view it was even sounding feasible and credible.

'I'll now be specific,' said the man behind the canine mask as he leaned forward. 'We're prepared to discover the identity of the Imp, tell you where to find him, provide you a weapon, and provide you an ample sum of money for you to complete your task. If your Imp is outside of the country, as he most assuredly is, we will provide you a false passport to travel on.'

'And in return?' asked Richard.

'In return you will kill two other people for us.' Richard froze for a moment, taken off guard by the type of deal he'd been offered. It would trouble him not at all to travel the world to kill a man who deserved it. But two innocent men? Two men whom Richard had nothing against? The concept was repugnant to him. Richard was a soldier settling a private grievance, not a hired assassin.

Yet there he was seated before those men. Here perhaps was the only opportunity he might ever have to find the Imp. He had to find out more. He recovered enough to speak calmly.

'Who are these two others?' he asked.

'Enemies of the republic,' said the voice. 'No names until we have an agreement.'

'Naturally,' said Richard. 'But no agreement until I know that you've located the Imp.'

'Of course, Mr Silva,' said the speaker, expressing no surprise in his tone of voice. 'We're gentlemen of honour, despite the fact that necessity obliges us to wear masks.'

Richard closely eyed the man behind the canine mask. Then he quickly looked around the room to again find that all eyes were on him.

'There are a few things that don't fit into place yet,' said Richard as he turned back to the speaker.

'Such as?'

'Why me?' Richard asked. 'It's no mystery how you got my name. But why bother with an outsider? If your organization is as sophisticated as you make it sound, why bother to bring in . . . a hired killer, which is in essence what you want me to be.'

'There are several reasons, Mr Silva,' said the masked speaker. 'First, you have no links to us at all. None. You could never prove that you've been here because you don't know where you are. Nor do you have any idea who *we* are. If you bungle either of our designated murders, you couldn't possibly lead anyone to us.'

'What about through Logan?' asked Richard.

'Who's Logan?' asked the speaker.

There was a pause. Richard smiled grudgingly. 'Go on,' he said.

'Yet, while you can complete these jobs for us and not ever be able to lead anyone to us, you need us for the murder you intend to commit. We consider you very sincere about your finding this Red sadist from Hanoi. Ideologically, we're pleased. That makes you even more acceptable to us.'

'I understand,' Richard said. 'But how do you know I won't take your money, your passport, and your information and just go after the Imp?'

'You won't,' said the speaker, struggling now with a longer cough.

'Why?'

'You're a patriot, Mr Silva, You wouldn't betray other patriots.'

'How can you be sure of that?' Richard asked.

The man in the canine mask leaned backward in his chair. He wrapped his arms together. 'We know who you are,' he said. 'And you know that we know who you are. You couldn't hide from us for long. I'm sure you understand, Mr Silva, that when it comes to defending our republic against her enemies there can be no compromise. A betrayal against us is looked upon as a capital offence. Do I make myself clear?'

Richard nodded. He let a few moments of silence fill the room. He wanted the other side to keep talking.

He considered the power and resources that these men obviously had. To find the Imp, Richard would have to accept their offer. Yet could he bring himself to murder their two victims? He doubted it. He would have to betray them and take his chances. The only alternative was to commit two murders.

'Well, Mr Silva?' asked the speaker. His voice had an upbeat tone. 'How does this sound?'

'Interesting,' said Richard.

'Interesting enough to become involved in?'

'Potentially,' said Richard.

'What seems to be your hesitation?'

'As I see it,' said Richard, 'the first step is up to you. Once you find my Imp for me I'll be ready to accept your offer. Not before.'

'In other words,' said the speaker, 'If we find him for you we would have your services for our other . . . jobs?'

'How much money are you prepared to give me?' Richard asked.

'I think we could arrange twelve thousand dollars,' said the speaker. 'One third now. One third after you complete the first assignment. And the final third when you complete your final assignment.'

'How about fifteen thousand?' asked Richard, beginning to enjoy the fine art of haggling with an employer. He never said that he probably would have accepted the assignment for no money at all, just for the information that would lead him to the Imp.

The speaker looked around the room as if searching for approval.

'An extra three thousand shouldn't be so hard to find for someone who's going to risk his life twice for you,' Richard said. 'You say your people are so high up in the government. So just get some money out of the Treasury.'

'I don't think you need to find humour in this situation, Mr Silva,' said the speaker.

'I'm not,' Richard replied. 'I'm merely asking to be paid properly for professional services.'

'All right,' said the speaker. 'Fifteen thousand. We'll arrange the instalments.'

'Now what about this passport?' Richard asked.

'It will be easily provided,' said the speaker. 'We simply have to take a photograph.'

'How do I know the passport is any good?'

'We're not children,' said the speaker with a hint of anger in his voice. 'We know what we're doing. You'll receive an expertly forged Canadian passport.'

'Canadian?'

'Another man used one for months,' said the speaker. 'But he got careless. He spent his money ostentatiously and he remained abroad. I would imagine, Mr Silva, that no one will ever know that you've been abroad. You'll perform your mission for us. Then you'll find your Imp. And that will finish the final part of your contract.'

Richard nodded. Silently he wondered how powerful twelve men who hid behind masks could be. The speaker wheezed another short intense cough.

'Very well, gentlemen,' Richard said. 'If you find me my Imp it would appear that we have a deal. As long as one final condition is honoured.'

'And what would that be?' asked the speaker.

'As soon as the third job is completed,' said Richard, 'I will sever all ties with your organisation. You will never again contact me or ask me to help you in any way. Despite the fact that we may be on the same patriotic side, I would imagine that this would be the safest path for both of us.'

'Mr Silva,' replied the speaker without hesitation. 'This is exactly what we had in mind.'

'In that case,' said Richard, 'when will I know if you can find the Imp?'

15

The late April afternoon in Paris was overcast, but there was a certain insouciance to the air. Mothers walked without topcoats as they strolled with their children in the Luxembourg Gardens or the Bois de Boulogne. The grass was green again. The earth was soft from the April rains. The men who sold balloons in the park had returned. And the children of U.S. Ambassador Kenneth W. Thatcher were still under the studious eyes of those who planned to kidnap them.

As had been the custom over the last few weeks, the austere black Citroën limousine bearing Barbara Thatcher, Lieutenant Simmons, and the two young Thatcher daughters was followed from the lycée Américain on the avenue Bosquet. On this particular day the children had been let out of school at 2.35. Those observing their movements noted that this time never varied more than five minutes on any day.

The men who followed the Citroën limousine used different cars each day. Usually they'd use small Simcas, Renaults, or a Citroën *deux-chevaux*, one of the ridiculously shaped automotive marvels that clutter traffic throughout France. Never was the following car in any way conspicuous or notable to Lieutenant Simmons. Those in the following car had taken every precaution to blend into the background.

On this particular day there were three men in the car following the Citroën limousine. Guisseny sat in the front seat with a watch in his hand as Savard drove. Klemeur sat calmly in the back seat, having observed both the children and Barbara Thatcher's breath-taking figure.

'The same route every day,' said Savard. '*Ça change jamais.*'
Guisseny said nothing. He observed everything.

Lieutenant Simmons, for reasons that were clear but un-
mentioned, never strayed from the busiest possible streets through
Paris. The lycée Américain was located slightly west of the geo-
graphical centre of the city. The ambassador's home was a regal
brick townhouse on the splendidly fashionable and busy avenue
Foch, one of the pinwheel of major boulevards that merge at the
Arc de Triomphe.

Each day Lieutenant Simmons would return the Thatcher
children to their home by driving across the busiest roads of the
Right Bank. He would leave the Left Bank where their school was
located by driving up the avenue Bosquet to the Pont d'Alma.
There he would cross the murky Seine and pass by the fashionable
Rive Droite shops on the avenue Marceau. Then he'd continue
northwest towards where the Arc de Triomphe stood at the centre
of the place Charles de Gaulle, or as the French people called it,
l'Etoile.

At l'Etoile the traffic never ceases. The car bearing the ambassador's wife and children would merge with the never-ending
traffic and travel a semicircle around the Arc and then drive down
avenue Foch until arriving at the ambassador's leased home just
past avenue Malakoff, the smaller private home that he kept in
addition to his official residence. At no point on that route was the
car ever out of the sight of hundreds of bystanders. The quietest
spot on the entire route was the starting point on the serene avenue
Bosquet.

And it was there, of course, that the kidnapping would have to
take place.

There, Anne and Cynthia would be taken in plain daylight
before scores of other witnesses, before the teachers of the school,
before the other children, and before the parents of the other children. That was why the kidnapping would have to occur quickly
and smoothly. All would have to appear normal. It would have
to occur before hundreds of eyes and yet the escape with the young
hostages would have to be perfect.

If Lieutenant Simmons, for example, reached for his gun at the
moment of the Abduction, he would have to be shot.

'*Voyez*,' said Savard to Guisseny as the black Citroën led them
down the avenue Bosquet and across the old white stone bridge
that was the Pont d'Alma. 'From here it's the same route each

87

day. It's getting so he bores us.'

'Don't follow,' said the Breton. 'There's no need.'

The black Citroën was allowed to disappear across the bridge into Right Bank traffic. The smaller pursuing car turned right on the Quai d'Orsay and the three men returned toward Saint-Germain-des-Prés and the student quarter near the Sorbonne. Although the car passed within a hundred metres of rue Rastignac, the Breton made no mention of the location. It was his secret, his alone. It would be there that the Thatcher children would be hidden and, under the proper circumstances, buried. And because he alone of the three knew of the old underground passages, it would be impossible to trace either him or the children there.

Guisseny asked to be let off on a corner of the rue Saint-Jacques just a few blocks from the Sorbonne. The street, like most streets on the Left Bank, was crowded with cars parked illegally bumper to bumper.

Then the Breton walked east past the Sorbonne for five minutes until he came to the old houses on the rue Rastignac. Had he walked west, he would have seen the zealous youth he knew from several Maoist cell meetings in Paris, Yves Ramereau.

Ramereau had just been thrown out of the small apartment of Françoise Durand for the most recent and most final time. He had barely been accepted back into Françoise's life again when a seventeen-year-old salesgirl at Au Printemps caught his eye. Tossing ideology conveniently aside, Yves's amorous attentions strayed from Françoise for still another time.

This time, Françoise told herself as she screamingly ordered Yves from her apartment, there would be no next time for him. No, this time she would find another man. Yves, she swore would never be allowed in her door or in her bed again. Nor would she again suffer either his literary allusions or his infidelities. This time she would change the locks on her door.

Yet as Yves strolled down the rue des Ecoles with his hands stuffed casually in the side pockets of a tattered corduroy jacket, he only had eyes or thoughts for a leggy young student who pedalled by him on a bicycle. Then, distracted for a moment, his gaze caught a man walking ahead of him on the other side of the street.

Yves recognised the man. André Guisseny.

Ramereau knew better than to say anything or let his presence be known. Instead he discreetly followed.

And, from a distance which lent anonymity to his presence, Ramereau was completely mystified when he saw Guisseny disappear into the ruined old houses on the rue Rastignac.

16

Richard rose late. He sat in his hotel room and pondered the idea of finding the Imp. He looked at the silent telephone.

Richard remembered a time in his life when the concept of murder had appalled him, back in college, back before his military career. Yet he sat in that hotel room waiting to discover – or decide – if he was to become a hired assassin. For a few moments on a balmy morning he was not certain if he wanted to go on with it. There were things in life beside murder and revenge. Yet there was also the Imp, never far from Richard's thoughts.

Richard winced. He remembered the sickening cracks of the pistol as it expelled the two bullets that ripped into DeMeo's brains, spilling them onto the slimy stinking ground of the outdoor prison. Richard recalled also the real Howard McKiernan.

Richard felt his arm and hand stiffening, not so much in revulsion as in anger. In fury. In hatred. Yes, he would continue in his own way to follow the orders of this organisation in Virginia. He had to. The Imp was an obsession.

It was the last time Richard ever considered turning back.

That afternoon Richard took a long walk. He wandered all the way from his hotel to the traffic circle at Twenty-third Street. Then he walked down Twenty-third Street, affording himself a distant view of the White House on his left and the Kennedy Center on his right. He went as far as the Lincoln Memorial.

Within the monument the huge stone Lincoln sat solemnly and silently, as if in angry contempt for what passed for government in present-day Washington. It flashed into Richard's mind that Lincoln, too, had been shot.

Richard's leg began to hurt. He found a taxi and rode back to the hotel. At seven that evening his telephone rang.

The voice on the telephone bore a southern inflection. Same place. Same time. Richard said he'd be there. They knew who the Imp was.

At ten thirty that evening the same car stopped for Richard at New York Avenue and K Street. Again Richard allowed himself to be blindfolded and driven in the back seat of a car. Within ninety minutes he found himself seated in the same basement. There were fewer men there this time. But those who were there were masked. The same canine-masked man behind a table addressed Richard again.

'Welcome, Mr Silva,' intoned the voice behind the mask. 'I believe the news is good. For both of us.'

'I'm listening,' said Richard.

'There's very little to hear,' said the speaker. 'First you have to look.' The man was lost in a violent uncontrollable cough for several seconds. Then he reached for a file on his desk. He opened it. From it he pulled a sheet of paper which Richard recognised. It was Kelly's drawing of the Imp. The speaker looked at it and then withdrew a photograph, a photograph that Richard couldn't see. Yet it was obvious that the man was comparing the two pictures.

'Please examine this,' said the speaker. 'See if there's anyone in this picture you recognise.'

The speaker handed the photograph to Richard. Richard took it and looked at it. There were several faces, mostly Oriental, in the picture. It was taken at a military installation somewhere and –

Richard's heart suddenly flashed in his throat. He saw what he was meant to see. His tormentor. The Imp. The photo had been taken within a prison camp in the north of Vietnam. There were several men in the picture, mostly Vietnamese. But the European face of the Imp stood out. Richard experienced an odd sensation, a thrill that he had never known before. For the first time, he had something on the Imp. His own heartbeat quickened but he remained outwardly calm.

'That's him,' said Richard, placing the picture down and looking up. 'That's him.' He felt his body tense. His palms, for a moment, were slightly moist.

'We know,' said the speaker.

'Who is he?' asked Richard.

The speaker paused. 'You realise, Mr Silva,' said the speaker, 'that if we give you that information, we expect you to accept our full agreement. We pay you fifteen thousand dollars at intervals to be arranged. In return, you kill two men for us and then one for yourself.'

'Agreed,' said Richard. 'And when the third murder is accomplished I will never see you or hear from you again. I never again even acknowledge that I know you.'

'That would be impossible anyway, Mr Silva,' reminded the speaker. 'You *don't* know us.'

'You have an agreement,' said Richard. 'Let's get on with it.'

'You'll have your weapon, your money, and your passport within a week,' said the speaker. 'And you'll not know the identity of the second victim until after the murder of the first.'

Richard nodded.

'Our photograph of your Imp is courtesy of a Canadian journalist who was allowed inside North Vietnam,' said the speaker. 'He's a publicly proclaimed socialist who obtains visas to the most difficult Communist nations. It's a genuine joy that he sells his pictures and information to a CIA contact in Montreal.'

Richard remained silent. The report and the photograph before the masked speaker had obviously been copied from some government file. Richard did not doubt that it could easily be done.

'I'm waiting to hear a name,' said Richard.

There was a pause. 'Names, Mr Silva, names. Names can be a problem. Your Imp. He's one of four people.'

'You'll have to do better than that,' said Richard. Outwardly calm, his entire body was tense in anxiety and anticipation.

'Patience, Mr Silva. Listen carefully. There is an intelligence dossier in government files about this torturer. It's based primarily on what you and other prisoners have revealed. And it appears that you are correct: the man is probably a European.'

'Get to the point.'

'The point is that a lot of intensive work has been done on this man. Yet no positive identity has been established.'

'Christ,' said Richard. His hands were sweating slightly. It almost scared him how badly he wanted to find and kill this torturer.

'But,' the speaker added quickly, 'a probable identity has been established. The field is down to four probable men. Of those four, as you'll see, one is most likely to be your man.'

'A name,' said Richard.

'You want a name? Try this one. Alphonse Rouen. Born in 1935 in Algiers. Father a French soldier, mother half Berber and half Spanish. His father shipped out with the army soon after he was born. His mother died of cholera when he was five. Grew up in a Catholic orphanage in Oran, which he ran away from in 1950. In and out of trouble with the French colonial police and army through the early fifties. Then joined the Algerian National Liberation Front in 1954. Fought as a guerilla in their war of independence. Loyal originally to Ben Bella but then loyal to the troops that overthrew him in 1965. Moved up in the army when Boumedienne took over. Travelled to Uruguay in 1969 and is believed to have continued on to North Vietnam from South America. That would put him there in 1970, or approximately when you were there.'

'Keep talking,' said Richard.

'He's a specialist in torture from his days in the NLF in Algeria.'

'And what was the name?'

'Alphonse Rouen.'

'Sounds like my man,' said Richard thoughtfully and impatiently.

'Think so?'

'Where is he?'

'Prison,' said the masked man. 'And he has been for a while.'

'Prison where?'

'Think for a moment,' said the speaker. 'When did you see him last? How long before you were released?'

'They didn't give us calendars in Hanoi.'

'Did you keep track of the time some way?'

Richard thought back. Some of the prisoners kept a makeshift calendar on one of the prison walls. There had also been a new prisoner, another airman, who had been brought in just after the Imp had disappeared. He brought with him the latest news from the United States, including the fact that the upstart Oakland Athletics had won the World Series. That meant that the Imp had departed by the mid-point of October 1972.

'Rouen was seen positively in France by the beginning of September of 1972,' said the masked man. 'That might rule him out.'

Richard shook his head. 'The Imp was still there in September.'

'Of course. That's why intelligence is certain that Rouen is not the same man. In any event, Rouen was arrested in France in December of 1972 for an attempted bombing. He's in a prison near Marseilles if you care to visit him. This picture was taken when he was arrested.'

A photograph was handed to Richard, one which had made its way through various channels from French police files to Washington and now – unofficially – to Virginia. Richard took the photograph and looked at it. He saw a small dark face which, despite an added moustache, looked somewhat like the Imp. Somewhat. But not enough.

Richard shook his head. 'That's not him.'

'No one else thinks so, either,' said the speaker. 'Try this one. Victor Andresik.'

'A Czech?'

'A Pole. A French Pole. Born in Warsaw in 1935. His parents moved to France, settling in Toulon. The information is sketchy. Lived in Vichy France with his parents during the war; normal French schooling with no apparent political activism. Andresik eventually served in the French army as a paratrooper. He was stationed in Algeria but was apparently loyal to the government when Algeria was granted independence in 1961. In any case, he returned to France with the army and went into police work, then intelligence work. He wouldn't even be considered here except for two factors.'

'Go ahead,' said Richard.

'He's a skilled interrogator, a *very* skilled interrogator. His sympathies are definitely not pro-American, either.'

'And?'

'And he was in North Vietnam at the same time as you.'

Richard nodded. 'Is there a picture?'

There wasn't. There was only a description that could or couldn't have fitted the Imp.

'He returned to France from Vietnam in November of 1972. That part fits. Want to hear the rest?'

'Why not?'

'Know where he is now?'

'Would I be sitting here if I did?'

'You can find him in the de Siblas cemetery in the town of Toulon. He's buried there.'

'Dead?' asked Richard, surprised.

'Well, he wouldn't be buried alive, I suppose. He died in a car crash along the Grande Corniche outside of Nice in December of

1972. Or so we're told, although the information seems fairly sound.'

'So you've got two others?' asked Richard.

'Kebal Adnanay. This one's a Turk transplanted to the Orient. A Marxist all his life, born in Smyrna in 1942. That might make him too young to be your man. There's a picture.'

The masked man handed Richard a photograph. Again a resemblance to the Imp. A close resemblance, a very close one. The picture was blurred, however, and showed Adnanay in 1966.

'A dedicated man. He disappeared some time ago and is very much wanted by his own government. He was involved in some left-wing labour disturbances among Turkish dock workers. Later left the country, going first to Egypt, then to Italy and then, it's believed, to Albania. Then off to China. Speaks French and is predictably anti-American. No military experience, so we don't know whether he's a torturer or interrogator or not. In short, he's a wild card, a question mark. We are, however, certain that he's still in China. He could have been to Vietnam and back, but we just don't know.'

Richard studied the picture.

'The man I had was older,' he said, 'And the man I had was a European, not a Turk.'

'Europeans, Turks same goddamned thing when they're Reds. It leaves one man. This one is the one you want.'

'Talk,' said Richard.

'We know a lot about this one. We can practically give you street directions to find him.'

'Why is he the right man?'

'Make up your own mind, Mr Silva,' said the masked man. 'But remember we wouldn't have brought you here for nothing. We have to fulfil our part of the bargain so that you'll fulfil the second, and the most important part.'

'Keep going.'

'This would appear to be your Imp, Mr Silva. His name is André Guisseny. Born in 1936 in Brittany in a town called Morlaix just outside of Brest. Marxist family. Marxist education. A union organiser in his late teens and early twenties. A revolutionary fanatic who for many years has been trying to spark some life into a Breton independence movement.'

'A what?'

'You know France. The usual left-wing factionalism and bickering. The people in Brittany, or some of them at least, fancy that they'd be better off as an independent country.'

Richard almost frowned. 'Like a Free Quebec movement?'

'Similar,' said the speaker. 'But with even less popular support. The movement is ignored by almost everyone except those who are in it. And like most movements, it has its handful of fanatics.'

'Continue,' said Richard.

'André Guisseny is very much dedicated to revolution all around the world, from Brittany to Africa. He studied in Moscow and later still was a mercenary for Lumumba in Africa. Later in Cuba and Bolivia. The Red grand circuit you might call it.'

'Any more?' asked Richard.

'Studied guerilla warfare and interrogation techniques in Moscow and perfected his lessons in field armies in South America. The Breton movement may sound half-baked to you, but it's serious stuff to him. This is what he thinks he's training for. No pictures, just descriptions and sketches.'

'When was he in Vietnam?'

'From late 1969 to late 1972,' said the masked man. 'We don't know what he was doing there. Perhaps you might have more insight into that than I.'

Richard paused for a moment, pressing his palm against his chin in concentration. 'And he speaks French, I assume?'

'With a regional accent that often makes him almost sound foreign to other Frenchmen. He's a European Marxist and he's one of the best free-lance torture specialists in their half of the world.'

'And what's the conclusion of the report?' Richard asked.

'This is your man, Mr Silva,' said the speaker. 'This is your Imp.'

Richard studied again the photograph he'd been handed earlier. There was no mistaking that face. Richard thought. According to the only intelligence work that existed on this subject – the intelligence work of his own government, he assumed – Rouen, Andresik and Adnanay were either unlikely, impossible, or both. Yet with Guisseny everything seemed right. Age, description, time in Vietnam, parentage and background.

'Where is he?' Richard asked.

'That,' said the masked man, 'is something that will be revealed after your first job is complete. He's in France and easily accessible. You'll be able to track him down and get close enough for both a look and a shot . . . if that's your pleasure.'

Richard pondered again for a moment. 'In other words, you won't assure me of anything.'

The speaker closed the file. 'The weight of evidence would point strongly to this man, this Guisseny. I'll put it to you frankly, Mr Silva. You started out on a mission of revenge, one with which we fully sympathise. This is as close as you'll ever get. If this Guisseny is not your man, you will never *ever* find your man.' The speaker paused to let his words sink in. 'Nor,' he added, 'is it likely that you will ever again find any group or organisation willing to offer the assistance we're offering.'

'How long do I have to decide?' asked Richard.

'You have right now, Mr Silva. You're either interested or you're not.'

Richard searched those shrouded faces in the room, those anonymous faces hiding in righteous secrecy behind the masks of children. Richard despised those faces without seeing them. These people wanted a hired assassin. They cared nothing for him, only for seeing their own missions accomplished. These were men with access to power and access to money. Now they wanted a hired gun who couldn't be traced. Richard searched those eyes in the thick silence of the room.

He could picture a pistol firing. He could see the head of William DeMeo split with a bullet. He could see that beautiful man's brains and life spilling out.

Richard glanced back at the file. And then at the picture of the Imp, the face that looked so much like Sergeant Kelly's drawing.

And he looked back to the eyes behind the wolf's mask.

'Well?' the man asked. 'Take it or leave it.'

Richard spoke.

'I'll take it,' he said softly.

There were masked smiles around the room.

'In that case, Mr Silva,' said the leader, 'we should turn to the first of your two assignments.' There was a pause. Then the masked man asked, 'Do you know the name Clifford Craig?'

Part Two

17

The details of Richard's first assignment were simple enough.

He remained in Washington for several more days. A Canadian passport, press card, and driver's licence were forged for him in the name of Howard McKiernan. He didn't ask from where the documents came. Nor did he care. He knew he was dealing with people who were powerful.

But how deeply their government connections ran was a matter Richard could only ponder. He did not like dealing with them and he did not relish what he was going to have to do. But the Imp remained a cancerous mental image.

Richard received his passport, press card, and driver's licence in a package left at the hotel. A day later another heavier package appeared. Richard knew what it was before he opened it.

He returned to his room with the second package and wedged the top of a straight-back chair firmly beneath the door knob in his room so that no one could walk in on him. Then he opened the package.

From the wrappings he pulled a black pistol, a 9 mm Walther PPK, an instrument designed perfectly for one use: shooting human beings. Richard found a silencer in the same package. He clamped it onto the nose of the pistol and then gripped the weapon in his hand, weighing it. Through his days in the air force he was no stranger to hand weapons; he was in fact an excellent shot. He admired the intricate workmanship and the coldly efficient mechanism of the German pistol. Fairly or unfairly, Richard had always felt that the Germans were experts at execution. Not that he objected. Not now. Several boxes of bullets were included in the package.

The serial number of the pistol had been filed off; tracing the pistol, should it ever fall into police hands, would be difficult. A professional filing job. Richard noted with a knowing smile. So much less to worry about.

There would, of course, be a matter of another gun, the one in France where he would probably be bound next in his pursuit of the Imp. That matter, too, was apparently taken care of. Richard had been given two addresses in Paris of men – professional men of still another order – whom he could see about purchasing a pistol. Richard memorised the names and addresses and destroyed the original slip of paper. He kept the names and addresses in coded form, however, in a blue note pad with which he always travelled.

Richard also had in his possession now a manilla envelope that contained extensive notes and clippings on the man Richard was assigned to murder, Clifford Craig. Richard was able to read of his victim's habits, lifestyle, tastes, and choices of friends and causes. Essential reading for any intelligent hired assassin.

Then there had been the subject of Richard's payment. The organisation argued for three payments, one after each job. Richard, reminding his new employers of their own statement that his body was his collateral, argued for one flat payment of fifteen thousand dollars. Richard argued long and hard. And vainly. A compromise was struck. Richard was to receive eight thousand dollars before the first hit and seven thousand upon making the second. What he did on his own time with his own project was his own problem.

So Richard waited until a third package was delivered to the hotel. This box contained nothing but cash, eight thousand dollars in unconsecutive, previously circulated tens, twenties, fifties, and hundreds.

There was one final detail: the information on where to find the Imp. This essential item was to be given to Richard along with the name of the second victim, after the shooting of Craig.

A key link in this first assignment, however, was a telephone number in New York City, a number that Richard could call each Tuesday and Thursday evening at ten o'clock. The number was a booth somewhere in the city. Richard could call it at the appointed hour on the proper days. On the other end would be a contact, a man who, once convinced that Richard had completed his assignment, would transfer to Richard the information on where to find the Imp. Richard was told that he'd never know whom or where he was calling. But he was free to make the initial contact whenever he wished to.

Richard checked out of the Marriott Inn. He drove north again through Maryland, past Philadelphia and to New York, arriving in the evening past the rush hour. Able to afford any hotel room in the city, he checked into the modest but neat and clean Gilbertson Hotel in the East Forties. He had taken the first step to bring him within pistol range of Clifford Craig.

Richard took no chances with the money he'd been given. On Friday he went from bank to bank, changing most of the smaller bills into hundreds. Then he entered a large First National City in mid-town and rented a safe deposit box. There he hid all his cash except for three hundred dollars. He hid, too, his pistol and a few boxes of bullets. The rest of his ammunition he kept in the trunk of his car. In turn the car was kept in the hotel garage. With the pistol and the money safely stored, fewer things could go wrong.

On a mild Saturday afternoon, Richard left his hotel room and walked through Manhattan. He wandered up Madison Avenue to the Fifties. He was ever conscious of the buoyant shoppers and strollers around him. They, and the bright store windows, welcomed the advent of spring. It was what people like to call a beautiful spring Saturday in New York.

Within this atmosphere, Richard considered murder. The murder of Clifford Craig, a man who'd done nothing to him. Richard had been armed for just that assignment and had verbally committed himself to the task. Yet now Richard considered the implications of pulling a trigger against a man whom, in a peacetime situation, he had nothing against.

Richard could kill a thousand Imps with no remorse. But an innocent Craig? He wondered.

Yet Craig was the vital inescapable link between Richard and the Imp's location. When Richard examined the situation from all angles there was very little choice.

He would shoot Craig. He had to. But he would do it his way.

A cab driver leaned on a horn at Madison and Fifty-fourth. The green walk sign exploded into a flashing red. Blood spurted from Captain William DeMeo's head. The Imp was back. So was Clifford Craig. So was the crowd along Madison.

The crowd. Craig had to be shot in a crowd. Of course. That

was it. What had Richard read about Craig? Something began to surface.

A crowd. The Philharmonic. Lincoln Center. Of course. Of course!

Two minutes later Richard turned into an optics store on Madison. He purchased an excellent small pair of high-powered binoculars. Now everything began to fit into place. Richard knew how and where. The question was when.

Richard's lonely mission continued through that Saturday night and through Sunday. He studied the clipping file on Craig. He reread a small, almost overlooked item from a New York *Post* column.

Clifford Craig, one of this city's genuine classical music enthusiasts, was among the first-nighters at the Philharmonic's new season. The former newsman and his wife never miss an important Philharmonic event. Betty Craig wore a red St Laurent gown which turned heads from the orchestra to the family circle. Mr Craig is currently turning heads in local Democratic circles with his unsecret desires to run for the U.S. Senate against Robert Armellin next year. Will city pols march to Cliff's tune? Smart money says yes.

Richard looked briskly through the theatre section of the Sunday *Times* until he found a Philharmonic schedule. Was it overstated how often Clifford Craig attended concerts? There was a Tuesday evening performance approaching with Bernstein making an appearance as the guest conductor. Though late in the season, it was an affair not to be missed by the Philharmonic's hard-core followers. Would Craig be there? On May 8? It was worth the gamble.

On Monday Richard went by the box office at Lincoln Center and purchased the cheapest of the few remaining tickets for Tuesday evening of the following week. Then he also took the occasion to examine the layout around the concert hall, where he might escape to if necessary, where he might fire from if he indeed had a shot. Meticulously he took mental pictures of the seating diagrams. He figured he could be accurate with the pistol up to ten yards, not much more. A shot at longer range could be off enough to ruin everything. Richard's shot – and he would get no more than one – would have to be accurate.

On Monday afternoon Richard returned to his hotel. A certain restlessness, loneliness, and anxiety was beginning to possess him. He began to feel the need to move from where he was, even at the expense of returning to Massachusetts to walk along the windy beach, bad leg and all. It was nearly May. The Cape was getting ready to open for the season, bracing itself for the warm weather influx.

Richard picked up the telephone in his hotel room. He dialled the business office of New York Telephone. He readied himself to sound as convincing as possible while telling a lie.

He asked for and was put through to a supervisor in charge of billing. Richard began to speak.

'My name is McKiernan,' said Richard, 'and I'm the reservations manager for the Goshen Hotel in San Diego, California.'

'Yes, sir?' she asked.

'What I'm calling about may seem a trifle odd,' Richard began. 'But I'm in New York on business and I thought I'd try to settle a certain hotel problem while I'm here.'

There was a pause that meant Richard could continue. It seemed, according to his story, that a number of calls had been made on his hotel's private line to a number in New York. Richard asked if the supervisor might be able to identify the number since the number was not recognised by hotel management.

'Sir, your local San Diego company can do that for you,' said the voice.

'Well, I'm afraid that hasn't worked,' said Richard. 'I've asked the local people to check on this and, well, I'm afraid they haven't been very speedy about it.'

'I'm sure if you remind them, sir,' the voice continued.

'What was your name again?' Richard asked.

'Mrs MacAndrew,' she said.

'And you're a supervisor?' Richard asked again. His voice was polite but increasingly firm.

'That's right,' she said.

'Are you at the offices at 140 West Street?'

'I am,' she answered.

'Perhaps I could come in and discuss this in person,' Richard said. 'I really can't stress the urgency involved here and, frankly, I'd just as soon not have this channelled through my San Diego office. The fact is that whoever made these calls probably works in my office. I might never receive your report.'

There was a peeved silence. Richard knew he was winning.

'Or perhaps,' Richard added, 'if this is beyond your capacity you might connect me with your superior.'

Again a silence. 'What was the number?' she asked.

Richard gave the number of his New York contact, the number of the anonymous telephone booth. He was asked to hold the line.

Two minutes went by. Then the woman's voice returned. 'Mr McKiernan?'

'Yes?'

'That number is in Brooklyn. A telephone booth.'

'I see,' he said. 'At what address?'

'I wouldn't know that without checking further,' she said. 'That's really all I can – '

'Mrs MacAndrew,' said Richard, 'this really could put us both to a lot of trouble. I could get a lawyer and a court order and cause the company a lot of complications about this. Or I could ask you to check further and call me back. I have a number in the city for the next few days.'

Mrs MacAndrew was far from enthusiastic. But she agreed. Richard left his false name and his room extension number. By charm, force, and persuasiveness, Richard got the woman to agree to check further and return his call.

Monday afternoon passed. On Monday evening Richard took the subway down to Bleecker Street and wandered through Greenwich Village.

On Tuesday morning, Mrs MacAndrew called back. More surprisingly, she was helpful. The number Richard had given was a telephone booth in south Brooklyn not far from the waterfront. Fifty-third Street and Second Avenue. Richard noted the location.

That afternoon he drove out to the area and examined it. The neighbourhood consisted of several shabby warehouses and was cluttered with endless battered or gutted cars. A poor Italian section was nearby. Richard made a call from the telephone booth and checked the phone number in the process. It was the same. It was from here, in this area that was so desolate by night, that his contact would come for any prospective telephone calls.

Richard examined the area for other telephone booths. He found none. The telephone company knew that almost any public pay phone in the area would be vandalised. Only this one booth, in the shadow of an abandoned shuttered bar but in the glare of a street light, remained. And even it had all its glass panes kicked out.

That same afternoon Richard returned to Manhattan. He went to the First National City Bank where his safe deposit box was.

He took with him a cloth portfolio case. He asked to be admitted to his deposit box and then was led to a private booth where he could examine its contents.

He removed five hundred dollars more from the cash, folding five hundreds into his wallet. Then he withdrew the pistol and tucked it into the cloth case. He withdrew one box of bullets and placed that in the cloth case with the gun. Then he returned the closed box to the bank. On his way out he cashed two of the hundreds into tens and twenties.

That evening at eight thirty, Richard again wedged a chair beneath the door knob of his room. He loaded his pistol, clicked the silencer into place, and made certain that the safety catch was securely in place. Then he carefully tucked the gun into his folio case. Taking his newly purchased binoculars with him, he went out again to his car, took it from the hotel garage, and drove southward down Manhattan. He followed the FDR Drive to where it merged with the Brooklyn Battery Tunnel.

He drove to Brooklyn, retracing his steps from the same afternoon. He drove his car with its Massachusetts licence plates to the second exit of the Gowanus Expressway. Then he followed Second Avenue past that telephone booth and beyond. The area was deserted. Not partially deserted, completely deserted.

Richard parked his car on Fifty-sixth Street, three blocks from that telephone booth. He stayed where he could just see the booth. Then he took out his binoculars and watched. And he waited.

He kept an alert eye open for any movement in the shadows near him. His gun was ready if necessary, the safety catch now off. His sixth sense – the survival sense that a man develops under combat and never altogether loses – was alert to any unpredictable or sudden danger. Richard hated this area. He hated it almost as much as he despised the masked cowards in Virginia with whom he was forced to play lethal games.

He looked at the clock in the car. Nine fifteen. He would have to be patient.

Thirty-two minutes later on that Tuesday night a car turned left off Second Avenue and pulled to a halt next to the telephone booth. No one came or went from that car. Its headlights were extinguished immediately.

Richard focused the binoculars but still couldn't see as well as he wanted to. He saw only a man sitting in the car, sitting in the car parked just a few feet from the booth.

The man was waiting.

The man was Richard's contact.

This man knew where Richard could find the Imp. This man was in possession of the information that Richard wanted so badly that he'd hired himself out as a political assassin.

Richard watched through the binoculars. He reached to the pistol next to him, reassuring himself that it was still there. Richard felt his pulse quicken.

It was almost ten o'clock.

He watched. He waited. Richard was excellent at waiting.

18

On December 12, 1969, beneath the grey ever-changing skies of Brittany, the seacoast town of Brest was rocked by a devastating explosion, the force of which had been unknown to the city since the last days of World War II.

Parked just outside the gendarmerie at Porte Touville was a white Volkswagen bearing Breton licence plates. At 3.37 on that cold afternoon a timing mechanism beneath the car flashed a charge to six closely bound sticks of dynamite. The auto erupted with an overpowering force that blew parts of the car for several metres in every direction, shattering windows and demolishing other nearby cars. Work thudded to a halt at the nearby *arsenal maritime*, the massive French navy yard in Brest harbour.

The lethal force of the explosion would have resulted in mass deaths had the car exploded within a crowd. As it happened the area was almost void of pedestrians when the bomb beneath the car was triggered. Five people suffered superficial cuts. Three people, one of whom lost an eye, were hurt seriously enough to require hospitalisation. And one police patrolman had the misfortune to be leaving the gendarmerie at the precise moment of the explosion. He was killed instantly.

The national outrage that followed the explosion damned modern terrorism and its disregard for human life. But the fire that ignited that fuse beneath the car had been kindled not by modern political extremism but by an aged conflict within France – a conflict downplayed by the French government and often met with smiles outside the départements of Finistère, Morbihan, and Côtes-du-Nord.

The cause is Breton autonomy. And within the jagged rocky coasts, the rolling plateaux, the moors, and the forests of the Breton peninsula, the cause is no laughing matter.

Ever since the Celts were driven down from Britain in the fifth century by the Angles and the Saxons, the population of Brittany – which derives its name from the Celtic for 'little Britain' – has been predominantly Celtic. And these Celtic people, for the last fifteen centuries a population within a larger population, continue even today a historical and occasionally bitter fight for independence.

The Bretons struggled first with the Franks and then with the dukes of Normandy and the counts of Anjou; later, inevitably, with the English before formal incorporation into France in 1532.

The sentiment for separatism among the Celtic people never completely disappeared. Nor did the Celtic language. Approximately 2,600,000 people inhabit Brittany today, a population equal to that of Paris. One million of them speak Breton, particularly in the *Basse-Bretagne* region, the westernmost tip of France. The language survives despite the fact that it officially does not exist, and is rarely read or written. It bears no relation to French. Oddly, a Welshman from the other side of the channel would have little trouble understanding Breton. In more ways than one, Frenchmen have never understood Bretons.

The Celtic regions of Brittany have been historically ignored by the rest of France. Despite the fact that the Bretons have borne terrible burdens in all of France's major wars, the province changed little between the time of Louis XIV and the advent of the twentieth century. Bretons never felt that they were part of the larger nation. Many Frenchmen shared this view. And, through the twentieth century, the notion persisted that Bretons – like the French in Canada, the Basques in Spain, and the Welsh and the Scottish in Great Britain – were the ignored stepchildren of the mother country. The more radical Bretons compared themselves freely to the other peoples colonialised by the French, the people of Algeria, Indo-China, Tunisia, Morocco, and Madagascar. And even moderate Bretons placed on their cars not the white oval plate with the black F to signify France as their country of origin, but rather a plate with the letters BZH, standing for *Breizh*, the Breton name for Brittany.

In 1965 a Dublin-based organisation called the Celtic League filed a document with the United Nations Subcommission for the Protection of Minorities. The paper pleaded for UN protection for the rights of autonomy and self-determination for Celtic people within England, Scotland, and, in particular, France. Other Breton nationalists tired of the more traditional channels of grievance. So in the 1960s two underground organisations appeared. One called itself the Armée Républicaine Bretonne (ARB). The other, which often overlapped the first in membership, called itself the Front de Libération de la Bretagne (FLB).

Although not nearly as prone to mindless terror as other liberation fronts or republican armies, these groups and other smaller sympathetic groups increasingly turned to random acts of violence throughout Brittany. Targets were anything vaguely governmental, from mail boxes to police prefectures. The movement probably had no more than a handful of zealots who were actually willing to take up arms. But of the approximately 2,600,000 people of Brittany, there were thousands who sympathised with the cause of the ARB and the FLB.

Among the more serious of the attacks on government installations was the bombing of the Volkswagen in front of the gendarmerie in December of 1969. Several people were hospitalised and one man was dead. This was an act that the French government, ever conscious of its honour, could not ignore. An intensive investigation eventually led to a group of young Breton nationalists who had manufactured the dynamite bomb and planted it.

Eight young men were arrested and convicted. They were eight French citizens, ranging in ages from seventeen to twenty-eight, with distinctly Franco-Breton names: Claude Kerjean, Malo Kertanguay, Pierre Locronon, André Trendez, Paul Mariaquer, Yves Quemeneur, Robert Cudenec, and Jean Le Barazer. Seven, through varying degrees of involvement drew sentences ranging from fifteen years to life. The eighth, Le Barazer, received four years for knowing about the bomb and doing nothing to alert the police.

The stiff prison terms handed out to these seemingly misguided but well-intentioned youths only worsened the nationalistic turmoil in Brittany. Rumours circulated that some of the principal Bretons involved in the bombing had escaped capture and detection altogether. Like good soldiers, so the stories went, the eight arrested youths had not revealed the names or positions of their commanding officers.

The stories were true. One of those to escape capture and detection immediately left France after the arrests began. He travelled abroad extensively, including a trip to Southeast Asia and Vietnam. Then he returned to France as a Marxist labour organiser, living in Paris and active in several leftist organisations. His name was André Guisseny.

19

Ten minutes past ten. The streets still dark and vacant. Richard stared through binoculars at the long American car three blocks away.

Then Richard saw the car's headlights go on. Seconds later the driver, tired of waiting before a silent telephone booth, backed the car onto Second Avenue.

Richard clicked the safety catch on the pistol and slipped the weapon back into the folio. As the distant car pulled just out of sight, Richard started the motor to his car. Then he turned the corner onto Second Avenue, leaving his own headlights off.

He would follow. And it was essential that he should not be seen.

As he turned the corner he saw the other car, three blocks ahead, moving toward the Brooklyn-Queens Expressway. Still at a distance through those forebodingly quiet streets, Richard kept safely back until the other car led him onto the expressway. Then Richard clicked on the lights of his own vehicle and pulled onto the same ramp.

The other car led him northward for several minutes to Queens from Brooklyn. Richard maintained a constant, cautious distance. He waited until the lead car flashed a right-turn signal. Richard drew just close enough to distinguish the licence number of the car. Then he dropped back again and followed. He was led across Queens Boulevard to Astoria.

Then across Astoria Boulevard. Traffic was thinner. Trailing would be tricky if the other driver paid any attention to his rear-view mirror. Like most drivers, he didn't.

8

The green sedan led Richard to a residential working class neighbourhood in Astoria, a street of conservative, modest two-family homes, the type of houses that people in Manhattan and New Canaan tell jokes about. Then the lead car, which Richard now recognised as a Pontiac, pulled into a parking place.

Immediately Richard halted his car at a light. He turned the next corner. He pulled into the first empty parking place by the side of the road. He moved quickly out of his car, jamming his pistol into his belt beneath his jacket, and walked quickly to the corner.

A man had stepped out of the Pontiac and was locking the car door.

The man was thick with a stomach that no doubt was no stranger to Queens taprooms. The man walked slowly to the two-storey house before which the car was parked. He did not look around, convincing Richard that the man had no idea he'd been followed. Richard watched as the man disappeared into the house.

It was ten forty-five. Richard looked at his watch. He wondered where the man had led him.

Richard returned to his own car and eased it quietly out of its parking place. Then he circled the block to find a better parking place in a more shaded area. He scanned the windows of the neighbourhood. Gradually downstairs lights were extinguished. Upstairs lights went on. Richard contemplated what it might be like to be married and have a job.

He chose a parking place that, he thought, would be relatively free of notice but would allow him to watch the Pontiac and the house. Richard sat and waited. Captivity teaches patience to a man. Richard had learned his lesson well. Gradually upstairs lights went off. It was one o'clock. The green car hadn't moved.

Richard waited ten more minutes, then put on a pair of light gloves. Then he got out of his car, this time leaving the pistol in the glove compartment.

He walked down the block to where the green car was parked. His limp bothered him slightly. He saw no one. With a gloved hand he picked up a large stone. He neared the Pontiac and stopped next to the small side window on the passenger side of the front seat.

He pressed one hand against that small side window to muffle the sound of what was to follow. Then with his other hand he slammed the rock against the glass. The pane crumpled quietly. Richard pushed the rest of it in and, working quickly, opened the car door.

Immediately he reached to the car's glove compartment. The owner of the car had made things easy. The glove compartment was unlocked and yielded a small billfold. Richard glanced inside it and saw that it held the car's registration papers. Glancing around to assure himself that he was still unobserved, Richard looked at the registration.

Herbert Lillis, 15–74 34th Street, Astoria.

It was the address at which the car was parked. The man, the driver, had surely been Lillis. The New York contact. Richard smiled. Other papers in the car bore the same name. Included were a few pieces of junk mail and an unpaid traffic ticket. The ticket was a month old.

'Damned scofflaw,' Richard muttered. Then he examined a couple of other scraps of papers. They were stubs from paychecks made out to Lillis from the New York City Fire Department. Lillis was a fireman. Richard noted the engine and firehouse number.

'Damned redneck smoke-eater,' mumbled Richard to himself. 'No respect for the law,' Then he returned everything to where he'd found it. He left the car and even locked the door, moving quickly away, knowing that Lillis would, on seeing the broken window and finding nothing missing, angrily chalk up the incident to vandals. It was past one thirty when Richard crossed the Queensborough Bridge and headed not towards his hotel but towards the East Sixties. There could be no harm, he reasoned, in scouting the area around Clifford Craig's home.

Richard, still pleased with the ease with which he'd found out the identity of his New York contact, circled that block of Sixty-seventh Street three times – paying particular attention to the building of Clifford Craig – before noticing that there was an embassy on that block. And that in front of the embassy were two police officers in an unmarked car.

Vecchio, from the years he'd spent in the Boston Navy Yard, had come away convinced that the only thing worse than a bad New York driver was a good Massachusetts driver. Thus when Richard's car with its Massachusetts plates crossed that block for the third time in five minutes, Vecchio watched it with more than token interest.

'Massachusetts,' grunted Vecchio. 'He's probably looking for the Brooklyn Bridge.'

'Why don't you go try to sell it to him,' suggested Lamont.

'Don't think I wouldn't like to,' said Vecchio. And the two cops silently watched Richard's car move to the end of the block for a third time. Then Richard, angry at himself for not having seen the police sooner, drove straight across Sixty-seventh until he turned and disappeared a block and a half away down Fifth Avenue.

'What the hell was he so interested in on this block?' Vecchio asked.

'Maybe he wanted a parking place,' said Lamont.

'Like hell he did,' said Vecchio. 'Look. There's not a single legal place on this block. He had to see that the first time he drove through. But he came through three times.'

'So maybe he's stupid,' yawned Lamont.

'Stupid, my grandmother's ass,' snorted Vecchio. 'He was looking at that number twenty-six building for something. Then he noticed us and he took off.'

'You sure are lucky to get so much to worry about,' said Lamont.

'Aah, go back to sleep, you turd,' grumbled Vecchio. But he wasn't ready to let the matter go. His imagination was at it again, wondering what a passer-by may or may not have been doing. When Richard didn't appear again that night Vecchio was ready to put the incident on hold. But just in case he ever thought he saw the same car again and wanted to be sure, he scribbled the licence number on the back of an envelope. Then, remembering that Theresia Hauser had entered her building with a man an hour earlier, Vecchio looked up to see if her light was still on. It wasn't. He felt a twinge of jealousy.

20

Guisseny met for a final time with Savard and Klemeur. The three discussed maps of their various routes of escape should things not go well on the avenue Bosquet. Despite the fact that Bill Simmons's guard might be relaxed, the three conspirators knew they were dealing with an experienced armed guard. Anything could happen.

They studied where Mrs Thatcher's car parked each day and they were aware of how she habitually walked out of her car to meet her two young daughters. Equally, they were aware that William Simmons usually stood at the car door with his back towards the north of Paris. Human beings are creatures of habit. And human habits create fatal human errors.

Guisseny pointed on a map to a railroad warehouse located on the rue des Poissonniers up near the port de Clignancourt in the Eighteenth Arrondissement. The warehouse, belonging to the Société Nationale des Chemins de Fer Français, was complete with a chain fence that didn't work, a few windows that had fallen victim to rocks, and a lock that worked perfectly when turned by a key provided by Klemeur, a former SNCF union foreman.

On Friday the eleventh of May the three covered for a final time each man's responsibility. Each was to carry a small pistol and an ether-soaked rag. Two cars, an intermediate-sized Renault and a similar sized Peugeot, had been stolen for the occasion. The Renault would be the car used at the avenue Bosquet. The Peugeot had already been hidden in the old railroad warehouse where it would not be used until the following Monday.

In the meantime, each man would dye his hair and perhaps add a false moustache to his appearance. Each in his mind would go over and over the plans for that Thursday. If everything went as planned Barbara Thatcher and her children would be helpless. Bill Simmons would never live to know what hit him.

21

On Thursday evening, May 3, Richard drove to a different telephone booth in Brooklyn. He had selected it for its proximity to the access point of the Brooklyn-Queens Expressway that the green Pontiac had taken the previous Tuesday. From this booth Richard could speak to Lillis, then wait for his car.

Tonight Richard would make his contact. And tonight Richard would assure himself that it was indeed Herbert Lillis he was speaking to.

At ten o'clock precisely Richard telephoned the number of his New York contact. The phone rang twice before being answered. The man answering knew who Richard was and knew why he was calling.

His voice on the other end was abrupt to the point of rudeness. He reminded Richard that no information about the Imp, the man said to be André Guisseny, would be forthcoming until Craig had been shot dead. The man was about to hang up on Richard.

'Now listen to me,' said Richard, 'and listen very carefully. There's an excellent chance that the hit will be made next Tuesday night. I can't guarantee the time but I'm going to want my information immediately afterwards.'

'I'm supposed to wait till I hear that he's dead,' the voice repeated.

'I'm aware of your instructions,' said Richard. 'But I want you to be by that telephone all night next Tuesday. Can you do that?'

The man on the other end agreed that he could.

'And I want you to be near a radio,' said Richard. 'I want you to listen to the all-news stations. There are two in New York. Do you think you can sit and listen without fucking things up?'

Again the voice grunted affirmatively.

'I'll be making the hit some time between seven thirty and midnight,' said Richard. 'You can hear it on the radio for yourself.'

'How do you know it'll be covered?'

'I'll worry about that,' said Richard. 'Just do what I say. I'm making sure that everything goes perfectly. Understand?'

Lillis understood. Richard sat in his car and watched the access ramp to the expressway. He waited until he saw the green Pontiac from the other night. Richard followed again, trailing all the way to Queens until the Pontiac led him to exactly the same parking place. Then Richard circled back to Manhattan. Now all Richard needed was Clifford Craig's presence at Lincoln Centre.

On the next day Richard returned to the First National City branch where he kept his money, taking out enough to pay his hotel bill in cash. Then he checked out of the hotel and drove northward to Massachusetts. He arrived at his sister's house in the middle of the afternoon. He warded off all questions from his sister. Downes himself knew better than to ask. Richard announced only that he was accepting a government assignment of which he couldn't speak. He would be leaving soon again, this time for a few months. Downes was visibly pleased.

On Saturday Richard disappeared again for the afternoon. He drove down the Cape until he came to a completely isolated area of the national seashore. He brought with him the Walther, the silencer, several boxes of ammunition, and a bag of empty tin cans. The wind across the dunes was still cold and the sky was a greyish blue.

Richard parked his car near an empty bicycle path and then walked to a desolate area of scrub pines among the sand dunes. When he was convinced that he was alone he put the pistol together, loaded it, and marked a spot on the ground.

He stepped off fifteen metres towards a clump of trees. Then from the bag he withdrew several empty cans, targets of five inches by three inches, roughly the area of flesh which Richard would have to hit. During his military service such a target at fifteen metres would have created no problem.

He set up the cans across the lower limbs of a scrub pine. Then he stepped back across those fifteen metres, returning to the spot he'd marked on the ground.

He removed his coat and folded it over his shooting hand in

a manner that concealed the pistol but allowed him freedom to shoot.

He held the pistol and squeezed the trigger slowly. When the pistol erupted, the kick of the gun came as a surprise, as it always does with an able marksman. The first tin can jumped from the tree limb. Richard turned his attention to the next four.

His second shot missed completely. Then, steadily, he removed the next four cans with five more shots. He reloaded the pistol and set up the cans again.

He continued for an hour. Finally he could pick off five cans with five shots. He backed up another ten metres and remained reasonably accurate.

On Sunday Richard repeated the procedure in a different deserted area of the dunes. Satisfied that he'd regained his lethal talent with a pistol, he sat down beneath one of the pines and cleaned the weapon, carefully protecting it from the sand and wind.

Richard returned by bus to New York on Monday. He checked into the Hotel Griffen on Lexington Avenue near Grand Central Station. He paid in advance for two nights. He carried little baggage and his same battered trenchcoat. On Tuesday he drew all his money out of the bank. Later that afternoon he rented a car and telephoned Air France to reserve a place on a Montreal to Paris flight for the following Thursday.

Then he made the most important call of the day, the one upon which all other plans hinged. He telephoned the office of Clifford Craig and, passing himself off as a Canadian journalist, asked if Craig might be available for an interview that evening. A secretary informed Richard that Craig had a prior social engagement.

'Oh,' asked Richard, 'then will I see him at the Philharmonic?'

The secretary hesitated enough to reveal to Richard that the answer was yes.

22

The interior minister of the French Republic presides over, among other things, a labyrinthine and sophisticated system of governmental intelligence networks. Some are excellent. Others are renowned for their leakiness. One English intelligence agent once commented that the three best ways to transform a secret into common knowledge were television, telephone, and tell a Frenchman.

Minister Renaud de Gaubert, interior minister in 1973, presided over this network of intelligence units from his office on the rue des Saussaies directly across from the Elysée Palace, the official residence of the President of the Republic. De Gaubert was aware that each of his units developed special loyalties within themselves. He was equally aware that most units functioned in blissful ignorance of all other units. Yet French intelligence somehow did manage from time to time to redeem itself with some highly efficient work, 'spying' being the dirty word for that work. It was no secret that the effort to watch France's enemies surpassed only the effort to watch France's friends.

France's intelligence units remain busy prowling through the private affairs and businesses of French citizens and foreigners both within and outside of France. Included is a domestic telephone tapping network.

Within these varied units and networks, however, there has always been a certain degree of élitism. The Renseignements Généraux, for example, the General Intelligence unit, which owns dossiers on politicians, Marxist professors, union leaders, writers, and other 'questionable' private citizens, is directly outranked by a bureau known simply as the DST. That bureau's full name, which is always written and rarely said, is the Direction de la Surveillance du Territoire. And it is headed by a career administrator named Jean-Claude Belfont.

The DST is the closest thing France has to a counter-espionage unit. As its name implies, it keeps the so-called internal security of France under constant surveillance. At airports, docks, customs points and border crossings as well as in *boîtes de nuit* and hotel bedrooms, the DST keeps tabs on those whom it considers undesirable. Anyone associating with those under scrutiny often becomes undesirable also, by a form of political osmosis.

But out-ranking both the Renseignements Généraux and the DST is the French Secret Service. Its agents, scattered around France and the world, engage in the most delicate missions of the French government. They are directly responsible to the minister of the interior who, in turn, is responsible to the President of the Republic for their actions.

During the early part of 1973 the minister of the interior was increasingly alarmed over one particular file on his desk.

The file concerned a Frenchman, possibly one in the employ of his own government, who had been travelling around the world as – among more official duties – a freelance torture specialist.

The man had appeared in various parts of Africa and South America and now most recently had surfaced in Southeast Asia. This was an intrigue that the French government could not allow to continue. Twice within the last few months American intelligence had inquired as to this man's possible identity. And de Gaubert, trying to keep the matter under control, had each time indicated that he did not know who the man was.

And in truth, he didn't.

But what the interior minister wasn't revealing was that he suspected that he – and he alone – did know. De Gaubert had narrowed the possibilities to a single man. Now all de Gaubert had to do was to make one or two key moves – moves that were still to be determined – to trap his suspect. Then the matter, while remaining in French hands, could be settled permanently. No need to involve other governments.

De Gaubert, the eldest son of a genteel Bordeaux wine farmer, looked at that file again, pondering what sort of move to make against this man. What a filthy bunch of people his ministry was constantly forced to deal with, he thought, But, he rationalised, even they had their uses.

23

By Tuesday evening, May 8, Richard had rented a small compact car and had packed his suitcases and left them in his hotel room. He kept all his money on him, mostly in large bills, That evening at six o'clock he left his hotel. He wore a trench coat that, due to the misty spring weather, did not seem out of place.

He carried the Walther, complete with silencer in place, tucked far back into his belt on the left side. He walked from his hotel to the garage where he'd left his car. Then he drove uptown, taking Eighth Avenue north through heavy traffic. Arriving in the vicinity of Lincoln Center within twenty minutes from leaving the hotel, it took several more minutes before he found a free parking meter on one of the cross streets north of Lincoln Center. It was not yet six forty.

Richard walked calmly the two blocks from his car to Philharmonic Hall. His limp was more accentuated now. The hip-bone hurt, as it frequently did in humid weather. But Richard wasn't thinking about his hip. He was thinking about Clifford Craig, the man he had to shoot. What if Richard missed?

He saw Philharmonic Hall on the other side of Broadway. He couldn't allow himself to miss, he told himself. He would have to get Craig even if it meant moving in so close that he could actually touch the man. There was no alternative.

He would recognise Clifford Craig easily. There was simply the matter of getting the proper shot from the proper angle. He walked to the bank of telephones across Sixty-sixth Street from Philharmonic Hall. He dialled the number in Brooklyn.

Lillis answered.

'We're on for tonight,' said Richard. 'You'll be there?'

'For as long as you say,' replied the voice.

The thought flashed through Richard's mind that this whole operation might be a setup of some sort. Would Lillis really have the information he wanted? Richard knew he had no real way to get back at the organisation in Virginia. Lillis and Logan, however, would pay a price for their roles. Logan might even be made to identify the others involved with him at the price of saving his own skin. Richard's mind jumped back to the present.

'Keep your radio on all night and sit tight,' said Richard. 'The chances are I'll be talking to you.'

Again Richard waited. The area around Lincoln Center became increasingly busy as darkness fell. Restaurant lights in reds and yellows were illuminated across Broadway. The traffic grew heavier. Car lights were more frequent. The sky grew darker. Richard watched faces going by him. Then he returned to the entrance area of the Philharmonic. He waited and watched. Clifford Craig and his wife arrived in a Checker cab at seven forty-five.

There was no mistaking that face. Or the voice. Richard was close enough to hear the voice.

Now holding his raincoat over his right arm, Richard reached beneath his jacket, tugging the gun from his belt. At first the gun wouldn't budge, some part of it snagged on his belt. Richard gave a firm tug and the gun came suddenly loose.

He watched Craig. The safety catch was now off the gun; Richard was close enough to shoot and he was ready to shoot. But the shot wasn't there. Not quite yet.

Like a hunter trying to stay downwind of a stag, Richard stalked Craig, watching from the corner of his eye and never moving more than twenty or twenty-five feet away. Richard knew he had only one shot; perhaps two, but only one that he could count on.

Craig approached the doors to the Philharmonic, then stopped, talking to his wife. She drew him away from the door for some reason, then opened her purse.

Mrs Craig drew a cigarette from her purse and lit it. She stood smoking for a minute or two. Richard moved around for position. The pistol was now clearly loose beneath that coat. Loose and ready to fire. Again he circled, moving for position. Craig smoked too.

But the crowd, the crowd that Richard knew was essential, was now Richard's enemy. Oblivious of him, the crowd was now entering Philharmonic Hall at a quicker pace. Little milling around now; people wanted to get to their seats. The path between Richard and Craig – the path that a bullet would have to take – was constantly obstructed by concert-goers. At one point Richard had a completely clear shot. He was even moving his arm – the coat still covering the gun – into position when a blonde woman in her twenties and her escort, a greying urbane man in his fifties – stopped right where the bullet would travel. Had Richard fired the blonde woman would have been hit in the right breast. Richard waited patiently. He moved a few feet to his right. Again, now ten yards from the Craigs, he had a shot. His shot. The *perfect* shot. Again he moved the pistol into position.

But now Mrs Craig stepped in front of her husband, sparing him for the moment. They each snuffed out their cigarettes and as Richard held his fire they stepped into another stream of people. They disappeared inside.

Richard cursed to himself. He clicked the safety catch back onto the pistol. He shoved the gun patiently back into his belt, kept the coat draped over his arm, and followed.

He was only a few feet behind the Craigs as he entered and gave his ticket.

He watched Mr and Mrs Craig and saw where they seated themselves. Then Richard walked to his own seat at the rear of the family circle. He found himself sitting next to a dumpy middle-aged woman who gave him a smile as he glanced at his programme. He smiled back and said nothing. He looked down into the orchestra area and saw Clifford Craig's head. Again he was conscious of the gun in his belt. A few minutes later the lights dimmed and Bernstein made his entrance. Richard waited through a performance of a Haydn symphony and Brahms' Second Piano Concerto.

Applause. Bows. The lights. Enthusiastic voices. Intermission. The Craigs rose from their seats. Again Richard watched. Then he moved quickly down the Philharmonic steps, spotted the Craigs again and followed. They walked outside among the milling crowd. They recognised some people and stopped with them to talk and smoke. Richard looked at his watch. Ten minutes past nine. Lillis damned well better be waiting. Richard had his shot. Now.

Richard turned slightly away from Craig, facing at a forty-five degree angle away from his target. He drew the gun from under his jacket and held it again covered by the draped raincoat. The shot was now so easy that it was embarrassing. He was no more than nine yards away. He was as inconspicuous as the next person in a crowd.

The gun was aimed. The safety off.

Craig was beside his wife. The two of them stood not more than fifty feet from the centre of the glass façade of Philharmonic Hall's south face. There were other clusters of people around Craig, some of whom recognised him. A few people stared, but in the prevailing fashion of Manhattan, no one openly acknowledged his recognition.

Craig dropped the butt of his cigarette and stepped on it with the toe of a well-shined shoe. Richard knew Craig would turn in a moment to return to the concert. For Richard the moment was now or not at all.

Richard fired.

At first there was silence within the din of conversation. Richard, turning away now and walking at a normal pace, heard shouts. He, like everyone else, turned in the direction of the shouts.

Craig was hit. Craig clutched his upper chest below the right shoulder. He staggered. He groped for his wife's lean body but he was falling. Richard's shot had been perfectly on target.

Richard heard Mrs Craig call her huband's name. Then more people started to yell. The man's hand was covering a huge bloodied mark on his upper chest. The blood had already oozed onto the whiteness of his shirt.

'Oh, my God!' someone – Mrs Craig – screamed. 'He's been shot!'

Craig staggered again and went down, clutching his bloodied shoulder. His face was pale and frightened. His wife propped up his head. More screams followed.

Richard had shoved that pistol far back under his belt. It remained hidden. Every instinct told him to turn and run. But he didn't. He remained inconspicuous within the disorder, standing and watching like any other bystander. And yet his body was bathed in sweat. He was terrified that someone might have seen just a flicker of the flash from the pistol. Richard's eyes searched the confused faces around him.

Richard saw two uniformed city policemen. They rushed in Craig's direction, attracted by shouts from where they stood on foot patrol. Richard heard a male voice yelling, 'Shooting, shooting!' Other people were running. The crowd round Craig gave way.

The police approached within twenty yards of Richard. He could feel his wet palms and his pounding heart. Eerily, the Philharmonic was lowering its house lights to call the audience back to the second half of the concert. The Philharmonic wouldn't wait for Clifford Craig. Or for Richard.

Some stragglers stayed and watched, as if transfixed by the sight of a famous man's blood. One cop stood and looked around, particularly upward towards the roofs. The other cop knelt beside Craig, saying something that Craig nodded to in response. Mrs Craig appeared on the verge of panic.

For a moment the standing cop looked directly at Richard. Richard felt his stomach leap, but he didn't flinch. The cop's gaze moved on. Then, like everyone else, Richard turned and walked back toward Philharmonic Hall.

The walk was painfully long. He feared that someone would stop him. No one did. He passed through a side door into the concert hall, then re-emerged from a front door a few seconds later. He never looked back. He calmly crossed Sixty-sixth Street and walked up Broadway.

Moments later he was in his car. Safe, and leaving the scene. He exuded a long loud sigh, relieving the incredible tension. His hands felt shaky on the wheel of the car.

But he had succeeded.

'It had to be done,' Richard kept telling himself. He had to find the Imp. This was the only way. He had winged Clifford Craig perfectly and intentionally.

Richard parked beside a fire hydrant near the Hotel Griffen. It was six past nine as he quickly went upstairs to his room, grabbed the suitcase he'd already packed, and returned downstairs to the front desk. He wondered if the desk clerk perceived any nervousness. Richard was trying to get in and out in a hurry. He briskly returned to his car.

Then Richard drove east across Manhattan, eventually turning onto the FDR Drive at the United Nations and heading south towards Brooklyn.

He flicked on the radio in his car, listening to one of the all-news stations, then the other. He waited impatiently as he drove. His hands again felt nervous on the wheel of the car.

'Maybe I should have called them myself,' he muttered. 'Damn them.' Then the bulletin he wanted came onto the car radio.

Former newsman and aspiring politician Clifford Craig had been shot at Lincoln Center within the hour. Craig had been taken by ambulance to Roosevelt Hospital. No report on his condition.

'Perfect,' smiled Richard. 'Absolutely perfect.'

A few minutes later Richard drove down lonely Second Avenue in Brooklyn until he came to the telephone booth at Fifty-third Street. A long green Pontiac was parked there. A man was in it.

Richard pulled off Second Avenue just a few feet from that other car. Richard saw Lillis watching him. Richard started to walk towards the booth.

'Hey!' called Lillis.

Richard stopped. 'What?' he asked.

Lillis eyed him suspiciously.

'I'm waiting for an important call,' said Lillis. 'Get away from that booth.'

Richard acted confused, pretending not to know what to do. 'Can you give me directions how to get back to Manhattan?' he asked.

Lillis still looked at him suspiciously. 'You lost?' he asked.

'Sure am, pal,' said Richard.

Lillis glanced backwards up Second Avenue. Richard could see Lillis's hands now. One of the hands was on the steering wheel. The other pointed at Fifty-second Street.

'Take this cross street to Third Avenue,' Lillis began. 'Then take the avenue until you come to an expressway.'

Richard stepped closer, as if to hear better. He was within ten feet. Richard moved a hand quickly. Lillis looked at him and froze.

Richard was pointing a gun at Lillis.

'Don't move,' said Richard, 'and you won't get hurt.'

Richard moved close to the car, holding the gun a few feet from Lillis's head. Richard glanced into the car and saw nothing in Lillis's lap.

'Put your hands on your head and slide over,' Richard ordered. Lillis obeyed. Richard quickly got into the car and sat in the driver's seat. He kept the gun low and aimed at Lillis's heart.

'Recognise my voice, Herbert?' asked Richard. 'I thought it might be fun to meet you in person.'

Shock, anger, and confusion were on Lillis's hard wide face. 'What do you want?' he asked.

'Information,' said Richard. 'I just shot a man, you know.'

9

'It's on the radio.'

'I know,' said Richard. 'But they haven't pronounced him dead yet. And you're not allowed to tell me anything until Craig's officially dead.' Lillis was silent. 'But I thought you'd change your mind if I were here in person.'

Richard leaned forward and reached under the driver's seat. He pulled out what had to be in the car somewhere. A pistol. Richard clicked the safety latch on and tucked the gun into his left-hand pocket.

'I want my information,' said Richard. 'I'll kill you if I don't get it.'

Lillis searched for a way out. He found none. He glanced down at the silencer on Richard's gun.

'How do I know you won't kill me anyway?' asked Lillis.

'You don't,' said Richard. 'But you don't have any other choice but to trust me.'

Lillis still appeared hesitant.

'I'm just trying to make a quick getaway,' said Richard. 'I hit Craig twice near the heart. He'll be dead by morning.'

Five seconds passed slowly. 'All right,' said Lillis finally. 'It's in my inside pocket.'

'What is?'

'Your information. It's written down.'

Richard looked at Lillis carefully. Then, holding the gun firmly in one hand, Richard reached into Lillis's inside pocket with his free hand. He withdrew an envelope. He dropped it on Lillis's lap.

'Open it and read it,' he said.

Lillis did, struggling with the French.

Richard's Imp was a man named André Guisseny. Guisseny, as had been explained in Virginia, was a French Marxist, union agitator, and labour organiser. Unpopular with his own government, he was occasionally under scrutiny by his own national police force. It had long been suspected, and never proven, that Guisseny had been involved in a 1969 bombing. At present, Guisseny was involved with a Marxist cell in Paris. He was frequently at a left-wing union hall on the rue Tournefort in Paris. It was at that address, according to the paper, that Richard might continue his search.

The note went on to mention two contacts in Paris, men from whom Richard might purchase weapons. A Monsieur Quinzani and a Monsieur Leduc.

Lillis looked up after reading. He was slightly calmer now.

'Do you want to know who your second victim is?' asked Lillis.

'I don't really care,' said Richard, taking the papers from Lillis's hand. 'I'm taking care of my own business. You and your pals can screw yourselves.'

Then curiosity nagged at Richard.

'But why don't you tell me anyway?' he added.

'You can read it for yourself,' said Lillis, motioning towards the paper with his head. 'He's a Congressman. From Texas. Name of Logan.'

24

At two o'clock in the afternoon on Monday, May 14, Guisseny parked his stolen Renault opposite the spot where Bill Simmons normally parked the black Citroën belonging to Ambassador Thatcher. Guisseny held up a newspaper and read it with apparent interest. His attention, however, was on the pistol in his lap, which the paper covered, and the watch on his wrist.

At twelve minutes past two, Savard appeared in a middle-class dark suit on the rue Sainte-Dominique corner of avenue Bosquet. Savard sat on a bench and nervously fed the pigeons.

Guisseny watched his rear-view mirror. Four minutes later, at sixteen past two, Klemeur appeared. He had checked the stolen Peugeot and found it to be where it had been left in the SNCF warehouse. Then he'd taken the métro over to the quiet Invalides area. Now Klemeur calmly stood at a waffle stand at the corner of Bosquet and the rue de Grenelle. He stood his position and began to munch waffles. Guisseny watched Klemeur and almost smiled. Nothing upset Klemeur. Nothing put him on edge. Unlike Savard, whose stomach was always in pain, Klemeur could calmly munch sweets while fully aware that he might be in a gunfight a few minutes later. Guisseny could have eaten well before a gunfight, too. Could have, but didn't. A man who covered everything, with a mania for perfection, Guisseny knew that taking a possible bullet in a full stomach could be fatal.

Almost simultaneously with Klemeur's first bite of a waffle, the black Citroën turned down avenue Bosquet. Klemeur continued munching. Guisseny watched cautiously. Savard felt his hands sweating.

The Citroën parked within a few feet of its usual spot. Guisseny watched with occasional side glances.

Five minutes passed. Then ten. Then, twelve minutes after the Citroën had stopped on the kerb, the iron gates of the school opened. Klemeur gulped down his waffle and turned towards the school. Savard emptied his bag of bread crumbs onto the sidewalk; there was a whirlwind of pigeons.

Then Klemeur and Savard, with the Thatcher children somewhere between them, started to walk toward each other from the different ends of the block. Their hands went into their pockets and they removed ether-soaked rags from foil. They moved toward the children from opposite directions.

Lieutenant Simmons opened his car door and stood as he always did, leaning forward on the open door and with his right foot on the sideboard of the open car door.

Barbara Thatcher began to walk towards the swarm of children. Other parents emerged and walked towards their own offspring.

Klemeur and Savard drew nearer. The Breton in the Renault folded the newspaper and placed his hand on his pistol. What was one American life compared with the entire cause of Breton nationalism, the cause of a people oppressed for centuries? Even if everyone on the avenue Bosquet died this same afternoon, those deaths would be worthwhile if they called world attention to the plight of the Celtic people of Brittany.

Anne and Cynthia were suddenly visible in the swarm of children. Klemeur and Savard moved towards them quickly.

Then Guisseny was out of his car. The pistol was in his hand. Lieutenant Simmons saw the two men shove Barbara Thatcher and grab the children. For an instant Simmons was so stunned by what he saw that he didn't react. Then he yelled 'Hey!' and went for his gun. Guisseny fired.

The gun dropped from the marine's hand. He heard Barbara Thatcher's screams and he heard the girls' screams. Other people were yelling and screaming and there was a sudden flurry around the gates to the schoolyard. But Bill Simmons, by the time he crumpled onto the sidewalk, had still not seen the man who'd shot him.

Savard and Klemeur each grabbed one child and smothered an ethered rag into each small wriggling young face. The children were unable to yell or resist.

Stunned and bleeding from the nose, their mother scrambled up from the sidewalk, panicked beyond reason. She howled for

Bill, then she looked where he lay, writing painfully on the asphalt edge of the avenue Bosquet. Instinct told her to pursue. She did.

She stumbled and rushed madly after her two daughters. Klemeur and Savard were already pushing the children into the Renault. In her unthinking frenzy, Barbara Thatcher, who had never fired a gun in her life, picked up Simmons's pistol.

Guisseny saw her. He fired twice. The children were already unconscious from the ether. They never saw their mother clutch the lower part of her abdomen. They never saw her hit the sidewalk.

Nor were they aware of anything else that happened that day. They didn't know how the Renault had disappeared from that normally serene street. Nor did they know how the car had disappeared into that abandoned SNCF warehouse. There the young wrists and legs were bound with coarse industrial ropes. Two gags were tightly tied into place. And both girls were stuffed into burlap sacks.

Working quickly, Guisseny, Savard, and Klemeur abandoned the Renault simply by leaving it in the warehouse. The two children were placed in the boot of the Peugeot.

Savard and Klemeur changed their clothes and left the warehouse for the airport. Two hours later they were out of the country. Later, under darkness, the children were unpacked but not untied at the rue Rastignac. That underground grotto was to be their temporary home.

Meanwhile, the kidnap vehicle, the stolen Renault, sat idly in the vast reaches of that battered open warehouse. But it was not being left there alone.

Long after Klemeur, Savard and Guisseny had departed with their two involuntary guests, there was movement from behind some rusted discarded railroad machinery. A man stood up, blinking his eyes at what he'd seen earlier and thinking that it was now safe to come out of hiding.

His face was unshaven and his breath stank of cheap red wine. His clothes were as unwashed and tattered as his body. His name was Christien Langlois but it had been years since anyone had called him anything as respectful as his own name.

The man was a derelict, one of the legions of *clochards* who populate the quais beneath the Parisian bridges or sleep in doorways or abandoned buildings.

Between noon and two the vagrant had begged enough money

to purchase a baguette of fresh bread and a bottle of nauseating red wine. Then he'd wandered among the railroad warehouses seeking a secluded spot to enjoy his good fortune.

He had tried the door to the vacated SNCF warehouse, and the door had opened. He had entered and had sat down in the shelter between the old railroad machinery and a wall. Gulping the wine, he had noted fondly that this would make an excellent home during the late spring rains.

Then he had heard activity, the sound of a car entering the warehouse. He'd remained hidden and had kept very still. And he had wisely kept very quiet.

But he had watched. And he had seen everything.

25

'*Et maintenant, messieurs,*' concluded an angry Renaud de Gaubert to the men he'd summoned to the urgent meeting at the Ministry of the Interior. '*Je vous ai mis au courant. La question qui se pose est que faire.*'

De Gaubert, a ferocious Gaullist who'd earned the Croix de Lorraine in World War II as a colonel in a North African paratroop division, was visibly furious. Those who worked beneath him in the Interior Ministry knew him not only as a tyrant but also as a megalomaniac. It had long been his contention that he should have been President of France.

De Gaubert was a man who functioned excellently within a ministry. If he were a tyrant and if he happened to be the furthest right in the cabinet, it was equally true that he attacked his job with unmitigated zeal and, in contrast with some of his predecessors, had turned the Interior Ministry into one of the more efficient branches of the French government. He hated nothing more than to be second-best or to be asked to do anything against his own judgement. But fortunately such instances rarely arose. De Gaubert could be trusted to make not only the expedient decisions in all matters but also the proper decisions. Thus the President of the Republic, despite personal antagonisms, could live with him. And therefore de Gaubert could put up with the President.

De Gaubert was very much a disciple of the first President of the Fifth Republic. Not only had he stood somewhat in awe of de Gaulle, but he fervently and arrogantly also believed in much of what de Gaulle had preached. In particular de Gaubert longed for a return of France's historical glory and independence, a return of the times when France could be not just a world power, but a symbol of the pinnacle of civilisation. In short de Gaubert believed in the glory of France in general and himself in particular.

And that's what infuriated him so greatly about the events of the afternoon.

Political abductions and street terrorism, ranted de Gaubert, were things to be expected in the banana republics of South America, *mais pas en France*. Two shootings and the abduction of the two daughters of a foreign diplomat, he continued, may have been something that three thugs would try this once in France. But his ministry, raved de Gaubert, would see to it that these and other hoodlums would never dare try such a brazen act in France again.

'As I speak,' said de Gaubert, 'this American man, this William Simmons, is on an operating table at the American hospital in Neuilly, as is the ambassador's wife. Our best physicians and the best American physicians are trying to save their lives.'

He leaned on the round conference table and looked at the silent faces gathered before him, the heads of various branches of the French police and government.

'I intend to see that these hoodlums are rooted out and brought to trial,' said the minister between clenched teeth. 'And if either of the children is harmed or if either of these two Americans dies, I intend to demand execution for anyone involved in this plot.' Execution still means the guillotine in France.

'And now this!' he snapped. 'This further insult to France!' He slapped a piece of paper down onto the conference table.

The paper was a written copy of a telephone message received by the American embassy in Paris and the chief prefecture of police an hour after the shootings and abductions.

The message was simple enough.

The two children were being held until the granting of two very simple demands involving the Breton nationalist movement. Further communication, when the time was right, would come via mail to the private office of Ambassador Thatcher.

But meanwhile, before the Breton demands were even announced, two simple prerequisites had to be met. First, word of this case would have to be kept totally out of the news media. And second, no investigation whatever was to be taken to track down the children. If the government failed to meet these prerequisites, Anne and Cynthia Thatcher would be executed.

'A news blackout on this squalid affair is already in effect,' said de Gaubert. 'It will suit our purposes as well as the kidnappers.' As for an investigation, one will commence immediately.'

The men at the round table eyed the interior minister carefully. Each man wondered what responsibility would be thrust on his department.

De Gaubert paced before them thoughtfully, as he always did when he was about to reveal unusual plans.

'The fact is, messieurs,' he continued, 'that this is a unique case, a situation that in its domestic and international ramifications we have never faced before. For this reason and for reasons of security, I am going to approach it in an unorthodox manner.'

De Gaubert leaned on the mahogany table. He looked squarely into the eyes of the DST director, Jean-Claude Belfont was the man in the room whom he trusted most.

'I want to keep this out of as many normal police channels as possible,' said de Gaubert. 'Therefore I am appointing an agent from my own ministry to head the investigation. His name is Charles Dissette. He will be reporting to me and to me alone. Is that clear?'

De Gaubert sensed the perplexed reaction around the room. No one had ever heard of Dissette. Nor did anyone seek to ask questions.

'He is a reliable man who has handled various affairs for me both in France and abroad. It will suffice to say, by way of background, that Monsieur Dissette is a remarkably skilled investigator, one of the best I've ever known. Of course,' added de Gaubert after a slight pause, 'your various police agencies will give this man what he needs to complete his investigation.'

De Gaubert searched the faces of the men around him. Each man was silent, each face expressionless. They knew the important decisions had already been made. De Gaubert asked for any questions. There were none.

Moments later, de Gaubert concluded the meeting. As the invited men stood and moved towards the door, however, de Gaubert caught the eye of the director of the DST. When Belfont responded the interior minister informed him that he wished a further word with him in private. The subject, Belfont was told, would be not entirely unrelated to the concluded conference.

Fifteen minutes later a moderately stunned Jean-Claude Belfont sat in the interior minister's private inner office. Belfont was finishing a close examination of that troublesome file from de Gaubert's office. The minister sat at his desk and waited. Finally, Belfont closed the dossier and looked up.

'There is really only one man who this renegade agent turned torturer could be,' said de Gaubert. 'But we must be sure. It is absolutely essential that our suspect be kept under very close surveillance.'

Belfont nodded.

'I want an agent of yours to observe him,' said de Gaubert. 'The agent we call "Corbeau".'

Surprise showed on Belfont's craggy face. 'Corbeau?' he asked. 'For this?'

'For this,' affirmed de Gaubert. 'I have to use a DST agent. I can't use one from my own ministry.'

Belfont nodded slowly and thoughtfully.

'Only you and I know who Corbeau is,' said de Gaubert quietly. 'I'd like it to remain that way.' De Gaubert paused for a moment, then continued with a tone of inevitability. 'Corbeau was placed in his present position for just such an eventuality. He's the man we must use.'

Belfont nodded.

'Contact Corbeau,' said de Gaubert. 'Give him his instructions.'

26

Richard twisted Lillis's car key counterclockwise in the ignition. The key snapped off, leaving a metal stub blocking the ignition slot. Then Richard, taking those written orders from Lillis, stepped from the car. He tore the telephone cord away from the coin box in the booth and, with the silencer still on his pistol, he shot out both of Lillis's front tyres.

Lillis was left unharmed, but with a great deal of walking before him.

Richard retraced his route back into Manhattan. In lower Manhattan, below Grand Street, he stopped and threw his own gun and Lillis's gun into the East River. Then Richard followed the FDR drive northward up the eastern ledge of Manhattan Island. He continued until he picked up Route 87, the New York Thruway, heading north from the south Bronx. He stepped on the accelerator but kept his speed consistently no more than ten miles beyond the speed limit. His destination was Canada.

Richard drove through the night, arriving in Montreal as dawn broke Wednesday morning. Feeling that he needed to reward himself for a job well done, he checked into a forty-eight-dollar-per-day room at a luxurious and towering modern hotel at the Place du Canada. His rented car he left on a quiet side street. And he registered under a new false name: William DeMeo.

It was six thirty by the time he arrived in his hotel room. The room itself had a short hallway at its entrance, a large closet on the left, and a private bathroom on the right as one entered. A large convex window afforded a view of the world's second-largest French-speaking city.

Richard took a hot bath, then prepared for sleep. He was now clean and deathly tired. But there was a vaguely unsettled feeling within him. He sat down on his bed and tried to place it.

He thought of Clifford Craig. He'd done Craig a favour, he decided. Craig had been marked for assassination. Any other man hired would probably have killed him. But Richard had had no argument with Craig. The wound in Craig's shoulder was merely a means to an end. Craig had been lucky, even if he might never know it.

Richard sat pensively on the edge of that bed. He thought back to the beginnings of this mission.

Washington. Logan.

That was it. He knew what was bothering him.

The name Guisseny, given by Lillis, checked. Time would tell how good the rest of the information was. But the further orders asked Richard to contact another man at another telephone. A 703 exchange. Logan's own organisation was arranging Logan's execution. Why? It didn't make sense.

Further, could Richard allow Logan not to know? In a vague sort of way, Richard owed Logan a favour. He looked at his watch. Seven ten. He crawled into the large comfortable bed and was asleep within minutes.

It was one o'clock the next afternoon when Richard awakened. He lay in bed for several minutes. The image of Craig falling kept recurring. Then Richard rose and ordered a meal sent to his room. That afternoon he took a brief walk around the city. He telephoned Air France to reconfirm his flight for 9.30 p.m. the next day. And he bought the afternoon papers and read a few paragraphs about Clifford Craig being shot. When he read the words 'police are investigating' he smiled to himself. No one could possibly know where he was.

That evening he stayed awake reading. And he made a decision.

Late the next afternoon he telephoned information in Washington, D.C. He acquired Logan's number.

He glanced at his watch. It was half past four. There was a good chance that Logan would be in his office. Richard dialled.

He got Logan's secretary who, upon being pressed, admitted that Logan was there but maintained that he was 'too busy' to come to his telephone. Richard insisted that it was a 'life or death' matter. He demanded that she tell Logan that Richard Silva was calling. A few seconds later a befuddled Logan switched onto the line.

'Silva?' asked Logan quizzically.

'That's right.'

'What the — Where are you calling from?'

'That's not important,' said Richard. 'I called to tell you something.'

Logan seemed hesitant, as if there were someone in his office with him. 'Sure, sure,' he finally said. 'Go ahead.'

Richard talked. He wasted no words. Logan listened in silence, then at last spoke.

'It can't be,' Logan said. There was another pause. 'Look,' he said. 'Let me call you back. Where are you?'

'That's not important,' said Richard. 'I owed you a favour. I'm signing off and leaving for Europe.'

Now Logan was practically yelling. He seemed panicked. He begged Richard for his location. He said he wanted to call back 'in private' as soon as he could.

Richard glanced at his watch. He gave in.

'I'm at a hotel in Montreal,' said Richard. He gave the number and the false name he was registered under. 'I'll be here for two more hours. Then I move on.'

Logan thanked Richard. He said he'd return the call. Richard was again nervous. He began to pack. Fifty-five minutes passed.

Then the telephone rang again. Richard picked it up, expecting Logan. It was the desk clerk.

'Sorry to disturb you, Mr DeMeo,' said the clerk in English. 'There's a man on his way up to see you.'

Richard bolted to attention.

'A what?' he snapped.

'A man,' said the desk clerk. 'He asked for you by name. He said you were expecting him.'

Richard stood in stunned silence, thinking of the two guns he'd prematurely thrown into the East River.

'Hotel regulations, sir,' said the clerk. 'I have to announce any visitors before they come up.'

It was suddenly clear to Richard. Painfully, anguishingly clear.

'The bastards!' he shouted, slamming down the telephone. Now it all made sense.

Richard whirled from the telephone and searched the room with his eyes. He bolted across the room and tore a lamp out of the wall. He ripped the wire and rubber electric cord from the lamp, doubled it and then knotted it twice at its centre.

Gripping the cord in his hand he darted to the bathroom. He

turned on a radio that was built into the bathroom wall. He turned on the shower full blast. He backed out of the bathroom and closed the door.

Richard opened the door to the hotel room and released the lock, leaving the closed but unlocked door the way a man waiting for room service would leave it. Then he backed into the closet in that short entrance hallway, the closet directly across from the bathroom door. He kept the closet door ajar so that he could just see out.

He heard the elevator arrive, but he couldn't hear footsteps in the hall. But then he did hear someone try the door. The door opened.

Richard froze, hardly breathing. He held the make-shift garrotte in his tense hands. He waited. A man whom he couldn't yet see had entered the room.

Five seconds later a man in an overcoat stepped into his view. The man had short hair, was solid but not large, perhaps five ten. With a good first shot, Richard knew he could take him.

Richard looked at the man's hands. Gloved. The right hand was in an overcoat pocket. The pocket bulged.

The man stepped towards the bathroom door, attracted by the radio and shower within. Richard felt his body soaked with sweat. His leg muscles were tense. He readied himself to spring. The man took another step towards the bathroom. The intruder was drawing something from that right-hand pocket.

Richard sprung.

He hurtled forward and crashed with full force into the intruder. He brutally knocked the man forward and took him totally by surprise.

The man went down hard. His head whacked against the full-length mirror on the hard wooden bathroom door. The mirror cracked against the human skull. Richard flailed at the man's head.

A small snub-nosed gun dislodged from the intruder's right hand and dropped to the floor a few feet away. The man groped for it, then was forced to protect his own head.

The man punched back as best as he could. But Richard had him pinned. And with every ounce of force he had. Richard struck savagely at the man's bleeding head. The intruder lunged again for the pistol.

Richard kicked with his right leg. His foot caught the gun and knocked it away. A fierce pain from his right hip shot through him. But with a quick motion of the hands he wrapped the lamp cord around the man's neck. The knotted part was flush against the man's Adam's apple.

Richard heard the sickening sound as the man gagged. The man writhed and punched upward. Richard tried to shield his face with his shoulder, but couldn't. Twice fists pounded against his skull with jarring intensity. But Richard had a death grip on his opponent's throat. He would not release. He pulled the cord so violently tight that he felt the veins in his own arms bulging.

The intruder's fingers dug at the cord. His face reddened with anguish. His eyes appeared swollen. His throat rasped a retching inaudible plea. Richard would not let go. The strangled man felt the world going dark around him until everything was spinning and then black.

Richard stood above the man he'd just killed. He mopped his brow with his sleeve. He breathed hard, gasping for breath and coughing slightly. For a moment he thought he was going to be sick.

But he wasn't. He locked the door to the room and sat down on the bed. He didn't know whether to be scared or exhilarated. He was both.

'Fucking bastard,' he muttered.

A few minutes later Richard finished packing. He dragged the dead body into the humid bathroom and dumped it into the tub. He locked the bathroom door from the outside and then jammed the keyhole with a broken pencil.

Then Richard took the elevator downstairs and checked out. His car was where he'd left it on a side street. He threw away the bilingual parking ticket on the windshield.

He drove to the airport, turned in his rented car, and checked in for his flight. He paid for his ticket in American dollars.

Then he waited until his flight was announced. Over and over he pondered whether he had a telephone call to make. When his flight was called, he rose. He went to the telephone.

He dialled Logan's number in Washington, reversing the charges and demanding to be put past the secretary. Logan, stunned again, came onto the line.

'Silva?' Logan asked. 'Where are you? I tried to call back and –'

'Shut up, Logan,' Richard said. 'I just killed the local goon you sent to get me.'

There was a pause. 'Silva, what are you – ?'

'Cut it, Logan, I've figured it all out.'

'What are you talking about?'

'You,' said Richard. 'I was never intended to get anywhere near you. I was to kill Craig and then be set up while trying to get at you. I would never have gotten close. I would have been blasted first. You people only had one person to kill and that was Craig. Very neat. And it might have worked.'

There was a revealing silence on Logan's end.

'Take care of yourself, Logan,' said Richard. 'When I get back, I *am* going to get you.'

Richard hung up. Later that evening Air France flight 008 lifted him away from North America.

27

Charles Dissette, small, wiry, and dark-eyed, sat impassively as de Gaubert concluded a twenty-minute summation of the day's events. De Gaubert included the few known angles that the police had on the crime and several reflections upon the manhood and ancestry of the three felons involved. He added that a total press blackout had been imposed upon the case.

Despite the lateness of the hour, Dissette was completely fresh. Nowhere on his angular face was there the slightest suggestion of fatigue. Indeed it was only now, past midnight, when he was capable of his most incisive thinking.

A humourless man with a meticulous memory for names, numbers, and details, he attacked any assignment tossed his way by the interior minister with a zeal that bordered upon a religious fervour. And if this man had any faults, as the interior minister knew, it was the fault of reaching beyond his proper authority in order to get a job done. Yet now, on this Thatcher affair, he was one step ahead of the interior minister already. As he sat crisply erect in a leather chair before the minister, Dissette was wondering why, out of hundreds of available men, he had been chosen.

Other men might have flattered themselves into thinking that their qualifications had set them apart. But Dissette knew better. He considered himself one of the best agents of the Ministry, but certainly not *the* best. And equally, there were always ulterior reasons why a particular man was assigned to a particular case. This was Dissette's first case within France in almost four years. Why?

'*Eh, bien,*' remarked de Gaubert as the monologue came to an end. Dissette hated all long talks except his own. 'Have you any initial thoughts?'

Dissette spared his superior his actual initial thoughts. 'You present me,' he said instead, 'with a virtually impossible situation. I am to find this man, or these men, although they may be anywhere in Europe. I'm to have these children returned alive although they may already be dead. I'm to run one of the most thorough investigations ever in the Fifth Republic and I'm to keep it a secret. And all I have to begin with is the fact that this may or may not have had something to do with some crackpot Bretons.' Dissette paused for a moment and added, 'Is that everything?'

'No,' replied de Gaubert. 'You're also to hurry.'

'Ah, yes. And I'm to be held responsible if the investigation fails.'

'I think,' said the Minister, 'that you've assessed the problem correctly.'

'I've never turned down an assignment and never would,' said Dissette without emotion. Dissette's accent was vaguely that of the South of France. Dissette had been born and raised in Valence.

De Gaubert almost smiled. 'I want you to use your usual office with the Police Judiciaire building,' he said. 'It will be necessary for you to make periodic reports on your progress. Perhaps once a day. Directly to me.'

'I'll need some sort of staff,' said Dissette.

'You'll have what you need,' said the Minister. 'And I'm also assigning another man to you by the name of Marius Dutronc. Dutronc will act as your top assistant and a liaison with the police.'

'Who is he?'

'A career man in the PJ. And a top investigator in his own right.'

'Is this . . . necessary?' asked Dissette.

De Gaubert sighed. 'For the politics of the situation it is,' he said. 'We'll need the full cooperation of the PJ and the CRS. Dutronic knows the right men in each department. Since I'm appointing you to head this investigation, I can't afford to have the PJ or CRS feel ignored. So I'm afraid Dutronc is essential.'

Dissette nodded. It didn't sound unreasonable.

De Gaubert reached to some papers on his desk. He pushed them together in silence and shoved them into a folder.

'These are the various initial reports from the police on the scene,' he said. 'Lists of witnesses who have been interviewed already and so on. I don't suppose there's much you can do before sunrise. Have you slept yet?'

Dissette shook his head.

'I suggest you try to,' said de Gaubert. 'You'll need it. For now, that's all.'

'No, it's not,' said Dissette casually.

The interior minister looked at him curiously.

'If I'm to work so quickly and so thoroughly on a secret project, I'll need one other item. A written security pass with your signature. I want security clearance and access to all police and intelligence files located in Paris. A clearance that will be at all times totally unquestioned.'

De Gaubert frowned thoughtfully.

'What do you need all that for?' he asked.

'To do this job thoroughly,' replied Dissette.

Several seconds passed as de Gaubert studied the man in front of him. 'I'll have it for you in the morning,' he said at length.

Minutes later Dissette found himself walking down a corridor of the Interior Ministry. He cursed his luck at drawing such a case. Despite his pleasure over being granted access to PJ and DST files, Dissette also knew that he would have to operate in full view of the interior minister at all times. There would be little opportunity to resort to more effective powers of stealth and persuasion. Yet he was stuck with this case. He would have to attack it with all his usual zeal.

As he walked towards his own office in the PJ building on the quai des Orfevres, Dissette was deeply lost in thought. Already the question of why this case had been dumped in his lap had passed from his mind. Instead he pondered different questions. Who was behind this shooting and abduction? Where were the children? If they were alive, where were they being hidden? If they were dead, where were the bodies buried? And how, with the entire world to search in, could he find either?

Dissette arrived at his office at two in the morning. Immediately he picked up the telephone. He had no need for the file on his desk containing names and numbers. Any important name or number Dissette knew. He began to dial.

His first hope for a lead would be police contacts in Brittany, contacts who might know whether any campaign of terrorism was rumoured or planned. The political angle could have been a smokescreen for a different motive, such as a cash ransom. But Breton politics would have to be a starting point. Police contacts would be tried first, then underworld contacts. The *barbouzes* would be tried, the petty criminals who would inform on their own mothers if the price were reasonable. And after that it would be necessary to try the organised gangs of hoodlums both in Paris or in Brittany: Corsican, African, Yugoslav, Italian, and French. If the kidnapping had been political, organised crime would be glad to help. They, too, had a stake in the status quo.

Dissette telephoned several dozen of his most trusted contacts in various parts of France, but particularly in Brittany. To each, Dissette skipped an apology about the hour and simply sketched the type of problem he faced.

By twelve minutes past four, he had completed his last call. He began to tire. So he pulled down the shade to his office window, removed his jacket, shirt, and pants and cleared several books and papers off an office cot. Then he lay down to nap, trying to get whatever sleep the rest of the world might permit.

28

'I suppose,' said Clifford Craig, 'that the best thing about it is the free publicity.'

The worst thing about it was the wound itself. That and the uncertainty of whether or not the unseen gunman might take another shot at him someday.

When Craig collapsed onto the concrete outside of Philharmonic Hall, not a single witness got a good look at Richard. Instead, with all attention drawn toward the falling Craig, Richard had been able to slip slowly and quietly through the crowd. Craig, clutching his bloodied shoulder in the confusion, had tried to stand. But his stunned wife had knelt by him, shielding his body with hers and holding him. A few seconds passed before she realised that her husband would live and that no further bullets were coming.

Craig was taken by ambulance to nearby Roosevelt Hospital, where he received emergency treatment for a gunshot wound. The bullet had entered his body exactly where Richard had aimed it: in the upper right chest below the collarbone. A few smaller bones in the area had been shattered, but the bullet had struck a non-fatal area. The wound was hot and painful. But it looked messier than it actually was. Two hours after receiving his emergency treatment at Roosevelt, Craig was able to contact his personal physician, Dr Henry Solomon. He was then transferred upon Dr Solomon's orders to Lenox Hill, where Solomon had admitting privileges.

The concept of his own mortality was something that Craig had never completely accepted. Now he had to. The bullet could have found his heart just as easily as it found his right shoulder. 'Who would want to kill me?' he asked himself over and over. Two days later, in Lenox Hill, he asked Dr Solomon the same question. 'Almost anyone who ever worked with you,' replied the doctor.

But witticisms didn't come quite as easily to the detectives from the Nineteenth Precinct who were assigned to the Craig shooting. Craig was a well-known man in New York, a television personality, and a possible senatorial candidate. From the outset, Detectives Patrick Sullivan and Michael Smith, both from the Nineteenth Precinct, had a plethora of possibilities to explore.

What Dr Solomon had said was true. Anyone who had worked with Craig might have had a desire to part Craig's hair with a bullet. Similarly anyone who had ever watched Craig on television might have had some real or imagined grievance. Or someone might have had something political against Craig. Sullivan and Smith, in other words, had their lists of suspects narrowed down to ten million people.

'What the hell,' said a confused and somewhat subdued Craig as he sat in his hospital room and talked to the detectives. 'I didn't see who did it and I don't know where the shot came from.' Betty Craig sat demurely in the room and remained silent, thinking only of how close she had come to losing her husband.

'What can I say?' continued Craig. 'I don't know who the hell might have done it. Maybe some prick was just out to fire a random shot and I happened to catch it.'

'Possible,' said Sullivan. And it was. Sullivan had been on the police force long enough to know that not all crimes have motives. Still, they insisted that Craig refrain from any public appearances and accept a police guard pending the disposition of his case. And that hurt almost as badly as the shoulder. No public appearances, the hospital for several days, and then a guard thereafter so that this same nut might not strike again.

The police weren't kidding about that guard. Already, on the night when Craig had been shot, they'd sent two uniformed men in a patrol car to Craig's apartment building for a routine inspection of the building's corridors. One never knew.

It was at that time, when the patrol car pulled up to Craig's building and two cops got out, that Anthony Vecchio, watching from his usual embassy position, recognised the two patrolmen and knew something possibly was up. But it wasn't until later that morning, when he returned to his precinct after his tour of duty, that he learned that the best-known resident of 26 East Sixty-seventh Street had been shot by an unseen gunman.

29

'Scared?'

The two little girls nodded. Their eyes were filled with tears. their stomachs felt nauseous, and their young bodies were bruised heavily. They emerged drowsily from their ether-induced sleep. They felt groggy, unable to stand.

And their wrists and ankles were bound. They were tied to chairs. There was a huge trunk a few feet away. A bare dim light bulb hung from the ceiling, wired to an area up above that squalid sub-basement.

The two little girls were in a damp, dark cellar that stank from a nearby sewer. Beneath their feet was soft, moist red clay. They wanted their mother. All they could remember was being seized brutally off the street.

Where was their mother? Their father? Bill Simmons? Who was this terrifying man?

Guisseny spoke to the girls in heavily accented English. He told them that they were not there because they'd done anything wrong. Rather, he told them, the country they were in and the country they had come from had caused a lot of people to suffer. Now those countries would have to fix their mistakes if they wanted the girls back.

The two girls, who had never known evil or malice before, were frozen with terror. Neither understood. Neither could speak. Cynthia started to cry again.

'You maybe not be here long,' said Guisseny. 'Maybe only days. If people want you back, they cooperate.'

He eyed the girls again carefully, trying to decide whether or not they were listening. He then spoke again. He told them there was no way for them to escape and that no one could hear their screams. But he said, gesticulating and showing them several strips of cloth, if they continued to cry or started to yell, they would be gagged.

Then he stood, gazing at what he considered to be the two insignificant offspring of an obscenely wealthy American capitalist. What were their lives compared with the historical exploitation of his people? What would these girls matter in twenty years? But if one extreme act of political terrorism could call attention to the plight of his people perhaps the fate of the Breton people would be vastly improved in two decades. The historical lessons of the years since World War II proved to Guisseny that political terrorism was a legitimate lever for political change.

Guisseny had already killed for his cause. Now he was ready to die for it. But Guisseny's death, unlike the deaths of his small captives, did not seem imminent. He would correspond with the Thatchers by mail. His demands would be untraceable. The police couldn't guard every post office box in Paris. And the terms of the ransom – pardons for the eight young Bretons imprisoned in the 1969 bombing in Brest – were not something that he would ever have to reveal himself to collect. He would ask for money, too, but not money that he'd ever plan to obtain. The cash request would only serve to distract attention from the first demand. He would no sooner take the chance of trying to collect a cash ransom than he'd take the chance of ever freeing his two young prisoners. The only real decision remaining about the girls was how they would die. Gunshot? Or suffocation?

Surely, he figured, the eventual and inevitable execution of the Thatcher girls would force the French government to take more seriously the cause of Breton autonomy. Surely, he figured, the government would have to act to avert similar future acts. Otherwise, no diplomat or his family would ever be safe in France again.

30

'Nothing.'

'Christ,' cursed Clifford Craig. 'Nothing at all?'

'Nothing at all,' confirmed Detective Patrick Sullivan. He and his partner, Michael Smith, sat near the hospital bed of Clifford Craig. Craig's influential friends in New Yorks politics had pulled a string or two. The detectives assigned to the Craig case were not from the West Side precinct that might normally deal with a Lincoln Center shooting. They were, conveniently, from the precinct nearest to Craig's home. The Nineteenth.

'So what's going to happen?' Craig asked, his irritation turning to anger.

'Sir?' asked Sullivan, a greying detective who rapidly approached his fiftieth birthday.

'What's going to happen to me?' Craig repeated. 'I'm leaving this goddamned hospital tomorrow and I'd like to start walking around this city again.'

Craig looked toward the drawn blind of the private hospital room. He felt another twinge of discomfort in his arm and shoulder. He looked back at Smith, brown haired, double chinned, and ten years Sullivan's junior. 'I'd like to venture out into daylight without wondering if the same maniac with a gun is – '

'You'll have your police guard, Mr Craig,' Smith offered. 'And – '

'Oh, fuck that,' cursed Craig. 'You know just what that's worth. You morons might just as well be working on the Judge Crater case.'

'What would you have us do?' asked Smith coolly.

Had this been a normal case, Sullivan and Smith could have conveniently let the matter go quietly to hell, but not so here. Despite Craig's rancorous behaviour and increasingly unbearable foul temper, Sullivan and Smith were stuck with this one, and they knew it. At seven o'clock the morning after Craig had been winged, the mayor had stopped by the hospital. Craig had friends in important places. And Sullivan and Smith were not, for example, terribly anxious to return to their previous assignments patrolling the Eighty-eighth Precinct in Brooklyn's Bedford-Stuyvesant, a section of New York known to the cops as 'The Planet of the Apes.'

'I'll tell you what to do, goddamn it,' snapped Craig. 'I want you to kick asses from here to Missouri to find out what happened to me. Or should I talk to the mayor again?' He can tell the commissioner that you two are having trouble.'

Sullivan and Smith left the hospital that day almost wishing that the gunman had been more accurate. 'This whole thing would be a lot more pleasant if that prick was dead,' grumbled Smith.

They returned to their precinct, stopping on the way for sandwiches at a delicatessen on Lexington Avenue. They were eating at their desks in the precinct when they heard a familiar voice.

'I have something,' said Tony Vecchio. 'Whether or not it's worth anything is what I don't know.'

Smith looked up. 'What are you talking about?' he asked.

Vecchio pulled up a free chair and sat down. He addressed Smith. Vecchio and Sullivan had never cared much for each other.

'I've been working graveyard in front of the fucking Egyptian mission,' said Vecchio. 'You know, that fucking Arab dump off Madison?'

Sullivan and Smith listened. Vecchio continued.

'Well, not much happens on that shift. Mainly you sit there and pick your nose. Or maybe your buddy's nose. Well, I was doing some thinking last night.'

'That's new,' said Sullivan.

'Now listen, Mike,' Vecchio explained. 'This guy who plugged Craig. Chances are that he might have been stalking for a while.'

'We've gotten that far without you,' said Sullivan.

'Yeah, right. But this you don't have. Five nights before Craig got plugged, Ike and I are sitting there in the middle of the shift when this red car from Massachusetts circles the block three times.

There's a guy in it. I didn't get much of a look at him but I saw there was one guy. A white guy.'

'And?' asked Smith.

'And what do you suppose this guy is looking at the whole time? Why does he circle the block three times? Because he's fascinated with one of the buildings on the block. Absolutely fascinated. Couldn't take his eyes off it.'

'Which building?' asked Sullivan.

'Twenty-six East Sixty-seventh,' said Vecchio. 'Craig's.'

Sullivan pursed his lips in thought and Smith merely looked at his partner. Vecchio glanced back and forth in triumph.

'Might not mean anything,' said Vecchio. 'On the other hand, this could have been your guy checking out his terrain. I'll tell you this. He was so interested in Twenty-six that he never saw Ike and me until his third time around. Then what happens? He looks right at us and acts real guilty. He drives straight this time and vanishes down Fifth. Now I ask you. Interesting or not?'

'Interesting,' conceded Smith.

'You said Massachusetts,' said Sullivan. 'You saw the licence?'

'Hell, Pat,' said Vecchio, 'I didn't just see the licence. I wrote it the hell down.'

Sullivan eyed Vecchio intensely, knowing how badly Vecchio wanted a detective's shield. Yet despite Sullivan's aversion to Vecchio, if this crazy Italian could break the Craig case for them, well, he'd kiss that Neapolitan face.

'Do you have the licence number?' asked Sullivan.

'Is the Pope Catholic?' answered Vecchio. He reached into his inside pocket and pulled out an envelope. He tossed it on the table.

The notation on it read: Massachusetts SH 1518.

Sullivan picked up the envelope and looked at the number. 'Okay,' he said, tacitly admitting Vecchio to the case. 'We call the state police in Boston and see where the number leads us.'

'Done,' said Vecchio.

Sullivan and Smith both looked at him.

'The car's registered to a Mrs Maureen Downes of Hyannis,' Vecchio explained. 'That's where we start. What the hell's her car doing circling Craig's block at two in the morning five days before he's shot? And who's driving?'

Smith and Sullivan half stared, half glared at Vecchio.

'Well, hell, guys,' he said. 'I wanted to give you a little lift.'

31

Richard Silva, equipped with a false passport, passed easily through French customs, took a bus into Paris and registered under the name of Howard McKiernan at the small, comfortable Hotel Corbet near the boulevard Pasteur. Although he'd managed to sleep a little on the flight, he was still tired.

'*Canadien?*' asked a small balding M. Lechêne, the concierge at the hotel. Lechêne copied the number of Richard's passport as he registered him. '*Alors, vous parlez français?*'

'*Un peu,*' replied Richard, rustily groping around in a language that he hadn't used in several years. '*Je suis anglais-canadien.*'

'*Ah, bon,*' replied the Frenchman, sucking on a pipe. '*J'étais au Canada pendant la guerre. Cette langue-là. Affreuse. Je n'ai pas compris un seul mot.*'

Richard smiled. Then he mounted a short spiral staircase to his thirty-eight-franc-per-day room. He carefully slid his wallet under his mattress. Then he bolted the door and undressed. He glanced again at the scars on his hip and leg, his lasting badge from Hoa Lo.

He flopped on the bed naked and for the first time in several days he allowed himself to relax completely. He was very much alone in a foreign city among people who spoke an alien language. He hadn't a single friend in Paris. It was possible that people were looking for him and could conceivably follow and find him. But what bothered him most was a growing sensation that he'd experienced in other hotel rooms: a sense of isolation. He was not part of anything that was happening around him. And he wouldn't be until this burden of finding Guisseny had been lifted. What Richard had convinced himself that he had to do had to be done alone. And yet the pangs of solitude were increasingly more painful. He thought vaguely of how nice it would be to have a woman. A few moments later, relaxed, he drifted peacefully off to sleep.

He awoke two hours later. He blinked sleepily for a few seconds. Then he remembered where he was and why he was there. He sat up. Surprisingly, the few moments of sleep had taken the edge off his fatigue. He felt better.

Richard dressed, took his passport, driver's licence, and money with him and left his room. He stopped in the lobby of the hotel where he changed a twenty-dollar bill into francs.

As he slid the French currency into his wallet he stopped.

His eye hit upon two small pieces of paper in his wallet, two official cards. His real Massachusetts driver's licence. His real United States Social Security card.

He should carry nothing, he reminded himself emphatically, that bore his real name. Yet neither document, he realised, should be destroyed. He didn't know when he'd again want to return to his actual identity.

He returned upstairs and placed both items in a large manilla envelope. He locked the envelope inside his heavy suitcase and wedged the suitcase into the top shelf of his closet.

He again considered destroying the cards but, for the time being, he didn't.

He then proceeded from the hotel.

The air of Paris was fresher and sweeter than that of New York, Boston, or Washington. There was an exhilarating feel to the city. Richard walked to a *tabac* and stood at the end of a long brass coffee bar. He ordered *café noir* and croissants. The bar and the tables to the side were filled with Frenchmen looking over racing forms. Richard glanced at a far corner of the *tabac* where a Pari Mutuel Urbain wagering window was both open and busy. Richard was tempted to throw some money on a horse just for the hell of it. Then he was served his coffee and croissants and promptly forgot about the PMU window. Nobody in the *tabac* thought it at all odd that Richard would be eating breakfast in the middle of the afternoon.

Richard walked from the *tabac* to the first bank he could find. There he changed five hundred dollars into French francs and deposited another five-hundred-dollars' worth of francs into a savings account that he opened on the spot. Later that same day he wandered over to the larger bank branches in the Eighth Arrondissement. In two separate banks he rented safe deposit boxes and split his remaining money between the two boxes. Each box that Richard rented he examined carefully. He made sure that either box, if necessary, could hold a pistol. But first he would have to buy one; he had the necessary contacts from Lillis.

After a satisfactory late lunch at a brasserie. Richard rented a small white Simca 1400. He parked the car near his hotel and set out on foot.

To orient himself, he purchased a map of the city. Then he began to walk, enjoying the freshness and tranquility of his new surroundings.

Only when he strolled by the Montparnasse Cemetery did Richard even remotely think of the homicide he'd come to Paris to commit. He continued to walk and lingered for a while in the Luxembourg Gardens.

He continued to walk north, finding himself soon crossing the Seine at the Ile de la Cité.

On his left was the Palais de Justice, housing the offices of the Police Judiciaire. On his right was Notre Dame. On impulse he walked towards the cathedral. As he approached he studied the intricacies of the cathedral's façade, its three ornate portals and its two glorious rectangular towers. He might have followed other tourists up into the towers, but within twenty minutes they would be closed for the day. For a few idle moments he studied the detail of the cathedral. As he turned to leave he noted that just below the towers, the green tile roof was a maze of bars and pipes. It was under reconstruction. Richard returned to his hotel, dined that evening in a nearby café, and then slept.

On the evening of his second day in Paris Richard went to an ordinary-looking café and brasserie on the rue Berger. He entered the bar, called the Café des Maritimes, and leaned against a long wood and brass bar. He sipped draught beer from Alsace and liked it.

Behind the bar was a jowly man who answered to the name of Philippe. Philippe was a jack-of-all-trades, bartender, waiter for the scattered tables on the sidewalk, and lord of the bottles behind the mirrored bar.

Philippe was also a go-between.

Richard fell easily into a conversation with Philippe. The bartender, in turn, noted Richard's heavy accent and hesitance in

French. Inevitably Philippe inquired as to what had brought Richard to the Maritimes.

'Monsieur Leduc,' said Richard. Philippe's expression barely changed.

'What makes you think you'd find him here?' Philippe asked.

'I was told I could,' replied Richard. 'I have . . . a transaction to make through him.'

Philippe sparred back and forth with several more questions. He eventually allowed that he might be able to relay a message to M. Leduc.

'How quickly?' asked Richard in French.

'That depends, monsieur,' said the bartender.

Richard peeled a hundred-franc note from his wallet and slid it across the bar to Philippe. Under such favourable circumstances. Philippe could get a message to M. Leduc within a few hours.

Richard left a simple message. His name was McKiernan. He was from Canada and wished to purchase a certain item from Leduc. Philippe said he'd have an answer that following evening.

Satisfied, Richard left.

On the next day Richard visited the union hall on the rue Tournefort. The hall had been mentioned in the information Richard got from Lillis in New York. It was said to be frequented upon occasion by André Guisseny, but when Richard entered only a few workmen and two youths who seemed hard at work shuffling memeographed papers in a small office were present.

Of each person encountered, Richard made several roundabout inquiries, introducing himself as a Canadian journalist. When he angled around to the name of Guisseny, all returned shrugs. The name, as far as anyone would admit, meant nothing.

That same afternoon, halfway down the block from the union hall, Richard seated himself at a sidewalk café. He lingered over a light lunch, then coffee, a few newspapers, a paperback book, and then two or three beers through the afternoon.

He appeared engrossed in what he was reading. But in fact, his eyes rarely drifted from the entrance to that hall. Yet he saw nothing of interest. Richard realised how many days this scene might repeat itself. He did not mind.

His thoughts again dissolved into his obsession with the man he was pursuing. He wondered what he'd do if the Imp appeared before him now while he was unarmed. Would Richard wait and return with a pistol, courtesy – he hoped – of M. Leduc? Or would he seize the opportunity as it presented itself and attack the man with anything handy, say a sharp knife from the café?

Richard tended toward the second alternative. He firmly believed that whoever strikes first usually wins. In this case, a good first strike with a knife to the throat would end Richard's long pursuit. Then he could begin to live again.

In the late afternoon, Richard returned to his hotel. That evening towards ten he returned to the Café des Maritimes. Philippe met Richard at a vacant end of the long wood and brass bar.

'Tomorrow at seven in the evening,' said Philippe. 'You will meet a man on the Ile de la Cité. By the statue of Charlemagne.'

'Monsieur Leduc?' asked Richard.

'His emissary,' said Philippe. 'He will make the arrangements.'

'How does he know what arrangements to make?'

Philippe blew his breath into a wine glass he was polishing and gave Richard an annoyed shrug. 'That, monsieur,' he said, 'is not for me to know.'

32

The man in the tan golf slacks and the matching wind-cheater lined up the ball with the head of his driver. He arced into a swing and drove the ball down the well-manicured fairway. It was a Friday afternoon in mid-May. With the exception of Congressman Logan and his guest, the golf course of the genteel Liberty Hills Country Club was deserted, But then, spring had only been in the air for a few days. The Virginia soil was still too damp and soft for most golfers.

'Not bad,' said Logan, observing the other man's shot. He teed up his own ball and lined up his shot. The other man, grey haired and with a Virginia accent, began to cough slightly – a chronic condition, not an intended distraction. Moments later Logan's ball followed down the long green strip.

The two men, out for a day of exercise, boarded a golf cart and drove after their balls. Their caddies followed on foot.

'What do you think?' asked Logan.

'Nothing to worry about,' said the other man. 'It's not as bad as it looks.'

Logan glared at the Virginian, studying the hard features and the closely cut grey hair. 'How can you say that?' he asked. 'He leaves Craig alive in New York, and then kills one of your locals in Montreal. Then he calls me from the airport and promises me my head on a plate. And it's not as bad as it seems?'

'No,' said the other man.

'Why?' snapped Logan, irritated.

'If Craig's smart he'll take the hint and stay away from that

Senate race. For our purposes he may be removed from the picture. As good as dead.'

'I doubt it,' retorted Logan.

'Second, Silva is powerless in Europe.'

'He was powerless in Montreal, too.'

The other man smiled. 'As soon as he tries to buy a gun, he's dead.'

'How?'

'It's been arranged. It will even look like suicide.'

Logan was unconvinced. 'I'll bet,' he said.

They neared Logan's golf ball. They were still alone as the cart crept to a halt. They stepped out. The tone of amusement was gone from the Virginian's voice.

'This time there will be two professionals,' he said. 'What's this unarmed Massachusetts kid going to do against two professional gunmen?'

'You tell me,' said Logan. 'Because he's coming back after me as soon as he realises that this Guisseny you sent him after – '

'Johnny Ray,' said the Virginian with a tight smile, 'he's not coming back. So forget it.'

The two caddies were approaching to almost within earshot. The Virginian hacked another cough.

'I could work something through State Department,' said Logan thoughtfully. 'We could get some "unofficial" French help to get rid of Silva.'

'Logan,' said the other man, 'let me worry about it.' He pointed to the ball as the caddies arrived. 'Your shot.'

33

Guisseny had almost forgotten. Children are human. They eat.

It was eight forty that evening when he opened the trap door leading down into that modern dungeon. The girls' hands and legs remained shackled to impede their movement. They could move around that filthy earthy pit, but movement wasn't to be encouraged or made easy.

As Guisseny lowered himself down and dropped the final foot or two to the clay below, the two girls – less groggy now – were again wide-eyed with terror. He stood there with a bag in one hand and a battery-powered lantern in the other. He glared at them. They were as terrified as they were tired. By this time all other nights their mother and father had kissed them good-night and had tucked them into warm clean beds. Never had they seen a cruel-looking man like this, a man who so obviously meant to harm them. Nor were little girls of wealthy American families in any way used to seeing rats.

'You hungry?' asked Guisseny in his heavy English.

The girls hadn't thought about food at all. But now that this man mentioned it, yes, they were as starved as they were terrified. Guisseny pulled from his belt a long butcher's knife.

Anne nodded, biting her lip and forcing back tears. Her younger sister was still too scared to move. Guisseny looked at them half in contempt and half in annoyance. Then he walked to them.

'Hold up hands,' he said.

The girls trembled and didn't move. Guisseny gestured with the knife and indicated that he was willing to free their wrists. The younger girl held up her wrists first. He cut the thick

165

ropes that had bound their wrists.

'I not make hurt you,' he said.

Guisseny reached into the bag. The girls shivered. It was cold and damp down there. And they were so scared.

Guisseny pulled from the bag a long day-old baguette of bread and half a kilo of cold meat. Then he pulled out a litre of milk in a triangular paper carton.

'Eat,' he said.

At first the girls were hesitant. Then, greedily and almost frantically, they ate. The grease of the cold meat coated their hands and the area around their mouths. It stained their expensive school clothing. The crumbs from the breaking crusts of bread tumbled to the damp clay floor. The crumbs would later be devoured by rats.

Guisseny waited until the girls had finished their meal. Then he made them hold out their hands. He bound their wrists again and this time gagged them with strips of cloth.

Then he explained to them as best he could in his broken English what was to happen next. They were to be sealed in that large trunk. And this would occur each time he had to leave that house.

It would be only temporary, he told them. He had to go out to mail a letter, a letter to people who could free the girls. As long as nobody interfered with him, he would be back immediately, they would be unlocked and in no danger.

But if anyone interfered with him, stopped him, or even delayed him, he would *not* be back that quickly. And the air supply in the trunk would last for fifteen to twenty minutes.

Anne tried to resist being put into the trunk. But the cloth gag muffled her shrieks and Guisseny slapped her across the face. He made sure that the gag was tight enough to stay in place but not so tight that it would suffocate her. Then he placed both of those young bound bodies inside the large trunk, smiled to them, and locked them in.

He placed the key inside his shoe. Then he pulled himself agilely up out of that cellar and into the sub-basement. Moments later he was on the street and heading towards a pre-selected mailbox on the boulevard Saint-Michel. There he would post the initial letter stating his demands and his position and his non-negotiable ransom demands. And if all worked well, he would be back in time to open the trunk. With at least four and a half minutes to spare.

34

Frederick and Maureen Downes were sitting down to dinner when two uniformed Massachusetts state troopers came to the door. The mere presence of two state policemen under his roof put Downes's heart in his throat. And worse, the police came in a blue and white state police car that couldn't possibly have looked more official. What, Downes wondered later, would he tell the neighbours? What, he wondered at the time, was this all about?

'Simply a few routine questions,' offered a state trooper named Archer. Archer, a tall, wide, imposing, blond man, was accompanied by a smaller darker man with a vaguely Latin face. The other officer's name was Leonard Russo. Both men wore heavy black service revolvers, which would have broken Downes's wrist had he ever tried to fire one of them.

'Routine about what?' asked Downes at the door.

'We'd prefer to explain in private,' replied Archer, 'if it isn't inconveniencing you.'

Downes exchanged glances with his wife and then admitted his two sudden guests to his home. Already the state troopers were on their guard. The red Dodge in question was parked in the Downes's driveway. And that car now represented more than a casual mystery to police in two states.

A Massachusetts check of the Downeses, in response to a request by telephone from New York City, had revealed that Mrs Downes worked in an insurance agency and Frederick Downes worked in a bank. Neither was new to the community, and neither was known to associate with anyone arousing the slightest suspicion. But perhaps most important, both had been at their respective jobs on the days surrounding the shooting of Clifford Craig. Unless their car was in the habit of driving itself, or unless one of them was in the habit of sneaking seven-hundred-mile overnight drives, someone else had been using that car.

'Mrs Downes,' said Archer, 'the red 1969 Dodge in the driveway is registered to you, is it not?'

'It is,' she said slowly and almost fearfully. She wondered whether she'd renewed her registration. She thought she had.

'Who usually drives it?' asked Archer.

'I do,' she said.

'I *never* drive it,' her husband volunteered.

'That's right,' she agreed somewhat reluctantly. 'I normally take it to work each day, leave it in the parking lot in Hyannis, and drive home.'

'I see,' said Archer. 'Where do you leave it at night?'

'Exactly where it is now.'

'Locked?'

'Locked.'

'Do you think it would be possible for the car to be used overnight and brought back by morning without your knowing it?' asked Archer.

'I . . . I don't see how it could be,' she said slowly, her brow furrowed with puzzlement.

'We'd hear it starting,' volunteered Downes. He was no longer concerned with the spaghetti that was growing cold and gummy on the table. What in hell was all this about?

'Won't you tell me what's going on?' asked Maureen. 'I think I have a right to – '

'The car that is out in your driveway at the moment,' explained Russo, 'was seen in New York City on the night of May third. The car appeared to be of a suspicious nature to a police officer on duty at the time.' Maureen Downes's mouth was wide open. 'And five days later a serious crime was committed that may or may not have been related to that time and place.'

'Serious crime?' asked Downes. Maureen was speechless.

'An attempted murder,' said Archer.

'We don't even know anyone in New York,' said Downes.

'What we'd like to know, Mrs Downes,' continued Archer, 'is where you think your car was on that particular night. And who might have been driving it.'

Maureen Downes was still unable to speak. All of this was coming at her too quickly. Frederick Downes broke the silence, turning towards his wife.

'Your brother,' he said flatly.

'My brother,' she said slowly and carefully, yet not measuring her words for their import, 'borrowed my car for a few days.'

Mrs Downes continued. She acknowledged that her brother, a former airman who had been a prisoner of war in North Vietnam, had borrowed the car upon occasion after returning home. He had made one trip to Boston and then a longer one to Washington.

'Washington?' asked Archer. 'What for?'

'I have no idea,' said Maureen Downes, almost snapping at the state troopers. 'He didn't say. It was his business so I didn't ask.'

'But it was government business of some sort,' volunteered Downes. 'He took some secret job through the government.'

'Secret job?' asked Russo.

'That's right,' snapped Maureen. 'And I'm sure that if you go through the proper channels of communication in Washington you'll be able to get in touch with him. I'm sure my brother has nothing to do with a . . . with an attempted murder.'

'We never said he did, Mrs Downes,' said Archer.

'No, you didn't,' she shot back. 'But that's what you're thinking. That's what the two of you came here to talk about.' She glared at the two uniformed officers. Her outrage rallied her courage and her sense of sibling loyalty. 'I have nothing further to say,' she added.

'Where's your brother now?' asked Archer.

Maureen Downes remained silent.

'Do you *know* where he is?' asked Russo.

The two troopers looked at Downes, who nervously returned their gaze and then looked at his wife.

'Richard Silva,' said Downes, 'to the best of our knowledge accepted a government job. Something requiring secrecy of some sort. He left here eight days ago and told us nothing about where he'd be going or what he'd be doing. We have no way of reaching him. He returned Maureen's car and then disappeared again.'

'And he didn't tell you what he'd done on these trips to Boston and Washington?' asked Archer.

'We didn't ask,' said Downes.

'Unlike some people,' said Maureen tersely, 'my brother does not run off at the mouth.' She blinked back tears. 'He could be seriously disturbed. I don't know. All I know is that he put up with unspeakable tortures in that prison camp. When he came back he was a different person. Hardened. More solemn. Quieter. He fought in a war while you were out enforcing speed limits. And now you come into my home and accuse him of murder. I'll tell you just one more thing: get out! Get out and if you want to talk to me again, come back with a warrant.'

None of the three men moved. Maureen Downes, enraged beyond reason, stood and bolted from the room, slamming a door behind her.

Twenty-two minutes later Archer was on the telephone to Anthony Vecchio in New York. Vecchio had been sitting patiently in the Nineteenth Precinct that evening waiting for the call, waiting to see where his lead was taking him. He spent the first ten minutes of Archer's call listening to the state police report and jotting down a few notes.

'A former airman POW, huh?' asked Vecchio, his interest thickening. 'And the guy's dropped completely out of sight on some alleged government business?' Vecchio issued a low whistle of intrigue. 'Fat chance.'

The lead could mean nothing and it could mean everything. But it definitely meant that this connection had to be pursued. And this Richard Silva, this vanished POW, would have to be found. By default, he had become the number-one suspect in the Craig case.

'I can check Washington to see if this turkey's really on Uncle Sam's payroll or not,' said Vecchio to Archer. 'But I've got no way of knowing what name he's travelling under. I doubt if he's using his real one if he's doing a disappearing act. You can't help me on that angle, can you?'

Archer said he couldn't adding that he also couldn't discount the fact that the Downeses might know more than they were so far willing to tell. 'My guess is that they're in the dark, too, though,' Archer concluded. 'But that's just that, a guess.'

'Got anything else on him?' pressed Vecchio.

'Nothing.'

'Nothing at all?'

'Nope,' said Archer. 'Unless you want to go into the fact that Silva's a scofflaw, too.'

'What?' asked Vecchio.

'Oh, nothing that helps you much,' said Archer. 'This turned up when we ran a check on the car with Mass Motor Vehicles. The guy picked up a parking ticket the day he was in Boston.'

'*A* parking ticket?' asked Vecchio. 'Just one?'

'Yeah. just one.'

'Shit,' said Vecchio. 'We got people down here who line their toilets and paper their walls with those things. Big deal.'

'Yeah, I know,' agreed Archer. 'But now that I think of it, maybe you can run a check on that licence in Washington and New York. It might give you some idea where else he's been.'

'Maybe,' said Vecchio thoughtfully. 'Hey. You don't have a record of that ticket in front of you, do you?'

'No,' replied Archer. 'Why?'

'I was wondering what area of Boston he might have been in. Got any idea?'

'To tell you the truth,' said Archer slowly, 'it struck me as odd, but it didn't mean anything to me at the time.'

'What didn't?' asked Vecchio.

'The ticket was picked up on Berkeley Street.'

'So?' asked Vecchio.

'Well,' said Archer, 'it's probably coincidence and I don't want to give you a bum lead since the address is right in the centre of town . . . '

'Keep going,' said Vecchio anxiously.

'But his car was parked only a block and a half from the main police headquarters for the whole city of Boston.'

35

On the next evening Richard arrived half an hour early by the statue of Charlemagne. Within his left shoe he had hidden twenty-five hundred-franc notes.

The huge façade of Notre Dame Cathedral was behind him. And as he saw no one resembling the man he was supposed to meet, Richard found a nearby bench and sat down.

He watched the area of the statue carefully. But he allowed his attention to drift to the cathedral. Richard looked skyward to his left. His eyes searched the twin rectangular towers of Notre Dame. For some reason he thought of the violent descent from sky to earth that he'd made in October of 1970.

And he thought of the Imp.

'Monsieur McKiernan?'

A voice addressed Richard from a few feet away. Richard's gaze shot from the twin towers to the man who stood next to him.

The man spoke in heavily accented English, an accent sounding more Italian than French. The man was wide and wore tinted glasses. He appeared muscular beneath a heavy jacket.

'You mistook the bench,' the man said, 'for the statue.'

'I was early,' said Richard. 'Sit down.'

The man shook his head. 'A bad place for business,' he said. 'I know a better one.'

'Where?'

The man grinned and held an open hand towards the cathedral.

'There?' asked Richard.

'Come,' said the man. 'Everything is arranged.'

Richard followed the man. They passed through worshippers and tourists and entered Notre Dame through the Last Judgement Portal. The stocky man Richard followed stopped momentarily in the vestibule and bowed to the cross. He turned to Richard. 'Follow me,' he said.

'Where are we going?' asked Richard, following but instinctively suspicious.

'Up,' laughed the man jovially. 'Closer to Heaven. Where we can talk in private.'

The man led Richard past several groups of tourists and up a flight of stairs that was prohibited to the public. The man motioned for Richard to go ahead of him. They then began to mount the winding stairs, which led two hundred feet upward to the outdoor walkway beneath the cathedral's south tower. The tower had been closed to tourists for over an hour. But this man knew his way around. As they climbed the endless spiralling stone steps, Richard's leg and hip began to pain him. The pain worsened.

'Tell me,' Richard finally said, stopping and turning on the dim steps. 'We're alone here. Why don't we discuss things now?' He looked at the race of the man behind him and suddenly liked it less.

'Impossible,' said the man. 'There's a man waiting for you upstairs. He will present you with your . . . your package.'

'A pistol?' asked Richard.

'That's what you wanted, isn't it?' the man answered.

Richard nodded, momentarily appeased.

'An odd place to discuss business, yes?' chortled the man with a false laugh. 'Not like America at all.'

Richard nearly froze. He felt a flash of nerves in his stomach but did not betray his sudden suspicion. *America?*

Richard continued to walk. Up ahead the dark steps were growing lighter. They were nearing the top, the two towers that were now lit by floodlights against the evening sky.

'Tell me,' Richard said to the stocky man behind him. 'You work closely with Monsieur Leduc?'

'Oh, yes,' said the heavy man, starting to breathe laboriously from the long climb. 'Very.'

'Then you know if he got my package?'

'Package?'

'The money,' said Richard. 'To pay for the gun. There's no point in my going any farther unless Monsieur Leduc has received his payment.'

'No, no,' said the man quickly between audible breaths. 'Monsieur Leduc received your money. It's all right.'

Richard, four steps, above the man, stopped and turned back towards him. 'You're sure?' he asked.

'I am.'

'He got the package this morning?' asked Richard. 'At the bar?'

'Yes,' the man said.

'I thought so,' said Richard. 'Good.'

Richard began to turn. Then he whirled as fast as he could on his bad leg and threw out his right foot. The foot crunched the hefty man squarely in the mouth and sent him backward, almost tumbling but able to brace himself against the grey stone wall.

Richard tried to rush past the struggling man but the thick body blocked Richard's escape. Richard threw a brutal punch against the man's nose.

But the man blocked him again, grappling his thick body against Richard. Richard pushed him down a few steps but still the man stayed upright.

And now the man's meaty fist was groping under his coat.

Richard broke away and fled upward, the only way he could go, towards the narrow walkway that led around those massive towers and the cathedral roof.

The man behind him fired. The sound rang deafeningly up the stone staircase.

When Richard burst through the turreted portal that led to the south tower platform and the walkway, he took the first man's partner by surprise. The second man was massive – broad and at least a foot taller than Richard. The man had been overlooking the outer ledge of the platform, keeping the gargoyles company.

Stunned for a moment when Richard burst from the portal, the man lumbered into Richard's path, blocking him completely. Yet Richard had the advantages of momentum, speed, and surprise.

Holding his head low, Richard charged squarely into him, gripping the larger man's arms with his own. With a powerful thrust of his bad leg, Richard brought a knee crashing upward.

The man doubled and bellowed in anguish, holding his hands to his groin. Richard crashed him against the low brick barrier that formed the ledge. Richard grabbed where the man's hand had been and yanked the man's gun from a hip holster.

The first man emerged from the portal, holding a hand to a bloodied mouth and nose. Richard fired at him. The man shot again at Richard at the same moment.

Both bullets missed. The stocky gunman ducked back into the stairs.

The larger man had gone down but had grabbed Richard's ankle. Richard jerked his foot away and fired again at the open portal. Then he jammed his second foot downward at the larger man's head, kicking the man brutally in the skull. He pulled free from the fallen man and ran, following the narrow stone passageway around the south tower of Notre Dame. A third bullet sailed several feet to Richard's left. Richard disappeared around first one corner, then another. He followed the passageway until it led to the area just above the green tiled roof above the nave of the cathedral.

Then he stopped. No one pursued. Seconds later Richard knew why. He had cornered himself.

Ahead of him was a massive gap in the passageway, a gap filled by a maze of pipes and bars. In the floodlights that lit the cathedral roof, Richard saw that the entire section plus the roof below was under reconstruction. He couldn't climb the face of the tower and he couldn't go over the ledge. And he couldn't retreat.

His eyes went to the automatic in his hand. He removed the clip quickly. He examined the weapon and counted five bullets. He pushed the clip back into the pistol and looked back around the last corner he'd turned. No one pursued him yet. But someone would.

He tried to imagine what must have been planned for him. Somehow, he reasoned, these men had intended to kill him up there. Maybe guns had been the last resort. Maybe, he thought, they'd planned to overpower him and throw him off the roof. A suicide.

Richard cursed the faceless men in Virginia. He looked at the pipes, bars, and narrow scaffolding of that reconstruction project. It was his only chance. He tucked his gun into a pocket. Gingerly, he began to climb onto the nearest bars.

In the glare of those floodlights, he pulled himself along. His hands were sweating furiously, making every grip perilous. Richard saw that the scaffolding and its adjoining bars led all the way to the apex of the roof.

If he could just get to the crest of the roof, maybe, just *maybe*, he could make his way to safety down the north side of the cathedral roof.

Painfully, he inched his way along until he was at last within an arm's length of the roof's summit. He pulled himself from the end of the scaffolding to the apex of the roof.

He exhaled a long sigh. He straddled the peak of the roof.

Then he heard a sharp crack. Something hit and shattered a tile six feet in front of him. He looked from where he'd climbed.

The first gunman, his hand still to a bloodied face, was firing the pistol at him. There was another crack. Richard saw the flash and the puff of smoke from the gun.

Richard crouched down low against the roof. He looked to the side that presented safety. He threw his leg over in that direction and prepared to crawl downwards, hoping he wouldn't fall into an uncontrollable slide.

As Richard tried to climb downwards, the gunman fired again. This time the bullet sailed close behind Richard, nicking him on the back of the calf and tearing a bloody surface wound across the flesh of his leg.

Richard ducked down to safety as another bullet sailed where his head had been.

For several seconds Richard remained motionless. He was too scared to feel the pain in his leg. Long ago in graver circumstances he'd conquered pain. And he'd also conquered the urge to panic. He remained still and coldly assessed his position.

Instinct told him to inch down the north side of the roof and escape across a north side walkway. There had to be one.

But Richard wouldn't obey instinct.

Instead he poked his head up and looked where the gunman had been. He saw the man retreating in the direction from which he'd come. If the man was going anywhere, he was going to find a vantage point overlooking the northern part of the roof. From there he could carefully pick his shots and kill Richard.

Richard again mounted the peak of the roof. Then he reached desperately for the scaffolding, pulling himself back where he could retrace his path. He pulled himself through the pipes and bars again, more sure of himself this time despite sweating palms.

His hip ached and the leg wound seared with pain.

He reached the first stone walkway and cautiously crouched in a shadow. He drew the pistol and held it before him. Quickly, trying to regain the element of surprise, he darted through the stone walkway in a low running crouch.

He moved cautiously around each corner of the rectangular tower until he reached the last corner before the portal leading to the long spiral stairs. It occurred to him that both men might be waiting for him on those steps. But when he looked around the last corner, he could see the larger man – the man he'd hit – propped in a sitting position against a stone wall.

The man was obviously still in considerable pain. He was looking the other way, to the north, in the direction in which his accomplice had gone in search of Richard. Richard was no more than thirty metres from the man. Thirty metres from the stairs and his escape.

The floodlights formed a shadow along the passageway between Richard and the fallen man. Half the passageway was well lit. The other half was in darkness.

Richard edged into the shadows. Then he raced toward the sitting man.

At the last moment the man turned his head and saw the on-rushing American.

But it was too late. Richard slashed the would-be killer across the skull with the nose of the gun. With a muffled and sickening groan the man buried his face in his forearms and slumped hard to his left.

Now Richard's escape was easy. He stepped carefully through the dark portal to the steps. He looked in first to see that no one was waiting for him. He moved down ten steps and found nothing. He stopped and listened in the semi-darkness.

He heard nothing.

He felt the burning in the back of his leg. He thought of the bullets that had been meant for his heart. He thought for a moment of the two who'd tried to kill him.

One was badly injured. The other was still alive. Untouched.

Richard turned and went back.

When he stood just within the portal he glanced toward the north tower. He saw the other man. Gun in one hand, other hand to his red, anguished mouth.

The man was walking briskly across the narrow stone walkway leading from the north tower to the south. He was approaching Richard but not looking toward him. The gunman's eyes were searching the roof. He was perplexed. Where was the American?

Bastard! Richard thought.

Richard waited in the dark portal. He crouched, stayed back a few feet, and used the steps and stone enclosures as a screen.

Richard barely breathed. He waited until the gunman was clearly visible, framed by the open portal.

Richard pulled the trigger.

The man slammed backwards and thudded against the stone inner wall of Notre Dame. The gunman's pistol leaped from his hand and disappeared over a ledge. The man crumpled. His hand left his face. He was motionless.

Richard examined the weapon in his hand. He'd come that evening to the Ile de la Çité to buy a pistol.

Instead, he'd earned one.

And he had four bullets left.

36

One way or another, Richard Silva would have to be located. That much was clear. Vecchio, Lamont, Smith, and Sullivan were all in accord. They wanted this man, at least for questioning.

Vecchio and the three other detectives could have gone through the proper channels and requisitioned Richard Silva's military records from Washington. Such a procedure can be anguishingly slow, however, and although a request was officially made, Tony Vecchio could think of faster ways to get what he wanted. He again telephoned Archer in Massachusetts.

According to what Archer had told Vecchio, Downes had seemed anxious to remove himself from any suspicion in a police matter. Downes, in short, had seemed more cooperative than his wife. So at Vecchio's suggestion, Archer went to work on Downes without Maureen Downes's knowledge.

Archer telephoned Downes at his bank. Would Downes, Archer asked, be able to help the police quietly but immeasurably in this case? Downes replied that he was wholehearted for law and order. What, he asked, would he have to do?

'What I'd like is a recent photograph of Richard Silva,' said Archer. 'Would you have such a thing?'

Downes didn't. But his wife did. Maureen had shot a roll of film not too long after her brother had returned home. Downes said he'd be happy to supply the police with a snapshot of his missing brother-in-law.

Archer said he'd pick up the photograph at the bank the next day and would keep it only long enough to have copies made. Then

Downes could return it before it was even missed. Downes, however, was not as concerned with the missing photo as he was with another detail.

'When you come to the bank,' suggested Downes, 'you couldn't wear your civilian clothes, could you?'

Archer said he could.

Twenty-four hours later the police in all the north-eastern states had a copy of the photograph of one Richard Silva, twenty-five years old, Caucasian, five ten, one hundred seventy pounds, no visible scars, walks with an occasional limp, possibly armed, and dangerous. Wanted for questioning in a New York City shooting. Probable location – unknown.

Vecchio studiously examined the copy of the photograph he'd received, trying to envision whether or not this was the same face he'd seen in the red Dodge a few nights earlier. It had been dark. He couldn't be sure. But who the hell else could have been driving?

So the New York police had a fresh picture and a cold trail. But while that picture was circulating, Vecchio had taken a further initiative. He had run a check in Boston, New York, and Washington of all hotel reigstration entries over the last month. He had asked if anyone by the name of Richard Silva had entered.

And again he had come up, as he put it, 'corpse cold'. He'd found nothing.

At the same time, he had had fourteen eastern states run checks on that car's licence plate. The check would turn up any violation – moving or parking – and would give Vecchio an added idea of where Silva had been at a given time. But again nothing. Even a check with a U.S. government personnel office, which might have revealed Silva had been placed in a job euphemistically referred to as 'sensitive', revealed nothing new. So all Vecchio was left with was a recent photo of a young man who'd stiffed him, with one of the coldest trails Vecchio could ever have imagined. But Vecchio accepted it as a challenge. 'You bastard,' Vecchio muttered at the photo one afternoon. 'You have to be somewhere.' Vecchio glared resolutely at that photograph and cursed at not knowing what name Richard Silva was now using.

But even as Vecchio was cursing at that photograph, other copies of the same picture had made the rounds of police stations and police desks up and down the east coast. They had been carefully examined in some areas and virtually ignored in others. But one spot where the photo received the attention it deserved was in

Boston's main police headquarters on Berkeley Street. Since Richard Silva had been in that area, it was strongly recommended that all officers take a close look at the photo. Most officers did.

It was late on a Friday afternoon when Detective Sergeant Kermit Kelly looked at the photo and suffered the shock of recognition.

'Son of a bitch,' Kelly muttered to himself as he read the copy underneath the picture. 'I'll be a son of a bitch.'

He reached for the telephone. Then his hand stopped. He was now possibly much more than a son of a bitch. Richard Silva might have involved Kelly in a major crime. Why, Kelly cursed to himself, hadn't he thrown that kid out of his office?

'Oh, fuck,' Kelly growled bitterly to himself. But his hand kept going. A minute later he had Tony Vecchio on the line.

Kelly introduced himself and inquired of New York City's interest in Richard Silva.

Vecchio explained. Briefly, but concisely.

'Wow,' said Kelly at length, shaking his head two hundred and ten miles away from Vecchio. 'I sure didn't know he'd go shooting at any Americans.'

'What *do* you know about him?' asked Vecchio.

And Kelly began to talk. He related the day Richard Silva had come to him with a story about imprisonment and a French torturer with an ironic nickname. Kelly told how this visitor had wanted to enlist government help in one way or another in finding this man. But first, the former POW had said, he'd need a picture. Only *then* could he go off to Washington to seek help.

'And like an idiot,' said Kelly, 'I believed him.'

'If it makes you feel better,' said Vecchio, 'under the circumstances, I might have believed him, too.'

But Vecchio's mind was beyond feelings of sympathy for Kelly. In a strange sort of way, some of the missing pieces were starting to fit together. This project of revenge that Silva had spoken of to Kelly. Was this the secret work he'd been enlisted to do? And whom had he been enlisted by? And Washington. His sister had said he'd gone to Washington. Now Vecchio suspected he might know why. It might very well have had something to do with this quest for retribution.

But where did Clifford Craig fit in, wondered Vecchio. Any involvement between Craig and Silva made no sense at all. At least, on the surface it didn't. But somewhere, reasoned Vecchio, there had to be a link. What was it?

'Sure, you might have believed him,' said Kelly, 'but I can't believe how stupid I was. I knew he was partially lying and yet I chose to believe the rest of his story.'

Vecchio asked what Kelly meant.

'Face and name,' said Kelly. 'No match. I make a living drawing faces and then seeing names matched to them. I looked at this face and I saw southern European ancestry of some sort. Italian, or even Spanish or something. The one thing that I make a study of is faces and names. I saw that face and then he comes at me with an Irish name, the name he must be travelling under.'

'Holy Christ,' said Vecchio anxiously. 'Do you remember it?'

'Yeah,' said Kelly slowly. 'I think so. I can hear the sound of it. Howard something. I remember Howard because that was my father-in-law's first name. And the last name. McSomething. McK . . . McKenzie. That sounds like it. Howard McKenzie.'

37

Vecchio's enthusiasm was rekindled. He brought the three other detectives up to date on his latest discovery and then informed the precinct commander of their newest titbit of information. The commander in turn informed the police commissioner, who in his turn informed the mayor. The mayor relayed the word to Craig, who in turn told his own police bodyguards that those incompetents at the Nineteenth had finally gotten the lead out of their pants.

Vecchio, Lamont, Smith and Sullivan then began contacting New York hotels asking if anyone by the name of Howard McKenzie was registered there at the moment. When the answer of no came uniformly to that question, they further inquired whether anyone by that name had been registered at any time over the previous month. The closest they came was a Herbert McKenzie of Tulsa, Oklahoma, who had been at the Americana's morticians' convention the previous week. Could that, the Americana inquired, be the man the police wanted? Vecchio, without any fear of contradiction, said it wasn't.

Now the manhunt grew. As Richard Silva became more likely as a suspect, the New York Police Department enlisted outside help. This time, since some sort of Washington, D.C. link appeared likely, the police in the District of Columbia were notified. The capital police would be requested, and they would comply to check hotel registrations exactly as the police in New York had done. The name Howard McKenzie was checked several times and, for good measure, so was the name Richard Silva.

And again, over the course of several days, nothing. Silva or McKenzie or whatever-his-name-was had again vanished. Still other locations on the outskirts of New York, Boston, and Washington were checked, as were likely stops in between. Over the course of several days hundreds of hotel registries were scrutinised and thousands of names were examined.

Still nothing.

The euphoria that Vecchio had felt on Tuesday morning had vanished by Friday afternoon. All four detectives were now trying to find some other link somewhere. The only one of the four who left the case for any amount of time was Sullivan, who took two hours off on Wednesday night to be with his family in New Jersey. It was his son's sixteenth birthday. After dinner, cake, and presents, Mrs Sullivan brewed her husband a pot of black coffee. Then he returned to the precinct, where he worked through the night.

Police in the District of Columbia, while not searching with as much enthusiasm, were equally busy and equally stymied.

Vecchio discovered that on the day Craig had been shot, Craig's office had confirmed to an anonymous caller that Craig would be at the Philharmonic that night. The discovery was worthless, however, since it shed no further light on the case. And Vecchio, who liked the girl's legs and short skirts, never informed Craig that his secretary had inadvertently aided in her boss's near assassination.

Then late that Friday afternoon, not long before five, Sullivan picked up the telephone to learn one further bit of information.

Police in Washington, on hearing the story of Richard Silva's meeting with Kelly, had taken a logical guess. Knowing that Silva had been away from the United States for three years they guessed where in Washington he might have begun in his search for help. Just as any good eighth-grade student would suggest, Richard Silva had contacted his congressman.

The Washington police had tried the Pentagon, but had found nothing there. C.I.A. offices in Virginia had refused even to listen to questions, and records of the Departments of the Army, Air Force, and Defence had showed no communication from a Richard Silva or a Howard McKenzie. And that was when one detective suggested that Silva might have begun with Irwin Coffin, Richard's own congressman.

A District detective called on Coffin and showed Coffin a picture of the sought-after man. To the amazement of the detective, Coffin told of his meeting with Richard Silva. Coffin remembered distinctly that Silva had used his actual name.

The detective listened carefully and then telephoned New York. Later, Vecchio called Coffin to make further inquiries. Where, Vecchio asked, did Coffin think Richard might have gone next?

'I couldn't possibly have less of an idea,' replied Coffin. Police procedurals bored him as much as POW nuts.

'Could you venture a guess?' pressed Vecchio.

'No,' said Coffin.

Vecchio thanked the congressman for his time and help, and hung up. 'Prick,' he grumbled. Again Richard Silva had appeared and then quickly disappeared. But sometime between the entrances and exits, Richard Silva had acquired a sophisticated weapon with a silencer. And similarly, Richard had to have gone somewhere in the interim. Was it during that time, Vecchio began to wonder, that Silva had decided to kill Clifford Craig? Where did that idea come from and where did the weapon come from? And, since he didn't seem to be in hotels, where was he staying? Vecchio was on his way towards an inevitable conclusion: somewhere Silva had found help. Had that help put him up to shooting Craig?

The rest of Friday passed, as did most of Saturday. Lamont and and Vecchio were in the Nineteenth Precinct late that afternoon when their telephone rang. It was long distance from a detective in Washington.

'What have you got?' asked Vecchio.

'Maybe nothing,' said the detective, 'but one of our hotel directories turned up something interesting when we double-checked it.'

'Go ahead,' said Vecchio.

'We found a name that fits right into the dates you gave us in the District. Right to the date at the Marriott Motor Inn at the Scott Key Bridge.'

'McKenzie?' asked Vecchio.

'No,' said the detective. 'McKiernan. Howard McKiernan of Hyannis, Massachusetts. But no one at the hotel remembers what this guy looked like. They see a lot of people, you know.'

'Holy Christ,' muttered Vecchio. McKiernan. McKenzie. It sure as hell *was* close enough. His mind was already running through the odds against its being a coincidence.

'I was intrigued when I saw the name,' said the Washington detective, 'so I made one phone call for you after I found this guy's address.'

'Yeah?'

'I called Hyannis to see if there was such a name at the address given.'

'And?' asked Vecchio.

'No such name,' said the detective. 'And the address is out in the middle of Nantucket Sound.'

38

It had been Dissette's understanding that he would be reporting directly and confidentially to the interior minister. He was therefore surprised two mornings later at eight o'clock when he reported to the small conference room in the Justice Ministry. There was a third man, Jean-Claude Belfont. Dissette knew him immediately.

Dissette did not know, however, the reason underlying Belfont's presence. Belfont was head of the DST, the branch of the Sûreté Nationale concerned with counter-espionage and the movement of political undesirables through France. Conceivably, the Thatcher case could involve Belfont's department. But it could just as conceivably involve countless others. Dissette, as he summarised the previous day's events, steadily moved to an unspoken conclusion. Belfont was there to observe him. And there had to be a reason why.

By eight thirty Dissette had moved the meeting to its final few points.

'In cases such as this, as you know,' Dissette said, 'the word of eyewitnesses is the most suspect of all clues. Yet this is almost all we have to work with since the abductors have yet to contact us. We have thus proceeded accordingly. We know, for example, that the vehicle used as a getaway car was a Renault sixteen registered to a Monsieur Jean Dubois of Versailles.'

Dissette noted the sudden attention that this fact elicited.

'Several witnesses reported part of the licence number,' Dissette explained. 'From this we pieced together the entire number and matched it with the prevailing description of the car. Most observers saw it as a tan Renault although one woman informed us that the children were swept away in a red horse-drawn coach.'

Dissette cleared his throat and glanced at those two granite faces.

'Our information on the car, in fact, corresponded with the report given us by Monsieur Dubois when he reported his car stolen. Our detectives called on Monsieur Dubois last night, questioned him, and informed him that the vehicle had been used in a crime. Monsieur Dubois is still under investigation, but at first glance it appears that he had nothing to do with this crime.'

Dissette watched the expression relax on de Gaubert's face. Belfont was totally impassive.

Dissette continued.

'There is an alarm out across France and across the other Interpol nations concerning this vehicle. While we don't expect to find it with anyone in it, determining the location of this car might give us obvious information as to where the kidnappers and their victims went. This much appears certain: the vehicle has not crossed the borders of France unless it had the luck to slip across one of the unguarded routes into Belgium. I would consider this unlikely, however. My own opinion is that this original car was abandoned quickly. A second car was then probably used. Where, this second car is, is as much a matter for conjecture as the location of the first car. Or, for that matter, as to where the Thatcher children are.'

Dissette reported that he had put in dozens of calls to various reliable police informers within Paris. The calls had turned up nothing. Similarly, various police stations and networks of spies in the political underground in the country had also been contacted. And again nothing.

'I have also seen fit to make several inquiries of those in our employ in Brittany,' said Dissette, 'on the theory that the Breton reference in that first message to the embassy was perhaps sincere. All but two of my Breton contacts have reported back to me. All seemed rather surprised that anyone in the Breton movement might have resorted to any sort of violence or terrorism at the moment. The Breton activists have seemed particularly docile lately. The sympathy for their cause still exists, of course, but the conclusion we can draw is that if Breton zealots were behind such terrorism, there would have had to be a very small number of them, a mere handful of fanatics who spoke of their plans only to each other. Perhaps it was only the three of them. I think the further conclusion there, gentlemen, is clear. If they were that small in number and that thorough in organisation, they have made themselves virtually untraceable.'

Dissette saw how his words were coolly received. He added, 'I hasten to add that this does not mean they cannot be found.'

Dissette continued with a discussion of what he knew best, the one hard set of facts that he had to work with. The bullets that killed the American marine had come from a German-made Luger, a powerful handgun and a reasonably accurate one.

'As you know,' he said, 'the wife of the Ambassador is still listed in critical condition at the American Hospital in Neuilly. I spoke with a doctor yesterday evening and discovered that Madame Thatcher will require another operation today. Something involving the removal of a bullet fragment from the base of the spinal column. And while the woman's condition leads us to believe that her life is no longer in danger, this second operation will determine among other things, whether she will be able to walk again.'

As Dissette concluded that sentence the door opened and Marius Dutronc, his assistant, entered. Dutronc sat quietly as Dissette concluded the meeting. Five minutes later, only the two investigators remained.

'Something new?' asked Dissette.

'A lot.'

Dissette nodded for Dutronc to speak. Dutronc withdrew a letter and an envelope from a plastic case he carried.

'The American Embassy,' he explained, 'received this message this morning.

Dissette eagerly grabbed the sheet of paper and the envelope it had been mailed in. The letter was formed by newsprint clipped from newspapers. Dissette cursed the kidnapper for his lack of originality. Just once, Dissette thought, he'd like to get a hand-written or typed ransom note.

He read:

The Thatcher children are alive, unharmed, and being held in a spot in Paris that will be impossible to find. They were seized by three men. Two have successfully left France. I correspond with you now as the one man in the world who knows where these children are. Any attempt to find me will result in the deaths of these children. This is not a threat. This is a fact.

189

If a search is organised for me, I will kill the children. I will be leaving my hiding place only to correspond with you by mail. At those few times the children will be sealed inside a large trunk. They will have twenty minutes of air. Any attempt to detain me will thus result in the deaths of those children within a third of an hour.

There is only one way to regain their freedom. The eight Breton patriots imprisoned for the 1969 Brest bombing must be freed. Then a ransom of 500,000 francs will have to be paid. The details of how this payment must be made will follow your release of the eight Bretons. The first demand is a prerequisite for the second demand. Both French and American governments will have to work together to free these children.

I am fully cognisant that the U.S. government does not pay ransom. That is why it is convenient that the ambassador is a wealthy capitalist. Five hundred thousand francs is well within his means. You must communicate with me through the newspapers. I await news of freedom for these Breton patriots.

'*Salaud!*' grumbled Dissette. He handed the letter back to Dutronc and asked that it be treated for fingerprints, if it hadn't been already.

Then Dissette examined the six-by-three-inch envelope. It was addressed by hand in block letters. The postmark was the previous morning in Paris.

Dissette thoughtfully eyed the stamps and the cancellation.

'I'm afraid,' said Dutronc, 'that he didn't give us much to work with.'

Dissette didn't answer for a full ten seconds.

'On the contrary,' Dissette finally said. 'He may have begun to tell us where he is.'

Dutronc was about to ask what Dissette meant, but this question was cut off when Dissette spoke again.

'Was there anything else?'

Dutronc nodded. 'It sounds better than it probably is, however,' he said.

'Go ahead.'

'They found Monsieur Dubois's car,' said Dissette. 'In an old railroad warehouse.'

'And?'

'There was a live body inside it.'

39

A thirtyish woman with thick glasses and dark hair pulled back into a bun addressed the meeting. This night's harangue concerned the methods with which the French auto industry kept certain unskilled marginal workers non-unionised while the larger mass of workers belonged to Marxist trade unions. Wasn't this enough, she implored, to shut down Citroën, Peugeot, Simca, Renault and – while they were at it – Michelin Tyre?

The union hall was half full. Richard's mind wandered. He considered the stinging flesh wound on the back of his leg. He'd dressed and bandaged the wound himself, but the discomfort remained. He glanced around the union hall. The polemics of the speaker bored him. He was there to look for a face. Not to listen, but to observe.

Yet as much as he was observing, he was also being observed. He had passed by this hall twice now, asking questions and persisting for answers. Some of those whom he spoke to took Richard at face value, believing him a journalist embarked on an assignment.

Others obviously were more suspicious. As Richard sat in the union hall that evening, he glanced around from time to time. Eyes were on him. An older man here, a younger man there. He was being watched. He knew it. He almost encouraged it. Someone here had to know Guisseny. If Richard persisted, if Richard were seen here often enough, perhaps one of Guisseny's friends would make the next move. Perhaps someone would want to know more about Richard before contacting the absent Breton.

Perhaps. Richard would persist. The next move was up to the other side.

40

Vecchio, Lamont, Sullivan, and Smith retraced their steps, starting late that Saturday afternoon exactly where they'd been on the previous Tuesday. They began with hotel registries, starting in Manhattan and working up and down the east coast.

Vecchio worked backwards from the day Craig was shot. He filled in the dates on a calendar. Richard Silva had been in Washington from April 9 to April 27. Similarly, Richard had been in Massachusetts at his sister's home on May 4, 5, and 6. Craig had been shot on May 8. The missing dates Vecchio wanted checked religiously in all hotel directories.

And this time the detectives scored.

The Gilbertson Hotel in New York was the first to make a positive report. A man calling himself Howard McKiernan had stayed there from the twenty-seventh of April to the fourth of May. Then he'd checked out, leaving no forwarding address. The home address he'd given had been the same Cape Cod one that had been used in Washington.

The Hotel Griffen reported back to Sullivan about two hours after the Hotel Gilbertson had reported to Vecchio. A man named McKiernan had stayed there from May 7 until May 8, the night Craig was shot.

Smith and Sullivan went to the Gilbertson Hotel and showed a picture of Richard Silva. No one remembered him enough to positively identify him as Howard McKiernan. 'I've been here four years,' the desk clerk said. 'By now everyone looks the same.'

Vecchio and Lamont did much better at the Griffen just off

East Forty-fourth Street. The evening man on the desk, Luther Rolland, positively remembered Howard McKiernan. Rolland was shown five snapshots, including one of Vecchio's brother. Without prompting, Rolland picked out Silva's picture as that of McKiernan.

'A good memory for faces,' commented Vecchio.

'Ain't nothing like that,' said Rolland.

'What?' asked Vecchio.

'I just remember unusual behaviour, that's all,' shrugged Rolland.

'What was unusual?' asked Vecchio.

'This guy McKiernan,' said the desk clerk. 'He paid in advance for two whole nights. Then along about ten o'clock Tuesday he comes back here like a wild man, packs up, and ten minutes later he's gone. That's unusual. Folks don't have that much money no more. Folks don't go buying rooms they ain't gonna use. This guy took off like the cops was after him.'

Rolland began to laugh at his own wit. Lamont and Vecchio remained perfectly poker-faced , but each smiled inwardly. For the first time, they knew positively that Howard McKiernan was Richard Silva. Now all they had to do was find him.

Vecchio continued to check hotels and boarding houses. But the suspicion grew that Richard Silva had either been taken in by accomplices or had quickly left New York. But how? Since Richard's car had been in Massachusetts on the night of the Craig shooting there were four other possibilities – bus, train, plane, or another car. No one, of course, would have gone far on foot. A boat was improbable but couldn't be ruled out. Airplane seemed the most logical alternative; therefore, Vecchio reasoned, Richard probably wouldn't have taken one. Meanwhile, Lamont began checking bus and train records to see if any name remotely resembling either of Silva's might turn up. None did. Bus and train travellers are anonymous.

Sullivan, Smith, and eventually Vecchio split the international airlines. Since both Congressman Coffin and Detective Sergeant Kelly had remarked that Silva might be tracking some unknown Frenchman, the three police investigators checked all passenger flights leaving for France since May 8. Yet they knew that Silva's name might have changed again, making him unrecognisable off a passenger list.

Saturday, Sunday, and Monday passed with no luck. Lamont had finished the train and bus assignments and was now constantly coming and going from the precinct, travelling to different sections of the city to check the various and tortuously long car rental records.

It was Smith who finally spoke on Tuesday night. 'Looks like our baby slipped away from us again,' he said. 'Balls!' The other men, frustrated, angry, and tired, were silent. Then they started over, each man checking the other's work, praying for something that had been missed the first time.

On Wednesday morning Lamont saved them. He located the record of the car that Richard had rented and then turned in at Montreal's Dorval International Airport. From there it was a simple matter of checking names on that day's flights departing from Montreal. It was Vecchio whose eyes opened wide with excitement early that afternoon. On the passenger list for Air France flight 008 the name Howard McKiernan leaped out.

Vecchio said only three words, but they were enough. 'We got him,' he said.

Further probing into Air France records revealed that Howard McKiernan had listed his occupation as a journalist and that his passport was Canadian. A simple check with Canadian authorities revealed that the passport, like the name and home address in Toronto, were fakes. Good fakes, but fakes nonetheless.

Accordingly, the FBI were notified.

The FBI, examining the case, concluded that Richard Silva had denied Clifford Craig his federally guaranteed civil rights (by shooting him), and possibly used a fraudulent passport, and had probably fled the state and country to avoid prosecution.

Based on New York State warrants, a federal warrant known as a 'you-fap' was issued for Richard Silva. The warrant's name was derived from its initials, UFAP. The letters stood, predictably enough for Unlawful Flight to Avoid Prosecution, something that Richard Silva was now believed, among other things to have done.

But now the warrant had to be taken one step further, to the Department of State in Washington. Papers for an extradition request were immediately drawn and sent by air to Paris where within hours they were delivered to the Sûreté Nationale.

The French police agents at the rue des Saussaies offices of the Sûreté Nationale took note of the charges against Richard Silva. 'Assault with intent to kill,' the Americans had generously termed it. Thus, for good measure, the dossier on Richard Silva was referred to the SN's Brigade Homicide.

Yet one other notation was made. Because Richard Silva

travelled on a false passport, the Direction de la Surveillance du Territoire (DST), the police agency that watches ports and border crossings, also received a copy of the dossier. A memo noting the case even arrived on the desk of the DST's chief, Jean-Claude Belfont.

Thus the involvement of Tony Vecchio and scores of other New York City police was at an end. No one yet knew what Clifford Craig had to do with the pursuit of a European torture specialist. But the entire affair had now burgeoned into a full-scale, all-out international manhunt.

41

At eight o'clock the next morning, having slept for no more than two hours, Charles Dissette convened a second meeting at the Justice Ministry. Again four men would be present.

Dissette was the first to arrive. He had fortified himself with black coffee and croissants and, although his stomach and nerves were in an uproar, he was both mentally and physically sharp. He tacked a map of Paris to a wall behind the oblong conference table. He laid several folders on the table before him.

The map would be functional. The folders were for effect. Dissette would work as he always preferred to work: without notes and relying on his incredible capacity for recall. His mind was such that it could remember tiny details or facts from years past, the alphabetical order of his class from his lycée, the licence numbers of all the cars he'd ever owned, the names of the men who'd served in the military service with him, or minor people in cases he'd been previously assigned to by the interior minister. The folders would merely support him in writing should anyone be foolish enough to challenge his memory.

Dissette nodded to Dutronc as his assistant from the Brigade Homicide arrived and seated himself. Moments later Dissette muttered a verbal greeting to the interior minister as the latter arrived.

Silently, as de Gaubert seated himself, Dissette cursed being brought into a case with overtones of internal French politics. Basically, Dissette hated both politics and politicians. He vastly preferred to be let loose with one of his usual foreign assignments, one in which he could avoid rigid supervision and employ his own methods. What was de Gaubert trying to prove by tying up an agent like himself with a case involving American children? Dissette had always suspected that the interior minister was something of a thumb-sucking idiot. Now Dissette was sure he'd been correct.

Yet he was stuck here. And he'd have to control his rage until much later that morning.

Then the final arrival, a man whose presence surprised Dutronc and de Gaubert, entered the room and took a seat. The man was Maurice Latour, the ministre des postes et télécommunications.

Dissette began.

He announced that Madame Thatcher had undergone a second operation the previous day. 'The bullet fragment was successfully removed from the base of the spine,' he said. 'I'm told that she has an excellent chance of being able to walk again. For that we can be thankful.'

There was visible relief in the room. One crisis, it seemed, was passing.

'We will turn our attention then,' Dissette continued, 'to the man – or men – who put her in the hospital in the first place. A correspondence was received yesterday. I'll discuss it presently. First, I'd like to explain where we are without this letter.'

Dissette eyed his audience and continued.

'The getaway car,' he announced, 'was found yesterday with a body in it.'

As his listeners leaned forward in unison, Dissette explained that the car had been located in an SNCF warehouse. 'However, the only recognizable fingerprints on the car were those of the owner, Monsieur Dubois. Those prints, I needn't add, are of little use to us. We did, however, find a live body in the car. It was that of a vagrant sleeping off a wine stupor when the car was located. The man is an alcoholic. We are, shall we say, drying him out. I think,' continued Dissette carefully, 'that this man has seen more than he would like to admit. I will personally be questioning this man. There are ways, as you know, of making even the most silent witness become vocal.'

Dissette's eyes caught subtle heightening of interest on the face of the interior minister. Dissette wondered what it meant, then continued.

'I have been in contact with the Sûreté Nationale. Their offices obtained for me the dossiers of the eight Bretons who are the subject of this attempted ransom. We have examined their files and are at present tracing down other people suspected of aiding them in 1969. So far we have found nothing, nor have we discovered anything from the many people we have who have links to Breton extremist groups. We have used all of our most reliable informants in Brittany and we've come across nothing. Similarly, we've scanned lists of thousands of Subversives whose files are kept by Renseignements Généraux. I've examined every name myself, the Daniel Cohn-Bendits, the Alain Fourriers, the Michel Duplasses, as well as those of lesser distinction and merit. Again, zero. Nor has an examination of all young girls leaving the country been able to turn up anything.'

Dissette was pacing slightly in front of his audience now.

'In short, gentlemen,' he continued, 'we have run through all our witnesses and checked all of our fingerprints. We have checked these eight convicts and we have checked their associates. We have used every spy and informant whom we trust. We have examined three or four times the name of every man or woman in France considered a subversive. And, gentlemen, we have found nothing.'

Dissette eyed a section of the map, weighed his words, and paused slightly.

'We may, however,' Dissette continued, 'begin to have some idea where the children are. We will have to take certain, shall we say, calculated risks. But if these risks are well taken and if I am allowed to continue this case in the way I see fit, I believe that we have an excellent chance of finding the Thatcher children and at least one of their abductors.'

De Gaubert could take no more without comment. 'Monsieur Dissette,' he broke in, 'could you kindly tell us what kind of risks you're talking about?'

'Certainly,' replied Dissette. 'I will be taking risks based on the little information that I have and the subsequent information that I will force our enemy to reveal to us.'

'Force?' asked de Gaubert.

Dissette gave a nod to Dutronc. At that signal Dutronc opened a folder and took out photocopies of the letter and envelope received the previous day. The photocopies were circulated around the table.

'This is our initial correspondence from this man,' said Dissette. 'And we will take care that it is not our last.'

Dissette then turned towards the map. With a forefinger he drew an imaginary circle around a section of Paris's Left Bank. The section was centred in the midst of the Fifth and Sixth Arrondissements. The occupants of the room hardly seemed in a receptive mood for a geography lesson. But they were about to get one.

'I think I've made my starting position clear, said Dissette. 'We are at rock bottom in this case. We are going to have to take the offensive and launch a counter attack of our own, one in which the enemy will be forced to play into our hands. Monsieur Latour,' Dissette said as he turned towards the postmaster, 'if I were to look at the cancellation on this envelope, what would I learn?'

All eyes in the room turned toward the postmark on the envelope.

'You would learn,' said the postal minister, 'that this letter was cancelled in Paris two mornings ago.'

'What else?'

'At the PTT station in the Fifth Arrondissement. On the rue Barsqué.'

'I see,' said Dissette. 'Now, how would it get to that postal station?'

'It would have to be dropped at the post office, left with the mail in a building, or dropped in a mailbox.'

'Now let's suppose, gentlemen,' said Dissette as he addressed the room at large, 'that I were a killer and a kidnapper. Would I mail a ransom letter at the post office where I might be seen? Or would I leave it with the concierge of my building so that she could see the address?'

Dissette felt a consensus of no to both rhetorical questions.

'No, I don't think I'd do either,' he continued. 'So Monsieur Latour, what alternative did that leave me?'

'A street mailbox,' said Latour.

'Exactly,' snorted Dissette enthusiastically. 'But now let's consider that message again for a moment. Let us assume that the sender, as he says, can leave his covert spot for only twenty minutes. That would mean, gentlemen, that he cannot be far away from whatever mailbox he chooses to use. Let's stretch the point for a moment.'

Dissette studied the interior minister as he spoke. He assumed de Gaubert was sceptical.

'Allow this man to walk at the absolute maximum ten minutes each way. Let's assume he walks briskly, taking two steps each second. I have calculated, messieurs, a man walking very briskly and with an abnormally long stride could probably do no more than cover seven hundred metres without breaking into a run. And a run would make him conspicuous, which is the last thing he'd wish to do. Reasonably speaking, this man would probably go less than this. He wouldn't cut so closely the time in which the children would suffocate. So I would calculate that this man would *have* to use a mailbox within seven hundred metres of his hiding place. Yet despite this, I will allow ample room for error. I will calculate that the man mails his letters as far away as a full kilometre from where he is hiding.'

'And what if he uses a bicycle?' asked de Gaubert. 'Or a car? Or boards a bus?'

'He wouldn't,' said Dissette, his eyes narrowing. 'I understand this type of man. He is treacherous. He is maniacal about details. He wouldn't depend on any form of transportation that would prove undependable. Consider the thought process, the psychology, of such a careful man. He couldn't possibly rely on anything except his own two feet.'

'All that aside,' said the interior minister, 'you cannot possibly believe him when he says he works alone. Someone could post his mail.'

'Conceivably,' admitted Dissette. 'But there's a reasonable chance that he is totally alone now.'

'Why?'

'The man we are dealing with is the evident mastermind of this whole ugly affair. He procured two other men – probably sympathetic politically – to abduct the children. But by now he has most likely dispatched these men out of the country before they could get in his way. I venture that our man is now alone, just as he says he is, making certain that everything is now completed properly.'

De Gaubert glanced at Marius Dutronc. Dutronc, the inspector from the Brigade Homicide, was silent, his face blank and his fingers steepled beneath his chin.

Dissette turned to the postal minister. He spoke with a calmer yet equally firm voice. 'How many street mailboxes are serviced by the rue Barsqué postal station?'

'One hundred and thirty-eight,' said Latour.

'And how many of those have priority pickups in the morning, pickups that would have allowed this letter to pass through for a ten a.m. cancellation?'

'Approximately half of them,' said Latour. 'Sixty-two.'

'So you'll want sixty-two police agents to monitor these mailboxes?' interrupted de Gaubert.

'That is exactly, monsieur,' said Dissette, 'what I do *not* want. We couldn't successfully hide a plain-clothes-man at each mail-box. Those children would be dead within a day. We will have to lure this man into corresponding with us as many times as possible. All mail placed in these mailboxes will be sorted separately and marked. I have already arranged for special collectors to cover *all* one hundred and thirty-eight boxes in this area. We must know immediately where this man is. And that we will know once he shows a pattern in his mailing procedures.'

'And once we know that?' asked de Gaubert thoughtfully.

'Once we're absolutely certain, we'll have two alternatives. We can cordon off the neighbourhood and turn it over stone by stone. Or, and this is vastly preferable, we could wait until we *spot* this man. Then we allow him to lead us back to his hiding place.'

'And how,' asked de Gaubert, 'do we compel this man to keep communicating with us?'

Dissette explained. 'Once again I have been in touch with our friends in the press. But this time I've asked them to run a false news story rather than suppress a real one. I've issued a false report through the Interior Ministry that the eight jailed Bretons are being considered for early parole due to 'extenuating new circumstances' in their case. The story appears prominently in this morning's papers. I would hope that we'd have a reply from the other side by tomorrow.'

'You're aware, I'm sure,' said de Gaubert, 'that not only are you completely out of order with such a story, but that France or any other civilised nation would never *ever* lessen a prison sentence under such circumstances.'

'True enough,' said Dissette. 'But I had no choice.'

De Gaubert raised his eyebrows thoughtfully and slowly nodded his consent. 'I have only one further question,' he added.

'Monsieur?'

'You implied that this vagrant, the one found in the abandoned car, might have observed something important. When will – ?'

'I intend to interrogate the man as soon as I leave here,' said Dissette.

'I hope you are more, shall we say, successful than the first police agents to question him.'

Dissette allowed himself a satisfied smile. 'He'll talk for *me*,' he said.

Dutronc glanced curiously at Dissette as the meeting concluded.

42

'There's no way around it,' said the man from Virginia. 'We're going to need French help.'

'Christ!' muttered Johnny Ray Logan. 'Christ and Christ again! Why couldn't you let me do it that way to start with?'

'It would have been easier my way,' said the Virginian in the dark brown suit, white shirt, and narrow tie. The man smoked furiously and coughed out the smoke. Neither enjoyed his expensive lunch.

'Yeah,' said Logan. 'Until it got bitched twice.'

'What are you so damned indignant about?' the Virginian retorted. 'You recruited him. A perfect nut to set up, you said.' He nodded sarcastically. 'Sure,' he said, drawing out the word.

Logan looked down to the plate in front of him and reached for his drink. He was silent in thought yet far from calm.

'It's done now,' said the Virginian. 'Now we've got to get him. Imagine if he ever gets back here.'

'Yeah,' said Logan, his eyes wide with anger and a trace of fear. 'I can imagine.'

'How can we get the French to help us?' asked the other man.

Logan explained. Since Richard Silva was now beyond the reach of any single man they could send after him to kill him, a certain unusual request would have to be made of the French government. The request, while unorthodox, would be far from unprecedented. It was the type of official favour routinely exchanged by the secret services and federal police of reasonably friendly nations. Essentially, Richard Silva would be branded by the Americans as both mentally unstable and a threat to American – and therefore Western – security. The secret service of France would thus be asked to terminate Richard Silva as a threat. Lethally and unofficially. Using the massive French government arsenal of wiretaps, hotel records, entry records, and passport controls, Logan explained, a man like Richard Silva could probably be found and tended to within days.

'And you can get them to do this?' asked the Virginian.

'I can make the request through State Department,' said Logan. 'But now we got a real nigger in the woodpile on this.'

'What's that?'

'A deal like this could only be worked if Silva had kept his nose clean in France,' Logan explained. 'From what you tell me, he killed one man and sent another to a doctor with crushed nuts.'

'Uh-huh.'

'So if the frogs find out who wasted someone on the tower of that church, they'll let their own police handle it. At least to start with.'

The Virginian thought. 'We've got to take the chance that they don't know Silva did that.'

'Do we? Why?' asked Logan.

'Because,' said the Virginian, 'I know people over at State, also. And they tell me it's not just a matter of getting to Silva and hitting him. It's a matter of getting him first.'

'First before who?' asked Logan. When it came to disturbing news, some days it sprinkled and some days it rained. But today it was pouring. 'Our friend wasn't all that careful with that job in New York. He left a trail.'

'A trail where?' Logan nearly swallowed wrong. This was going to be a triple martini lunch.

'A trail right behind him,' said the other man. 'State Department got a request from the New York police. They want a Richard Silva, alias Howard McKiernan, for "questioning" in the attempted murder of one Clifford Craig.'

Logan sat with his mouth gaping open. The other man ground his teeth together.

'They've got a bulletin out for him to the French police. The cops in Paris, if they're not too busy, will be looking to pick him up. Then they'll put through the extradition and, presto, if they take him alive he'll be right back in New York. Now,' said the Virginian as he leaned forward, 'what do you suppose he's going to say when they ask him why he shot Craig?'

Logan, becoming frightened, searched for the silver lining. 'I don't think he's much of a one to talk,' he said.

'Only when he doesn't want to talk,' said the Virginian. 'Wait till he decides to save his own neck. Suppose he goes for a reduced sentence. Suppose he tells about your office. Suppose he figured out where he was in Virginia. Jesus Christ, Logan, if this guy lets the lid off, we'll all be running for cover.'

Logan felt suddenly but genuinely sick to his stomach. 'I'm convinced,' he said slowly. 'I'll pull the strings this afternoon.'

The Virginian studied the congressman. 'What exactly do you have to do?' he asked.

'I can arrange an intelligence file to be sent through State Department,' said Logan pensively. 'It goes to some frog outfit like an SDT or DST or something.'

'And?'

'And one of their men arranges an execution. No questions asked.'

The Virginian cleared his throat noisily.

'You better hope that frog secret service hits this Silva bastard before their own cops take him alive.'

'They'll get him,' said Logan. 'He can't hide from the entire French government.'

43

On the next afternoon Richard again passed by the union hall on the rue Tournefort. He asked questions. He saw a few of the same people. And that evening he attended a noisy meeting of certain non-unionised auto workers from a local Citroën plant. Richard didn't understand their grievance, nor did he try to. Instead he searched the faces in the hall.

He recognised no one. But beneath his jacket, tucked into his belt, he carried his newly captured weapon.

On still the next afternoon he again was in the vicinity of the union hall. He glanced around it and actually received familiar nods from one or two people. Then he retreated to that same café half-way down the block. He was seated there for no more than twenty minutes when someone reached to an empty chair at Richard's small table.

Richard looked up into the face of Yves Ramereau.

'What is it?' Richard asked in French.

'You're a journalist, you say,' the visitor said in French.

'I am,' said Richard. He allowed Ramereau to sit down. 'And you?' he asked.

Ramereau shrugged innocently. 'A student,' he said.

'Of what?'

Ramereau eyed the foreigner closely. 'Life,' he said. He paused and added in English, 'People.'

Richard leaned back in his chair. 'I have the impression,' he said, switching to his native tongue, 'that you want to talk to me.'

'Who are you?' Ramereau asked bluntly.

Richard explained his false Canadian identity.

'You speak French like an American,' Ramereau said.

'Canadians and Americans speak English the same way,' said Richard. 'So they learn French with the same accent. Satisfied?'

'No,' said the Frenchman.

Richard tossed out his false passport and his press card on the café table. Ramereau leaned forward but made no attempt to examine either document. He considered Richard highly suspicious but not necessarily dangerous.

'Why are you looking for André Guisseny?' he asked.

Richard explained his alleged motives. 'Do you know where Guisseny is?' he finally asked.

'I might,' said Ramereau.

'What does "might" mean?'

Ramerau chose to taunt him.

'Ever read Balzac?' the Frenchman asked.

'No.'

'The old man in *Père Goriot* would recognise Guisseny's street,' Ramerau taunted. 'But you wouldnt'. North Americans have no sense of literature.'

'Do you always talk in puzzles?' Richard asked.

'Only when I choose to.'

'Why don't you repeat the last puzzle?' Richard said. 'I'm not sure I got it.'

Ramereau declined to repeat the allusion to Rastignac, a central character in *Père Goriot*.

'Well, if you won't repeat it,' said Richard, 'why don't you tell me straight out where I can find Guisseny?'

'Why don't *you* tell me straight out who you really are?' asked Ramereau, the anger in his voice poorly disguised. 'And what you really want.'

Richard looked his adversary in the eye. 'Guisseny has been in France, Africa, South America, and Asia for his causes,' said Richard. 'I need to talk to him. About his past and his future.'

Ramereau furrowed his brow, taking Richard more seriously now. 'How did you know where he's been?' he asked.

'It's my job to know those things.'

'I'm sure of that.'

'I'll pay,' said Richard slowly, 'for the information that will lead me to him.'

'You *must* be American,' smirked Ramereau. 'You think everyone can be bought.'

There was a tense moment. Then Ramereau relaxed slightly. From his inside jacket pocket he withdrew an envelope. On the back of it he wrote Richard's name and hotel location. Then, on a separate piece of paper, he scribbled a name and an address, a public square in Montmartre. Richard took the paper.

'So you want to find Monsieur Guisseny?' asked Ramereau cryptically.

Richard nodded.

'Then,' he said, motioning to the paper, 'you must ask this girl.'

44

Dissette presented himself at the main prefecture of police at a few minutes past noon. The object of his concern was Christien Langlois, the vagrant found sleeping off a stupor in the SNCF warehouse.

Langlois, sobered, fed, washed, and held as a material witness, had maintained a consistent silence over what he'd seen in that warehouse. Questioned first by the arresting officers and then by Dutronc, he insisted he'd stumbled into the unlocked warehouse, found the car, and curled up in it. Despite relentless questioning Langlois hadn't swerved from his story. The man simply didn't care to talk.

Then Dissette had taken charge, requesting that Langlois be held pending Dissette's personal interrogation.

Dissette escorted Langlois to an isolated interrogation room in the basement of the prefecture. The room contained no more than a desk, a pair of straight-backed wooden chairs, a stool, and a ceiling light. The walls were cement and thick; the door was solid oak. Dissette had not brought Langlois to such a room by coincidence. The room was soundproof.

Dissette sat Langlois on a wooden stool before the desk. Dissette sat on the desk and looked at his prisoner.

'*Et maintenant, Christien,*' Dissette began, 'you and I are going to share our secrets with each other.'

The vagrant looked up at the police officer. Dissette's eyes were dark.

'I have no secrets,' replied Langlois, experiencing a new

palpitation of fear. He longed for a drink. 'I've told everything I know.'

'I don't think so,' said Dissette. 'I think you saw the men who came with that car. I think you saw what they did and what they looked like.'

Langlois hesitated. '*Non*,' he said. '*Rien*.'

Dissette grimaced slightly. He spoke softly, yet tersely. 'Christien,' he said, 'I'm going to make it very uncomfortable for you until you tell me everything you saw.'

'*Rien*,' Langlois repeated.

Slowly Dissette slid off the edge of the desk. He walked slowly to the nervous man. He stood in front of Langlois. The vagrant, a man in his fifties, looked up at the ramrod-erect investigator.

Dissette's hand moved so quickly that Langlois never saw it coming. The palm smacked across Langlois's face from the left, then backward from the right.

The bum's eyes were wide with shock.

'No! I saw nothing!' the prisoner exclaimed. 'Nothing!'

Dissette grabbed the man by his shirt. He gripped him, jostled him, and lifted him from the stool.

'Liar!' roared Dissette. 'Liar!'

'No!'

Dissette dropped him and boxed him on each side of the head with a fist. Dissette knew how much the man could take without being permanently hurt. He pummelled the head four or five times. Langlois tried to protect himself with his arms. Dissette pushed the arms away and grabbed him by the scalp, slanting his captive's head back. Dissette held up an open hand and prepared to chop downward.

'Enough! Enough!' screamed Langlois.

'No,' said Dissette through clenched teeth. 'Talk.'

Dissette's hand struck again, viciously now, across the man's face. A cut appeared above the man's left eye. Now the bum was terrified, trapped in the small room with an apparent maniac. Blood began to pour from the cut.

'Please,' begged Langlois. 'Ple – '

Dissette chopped the man to the left side of the jaws. The blow rattled the man's teeth. Another upward chop on the other side of the face drove the jaws upward and forced teeth into the tongue. The vagrant's mouth started to bleed.

'Please! Please!' begged Langlois, trying to lean away from Dissette. But now Dissette brutally grabbed the man's throat, gripping it with steel fingers. Blood poured into Langlois's left eye from the cut above his brow.

The vagrant was breathing hard, panting, and wanting to scream. Yet he knew a scream would be useless. He had no defence. The entire left side of his face was bloodied.

Dissette glared at his captive. He released the grip from the man's throat. He reached to his own waist, loosened his belt and pulled it off. He doubled it over, knotting it before his prisoner's eyes and allowing the buckle to reinforce the knot.

'All right, Christien,' said Dissette. 'I'm ready to listen.'

Langlois stammered, then began. 'There were three men,' he said. The vagrant held a trembling protective arm before him. He continued. 'They had two cars. And two little girls . . .'

45

Yves Ramereau found Françoise at her usual spot at the place du Tertre. He moved quietly to a position behind her, thinking she'd not yet spotted him.

She spoke without facing him. 'What do you want?' she asked.

'A favour.'

She turned and looked him in the eye, giving him a hard stare that he'd never seen from her before. 'Forget it,' she said.

'The favour,' he continued after a slight pause, 'involves our political beliefs.'

'Not ours,' she countered. 'Yours.' She returned to her canvas, but he had already subverted her concentration.

'I want you to do something important for me,' he said.

She turned. 'Perhaps you didn't understand,' she said. 'I'm not interested in you, your politics, or any favours you need done. Leave me in peace and do me the service of never coming back here.'

She tried to recommence her work.

'Do you speak Canadian?' he asked.

She turned again, annoyed and distracted. 'What?'

'Canadian.'

'Canadian what?'

'There's a Canadian man coming to see you,' he said. 'I want you to find out who or what he is.'

She went back to her canvas.

'He's been hanging around the union hall. Asking questions. About Guisseny.'

'Good for him. If he comes to me, I'll tell him the answers.'

Ramereau grabbed her by the left arm and spun her back to him.

'If he comes to you,' he said between clenched teeth, 'you'll find out exactly who he is. Then you'll tell me.' He twisted her left wrist, applying pressure. She attempted to swing her paint brush at him with her free hand. He blocked her thrust, though paint spattered near his eye.

He glared at her with wide angry eyes. She was essential to discovering who this Howard McKiernan really was. There was no way that Ramereau would permit a woman to avoid her duty to either him or his cause.

He spoke just loud enough for her to hear. 'Either you find out who he is for me,' he said vengefully, 'or I'll see that every canvas you own is destroyed.'

He released her smarting wrist. Her eyes burned at him.

'Do you understand?' he asked.

She retreated from the urge to spit in his face.

She had no doubts that if she defied him, she would indeed lose every canvas she owned.

46

Dissette had moved out of his apartment and into his office. He slept there on the cot when he slept at all, he took his meals either there or at a local café. He shaved there, he kept a few changes of clothes there, and he used the washrooms there. He told himself, by the third day of the Thatcher ordeal, that he would somewhere that day find a spot to take a shower or a bath.

But on this morning, despite an acute case of late-night insomnia, Dissette opened his eyes at ten past eight quite naturally. Since it was raining heavily, he couldn't even accuse the sunlight of sneaking through the office blinds to wake him.

What had actually roused him, and what had contributed to his sleeplessness for the better part of the night, was the growing doubt that he was on the right course.

He couldn't wait for the mail to be delivered. Accompanied by a bleary-eyed Marius Dutronc, he arrived at the Fifth Arrondissement PTT station on the rue Censier. It was there where the mail from street boxes in the entire Fifth, Sixth, and northern Thirteenth Arrondissements would be sorted and forwarded. And it was there where Dissette would hope for a break.

He got one.

Waiting for Dissette and Dutronc at that postal station was the morning's entire pickup of mail. There were more bags than either man wished to count. Yet, as arranged with the station's postmaster, every bag was marked. Smaller bags within the larger bags were labelled, too. The origin of every single letter picked up had been duly noted. Every single pickup was in its own postal bag, kept separate from all others.

And so, at a few minutes past eight that morning, Dissette and Dutronc began their laborious search for a single letter that might not have been there at all.

The minutes passed slowly, painfully. Nine o'clock arrived. Then ten.

It was Dutronc who was suddenly to exclaim, '*La voilà!*' to his superior. And there it was, indeed. Dutronc held it aloft. The second letter from the kidnapper, mailed from a small red-and-blue iron PTT box on the rue Vauquelin.

'God in heaven!' exclaimed Dissette in joy. His whole maligned scheme might hold water after all.

At ten thirty that morning Dissette met with de Gaubert in the usual conference room. Dissette showed the letter he'd intercepted. Then he humbly announced that it had appeared, as he'd predicted, in a mailbox in the Fifth Arrondissement.

'Accordingly,' said Dissette, 'if my predictions are correct, the abductor and the children can be found within one thousand metres of that PTT box. Observe.'

Dissette had already measured off a strand of string that represented one kilometre on the scale of the map behind him. On one end of the string he placed a felt-tip marking pen, point to the map. The other end he held with his finger, precisely at the spot where the rue Vauquelin mailbox was located.

Then, holding the finger in place, he drew a huge circle on the map, stepped back from it to consider it, and then turned to de Gaubert.

'Monsieur,' he said, 'that area within the circle represents about three point fourteen square kilometres of city blocks. Not a large area at all. I would suggest,' continued Dissette, 'that if my theory proves accurate, the man we are looking for is within this circle at this very moment.'

Dissette allowed his words to sink in. There was a silence in the room.

'Accordingly,' the inspector continued, 'I have issued a false story to the newspapers. The story will state that pardons are being considered for *only* four of the eight imprisoned Bretons.' Dissette paused and, with a nuance of a smile, continued.

'I want our friend to have to write to us to turn down any compromise,' he said.

47

'I can't help you,' she said.

Richard stood on the edge of the place du Tertre watching Françoise Durand sweep her brush across a canvas. She stood with her back to Richard and did her best to ignore him.

'Does the name André Guisseny mean anything to you?' he persisted.

'Nothing,' she said. 'Now go away.'

'I was told you could help me,' he said.

With anger evident in her eyes, she turned towards Richard and set her brush down at the easel. She studied his face.

'Look,' she asked, 'what is this all about?' I want nothing to do with it.'

'I'm looking for a man named André Guisseny,' he said. 'I was told that – '

'You were told that I could help you find him.'

He nodded. 'Right.'

'I'm curious,' she said thoughtfully. 'You said you're a Canadian. You've never met this man. Why are you looking for this one man?'

'For a newspaper report,' he said. 'I explained before – '

She looked at him with an expression that told Richard she was weighing how much to say.

'I know nothing,' she said. 'If someone said I could help you, someone played a joke on you.' She shrugged. 'Talk of something else.'

'Ever read Balzac?' he asked.

'What?'

'Balzac,' he said. '*Père Goriot.*'

'What about it?'

'You've read it?'

'When I was in lycée,' she said. 'Long ago. But what – ?'

'What part of Paris would old Goriot recognise?'

She thought for a moment, amused by the seemingly harmless line of questioning.

'The Latin Quarter, I suppose,' she said thoughtfully. 'The . . . the Faubourg St Marcel, isn't it?'

He smiled. 'If you say so,' he said.

She tried to return to the canvas she was painting. But she was quickly aware that this foreigner was not to be so easily satisfied. He was now inspecting her other paintings, perusing them as a prospective buyer might.

'Where *is* the Faubourg St Marcel?' he finally asked.

'In the Fifth Arrondissement,' she said. 'As any city map would tell you.'

'It's easier to ask a native,' he replied. He moved from one canvas to the next. She noticed his limp. Now she too was curious. Who was he?'

'Want me to give you directions how to get there?' she asked.

'No,' he said. 'What I'd really like is for you to show me.'

'On foot?'

'I have a car,' he said with a sincere smile. 'And I'll buy you dinner if you come with me.'

She looked at Richard carefully. Then she thought of her canvases, the ones that Ramereau had promised to destroy if she didn't find out more about this foreigner.

'I leave here at six in the evening,' she said. 'I'll wait for you.'

48

The director of the DST sat in his office and opened the dossier marked urgent. It had arrived on his desk during his lunch hour.

Belfont pulled out several sheets of paper, recently arrived by diplomatic pouch from Washington. He studied the contents.

Belfont's counter-espionage agency was being asked to pass on to the interior minister an American request for help. The Americans, for unnamed reasons of national security, wanted a man named Richard Silva – an American national travelling in France under a false name and false passport – found and, if possible, destroyed.

Belfont pondered the request. He might have okayed it and sent it along to the interior minister's office, but instead he dwelt for several seconds on the name of the man involved. The DST director dealt with dozens of names per day, hundreds per week, and thousands per month. Yet this one crackled with a distant familiarity. Why?

Belfont thought again. Then he realised that three days earlier he'd seen the same name on a confidential memo from the Sûreté Nationale. Ever on guard for hidden implications, Belfont reviewed that other memo.

An hour later Belfont was in the office of the interior minister.

The minister was holding what Belfont had brought him, the DST request from the Americans and the SN folder on Richard Silva. The intelligence request for the location and elimination of Richard Silva had been unusually – and perhaps intentionally – sketchy, much less specific than the U.S. State Department order for Silva's arrest and extradition. Yet the first request had been made with no apparent knowledge that the second would follow. And even more unorthodox, the second request did not necessarily cancel the first. It was as if the American agency that issued the first request was never to find out about the second.

'I know you have headaches enough with the Thatcher affair,' apologised Belfont. 'But why a routine request for a would-be killer? And then a high-priority request for the termination of the same man?'

De Gaubert showed no expression at all. Considering the turmoil his ministry had been in in the last few days, he was tempted to ignore the matter and let his secret service agents handle Silva. But de Gaubert also knew Belfont. He recognised what Belfont wanted – a chance to investigate. And since he'd need Belfont's good will particularly in the next few days, he decided to humour him. After all, it was Belfont's agent Corbeau whom de Gaubert had borrowed in his investigation of a freelance French torturer.

'I won't pass this along to the secret service yet,' de Gaubert said. 'I'll hold it for a few days. You can investigate.'

Belfont smiled. 'Thank you,' he said.

De Gaubert looked at his colleague. 'What exactly do you plan to do?' he asked.

'I'm going to telephone the New York police immediately,' said Belfont. 'I want their full file on this Silva. I'd like to know whether he might be of some . . . informative use to us.'

De Gaubert nodded. He did not dislike the idea.

'Let me know what you find,' said the minister.

49

'As far as I could discover,' she said, 'he's exactly who he said he was.'

Ramereau looked at her in disgust. His hands were in the side pockets of his ever-present tattered corduroy jacket. She returned his gaze with animosity.

'That's the best I can do for you,' she said. 'Now why don't you leave me out of this?'

'Damn you,' he said.

Françoise had spoken with Richard for more than four hours. They'd driven around the Left Bank, mostly the student quarter and the Fifth Arrondissement. Then they'd dined not far from his hotel in the Seventh. He had gone into elaborate detail describing his non-existent newspaper work in Toronto. He referred constantly to his need to contact this Breton named Guisseny.

She had not disliked him. Yet she'd told him nothing. In response to her questions on his own background his story had never wavered: born and raised in Canada, now assigned to a story about Europeans who'd aided the North Vietnamese cause.

'His story was always the same,' she said. 'If you want more work done on him, have someone else do it. I'm incapable.'

Ramereau sat down on the bed in her apartment. He fleetingly thought of demanding sex from her. He would have found it an excellent way of re-establishing his dominance and of alleviating his anger. Instead, she spoke.

'The only other thing he was interested in,' she said, 'was Balzac.'

He looked up. 'What?'

'Balzac. *Père Goriot*,' she said.

'What about it?' he snapped. He felt a rumble of fear in his stomach. The North American *had* understood his vague allusion to the rue Rastignac.

'He kept asking about the book. About street locations. About recognising streets.'

'What did you tell him?'

She was afraid of him, knowing his temper. 'Nothing,' she lied.

He moved quickly to her and grabbed her by the shoulders, shaking her as if to dislodge the truth.

'Tell me!' he demanded. 'What did you tell him?'

'Nothing,' she repeated, her fear of him increasing.

He looked her in the eye. He sensed the lie. He pulled away his hand and then smashed her across the face with an open palm.

'I didn't tell him anything,' she pleaded, her voice breaking, her eyes wet. 'I haven't read the book.'

'Then why did he keep asking?'

'How would I know?' she asked, her cheek hot and painful from his blow. 'You tell me. You have all the answers.'

He released her and glared at her for a moment before moving toward the door.

'Damn him,' he cursed. He reached into his inside pocket and withdrew several papers. On the back of an envelope he found Richard's hotel address. 'Now,' he muttered, 'he'll have to be stopped.'

50

Richard found an English-language bookstore on the rue de Rivoli. There, still intrigued by Ramereau's cryptic allusion, he purchased an English version of Balzac's *Père Goriot*. He planned, on returning to his hotel, to read the book and make notes on each locale mentioned. He already had a map of Paris to spread out beside him as he read. Richard was convinced that he was on the proper track. Something soon would have to make sense.

But on his return to the Hotel Corbet, he was called aside by M. Lechêne, the day concierge.

'Ah, monsieur,' said Lechêne. 'There is a gentleman here to see you.'

Instantly Richard was on guard, conscious again of the weapon he carried.

'Where?' he asked.

Lechêne motioned to a small anteroom beside the main lobby of the hotel. Lechêne led Richard to the room and then stopped short. The room was empty.

'He was here just five minutes ago,' said Lechêne quizzically. 'I was away from my desk for just a few moments. No one left the hotel. Maybe – '

Instantly Richard bolted towards the stairs. As fast as his bad leg and hip could carry him he raced up three flights. He ran down the corridor and saw easily that his door had been forced in.

Richard heard movement in his room. He burst in.

Ramereau. In the midst of searching the room, searching for Richard's actual identity.

'You!' snapped Richard bitterly. Ramereau had a desk drawer in his hands. Richard slammed the door and blocked the intruder's exit. Then, suddenly sensing the opportunity to force information from Ramereau, he allowed himself a slow sly smile. 'Find what you were looking for?' he asked.

Ramereau, unintimidated, smiled back. 'I did,' he said calmly.

Richard was silent, his amusement gone. Ramereau held aloft the envelope he'd torn open. Richard's suitcase, where the envelope had been, lay broken open on the bed. Ramereau proudly showed the driver's licence and social security card that had been in the manilla envelope.

'Who would Richard Silva be?' asked Ramereau. 'You, perhaps?' Ramereau grinned and tauntingly let the documents drop to the floor.

Incensed, Richard grabbed for the gun in his belt. But at the same moment Ramereau pitched the desk drawer at Richard. Richard managed to duck and throw up both arms to defend himself. But the hard corner of the drawer hit Richard with full force in the left temple. The impact staggered him back against the door. Ramereau was on him, trying to push by, to escape.

Richard grabbed Ramereau by the shirt and yanked him back. But Richard was off balance and halfway to his knees. Ramereau kicked at him and flailed with his fists. Again he caught Richard on the left side of the head. Ramereau wasn't a large or strong man. But he was stringy and agile. He couldn't be overpowered.

A knee thumped Richard sharply on his left hip. Richard gagged as a sharp pain shot through his body. Ramereau shoved Richard hard against a dresser and broke free.

Richard groped for his gun. He yanked it from his belt and released the safety catch in the same movement.

'Hold it!' he roared.

But Ramereau was through the door. Richard lurched through the door and fired wildly as Ramereau bounded towards the stairs.

Richard attempted to pursue. But his hip had been hit hard. His leg wouldn't respond. Richard staggered down one flight of stairs and in vengeance fired a second time.

The terrified Ramereau heard the bullet whistle by his shoulder. But, leaping down the stairs so fast that he almost stumbled, Ramereau continued. Down to the first floor. Then out through the lobby.

Richard followed to the lobby. But Ramereau was gone. Lechêne, his eyes wide with fear, stood speechless behind the con-

222

cierge's desk. He did not understand. Nor did he wish to.

Richard, however, understood what Lechêne tried next. He grabbed his telephone and dragged it by its long cord into the next room. He bolted the door behind him and dialled the police.

'Christ!' exploded Richard. He had no choice. He climbed over Lechêne's desk and slammed against the bolted door. He put a shoulder to it, preparing to shove it in. Then he saw the long telephone cord leading beneath the door.

Richard grabbed the cord and pulled. It snapped from its connection in the wall. Lechêne was disconnected. But Richard had bought only a few minutes.

He raced back upstairs, His body ached, his hip throbbed, and he knew that his forehead was bruised if not gashed. And he'd never be able to stay at this hotel . . . or any other under his new assumed name.

Richard spent less than ninety seconds throwing everything he owned into his suitcase. He ran back down the stairs. He heard Lechêne's door slam again. He didn't know whether the hotel keeper had summoned police yet or not.

But it didn't matter.

Richard walked calmly on to the street, though bathed in sweat. He cut through two side streets until he was convinced that no one followed. Then he disappeared into the métro.

He felt his forehead on the left side. No blood, but a wicked smarting bump. He cursed wasting two bullets. And he cursed Ramereau.

Yet now he had to find him. Quickly.

Richard had no doubt where Ramereau would go next.

To Guisseny. To warn him.

51

'There can be no compromise,' Guisseny wrote in his next correspondence. 'All eight men must be free or the children die.'

The note was again constructed of letters clipped from a newspaper. It was tucked in a stamped envelope.

Guisseny placed the envelope on the table with a gloved hand. Then he opened the trap door and let himself down into that subbasement. The girls were tied to two heavy chairs.

Though the girls had already lost weight in their captivity, they were not yet numb to terror. They had been fed twice that day, milk and bread each time. They had not been allowed out of that underground room since their abduction and a stench was building down there. When they'd had to excrete, Guisseny had only pointed to earthy corners of the room and laughed. By the third day the smell was acrid and nauseating.

Guisseny grabbed Anne roughly and gagged the terrified eight year old first. He pointed to the trunk and indicated that he'd again soon be going out. Cynthia was next. Her hands were already tied. But as Guisseny went to gag her again, the terrified girl sank her teeth into his wrist. With his free hand he walloped her across the face so hard that for an instant he thought he'd broken her neck.

He managed to gag her and shove her into that trunk with her sister. The trunk was slammed shut. Muffled sobbing could still be heard. Why *not* kill them, he thought again. By now they practically deserved it. Maybe he just wouldn't feed them. Let them starve.

He hoisted himself up to the ground floor and replaced the heavy trap door. A few moments later he was outside.

This time he went to a mailbox on the rue Rémusset, a walk of less than two hundred metres from the rue Rastignac. For a fleeting second as he posted the letter he wondered if there was any way in which his mail could be traced.

Surely, he thought, it couldn't be traced without the government's staking out every mailbox in Paris. Hadn't he last time posted his letter a full four hundred metres in the other direction? He wouldn't correspond all that often, anyway. No one was going to lure him into doing that.

But just for good measure he stood for a few moments after mailing the letter and walking from the box. He turned and watched for three full minutes. No one rushed to open the mailbox. He grinned. Maybe he was getting paranoid. He turned and walked briskly back to the rue Rastignac. Another few minutes and the girls would start to suffocate. Would it really bother him, he wondered.

He was turning down his street, just a few metres from that invisible entrance, when he heard his name called. He whirled.

He saw Ramereau hurrying towards him. Not this, he thought. Not this above all. Any intrusion could prove catastrophic.

'I've got to talk to you,' Ramereau exclaimed. 'It's important!'

Guisseny thought of the girls in the trunk. This was just the type of interference that would kill them. 'Not now,' he snapped. 'I'm in a rush.'

'To where?' asked Ramereau.

'None of your business,' said the infuriated Guisseny. 'Get lost or you'll ruin something crucial.'

'For the movement?'

'Get lost!'

'Where are you going?' gloated Ramereau. 'Those old houses?'

Guisseny froze. Then he turned and looked carefully at Ramereau. 'What old houses?' he asked.

'The ones on this street,' said Ramereau. 'That's where you've been, isn't it?'

'Why do you think that?' asked Guisseny calmly.

'I followed you one day,' said Ramereau, proud of his skills as a sleuth. 'I saw where you went.'

'Was anyone with you?' asked Guisseny.

'No, I'm the only one who knows. You can trust me, I – '

'You say you have something important to tell me,' said Guisseny.

Ramereau nodded. Guisseny masked his anger. 'Then you must leave me now and meet me later.'

'It's important,' reiterated Ramereau.

'All right, all right,' said Guisseny. 'I know your address. Be there at eleven this evening. Be alone and don't tell a soul I'm coming.'

'Can't I tell you now?'

'Not now!' raged Guisseny. 'Later! You must be there later and you must let me go now!'

Guisseny didn't even wait for a response. He turned and ran, moving as quickly as he could back to number 11 on that street. He pushed through the old door and shoved it closed behind him. He stumbled through the rubble and down into the passage that led beneath the houses and the street. If Ramereau followed him now, he thought, he'd have to kill him immediately.

Guisseny fumbled his way to that sub-basement and clutched the trunk key from his shoe. He unlocked and threw open the trunk.

They were alive. Coughing through their gags, but alive.

He unbound their mouths. They gasped for air. They stared at him, mute with horror.

For the first time, he almost pitied them.

52

Richard proceeded quickly across the city. He had to avoid the police. But he also had to find Ramereau. Immediately. Before Guisseny was forewarned.

Richard went first to the gare St Lazare. He checked his suitcase in the station, then set out on foot to the inexpensive and inelegant hotels northward behind the train depot. Richard was relying on instinct now. But he had an idea that might see him through.

Richard walked until he came to a hotel that seemed to be in a suitable state of decline.

He entered the lobby. A fat unshaven man in his forties manned an old desk. The lobby needed paint, just like the hotel's exterior. Richard inquired about rooms.

'By the day?' asked the hotel keeper in French.

'*Par jour*,' affirmed Richard.

The man looked at Richard closely, particularly intrigued by the fresh battering that Richard's face had taken. But hotel keepers know better than to ask silly questions.

The man threw open a register. Richard looked around to see that no one else was within hearing distance.

'What I'd like,' Richard said in subdued tones, 'is to have a room without signing anything.'

The fat man looked up. He laid down the pen beside the register. He explained gutterally that Richard's wish was both illegal and impossible.

Richard withdrew his hand from his pocket. He laid two one-hundred franc notes across the hotel register.

'*Des ennuis avec la police, eh?*' smiled the man.

'I lost my passport,' said Richard.

The man looked at the money. Richard continued to speak. 'Two hundred francs today. One hundred francs each additional day. Cash. No questions. No explanations.'

The man noted that if discovered, he too would be having difficulties with the police. But seeing as no one would ever know . . .

His hand moved towards the money.

53

At eight thirty that evening, the agent called Corbeau went unnoticed as he walked into a crowded *tabac*. He proceeded directly to a public telephone. He removed a *jeton* from his pocket, dropped it into the pay telephone, and dialled.

On the other end, the telephone rang in the residence of Jean-Claude Belfont. The director of the DST heard a recognisable voice on the line.

'*Ici Corbeau,*' said the voice.

'What's wrong?' asked Belfont.

'I'm not getting anywhere,' said Corbeau. He looked each way in the *tabac*. Then his gaze carried out past the sidewalk tables and across the street to a red-brick apartment house. Corbeau had just left the building, having entered and searched a private residence.

'I got into his apartment, searched it up and down and found nothing,' said Corbeau. 'Absolutely nothing.'

Belfont let out a long pained sigh. He tried to think.

'I've been watching this bastard day and night almost every minute for days now,' continued Corbeau. 'And we're not going to prove anything against him this way.'

'Can you suggest something?' asked Belfont.

'Find someone who can identify this torturer. One way or another.'

'Impossible,' said Belfont. 'We'd need an American, one of his victims. To start with, we don't have one. And even if we did. we wouldn't want an American involved.'

Corbeau was thoughtfully silent on the other end. 'I'll stay with it until hell freezes over,' he said. 'But it doesn't look promising.'

Belfont sighed. 'Do what you can,' he said. 'I'll talk to de Gaubert again if nothing happens within another week.'

The two men signed off. Corbeau disappeared from the *tabac* while Belfont, at home, lounged pensively in a leather easy chair.

Three hours later another man, known to both Corbeau and Belfont, passed by the same *tabac*. He enjoyed Alsatian beer and sandwiches before returning to his home across the street. The man was quitting early that night due to the strenuous hours he'd been keeping of late.

The man was Charles Dissette.

54

That night Guisseny was for the first time diverted from his carefully made plan. He would have to go out to remove Ramereau as a possible lapse in his security. Worse, he would have to deal with Ramereau without sealing the children inside that trunk. It would take him at least an hour to get to the Thirteenth Arrondissement and back. The children would have to be tied and gagged. But they couldn't be locked in the trunk.

Toward ten that evening, Guisseny descended into the sub-basement prison. He explained in his impoverished English that he would be tying up the girls but wouldn't be locking them into the hated trunk. Then he looked for the best rope he could find for his purposes. All he had was a sturdy thick hemp, something better intended for use in pulling in the sails of a ship. He gagged the girls and tied their legs and wrists painfully tight. And he left them in semi-darkness in that stinking grotto.

Then he loaded his pistol, the same weapon that had cut down Barbara Thatcher and William Simmons. He tucked the gun under his overcoat and left via the métro for his rendezvous with Ramereau.

Within minutes, Anne's agile young wrists had slipped from the thickly knotted rope that had held them. In a frenzy she undid the gag and the painful ropes on her ankles. She rushed to her sister and undid her, both of them experiencing a terrifying yet exuberant sense of freedom. Then they looked above them.

They could see a dim ring of light around the contours of the trap door. If only they could get up there!

Guisseny was early. He arrived in the warehouse district of rue Pierre Levée at ten thirty. It was not yet ten forty when Ramereau opened the door of his loft apartment and admitted the Breton.

The streets outside were quiet. Ramereau's building, being commercial, was empty. A caretaker watched the premises during the day, but was home in bed at this hour.

Guisseny seated himself in a shabby chair as he eyed the room around him. Ramereau spoke, noticing that Guisseny had for some reason worn a light pair of gloves and had not yet removed them.

'You're not going to believe what I have to tell you,' Ramereau began. But Guisseny had not come to listen.

'Why did you follow me?' asked the Breton coldly. 'That was stupid. I resent having been followed.'

'It was important,' replied Ramereau.

'Nothing could be more important than what I'm involved in. No one was to know my location. No one!'

'Why don't you let me in on things?' asked Ramereau. 'It would be so much easier.' He was about to tell Guisseny about the North American when he heard a click. He turned to face the Breton. Then he froze.

The expression on his face was quizzical. He saw the gun but didn't understand. Guisseny offered no explanation.

Instead, the Breton pulled the trigger twice. Two sharp and resonant blasts exploded from the barrel of the gun.

Ramereau felt two blazing hot pains rip through his chest. He staggered backwards and thudded against a closet door. His eyes were wide in incomprehension and terror. He slumped downward and fell.

One bullet had nicked the left ventricle of Ramereau's heart. But Guisseny took no chances. The Breton rose from his chair and walked to the fallen younger man.

Ramereau's eyes were still flickering. Guisseny pulled back Ramereau's head by grabbing the hair. He pushed the gun into Ramereau's face and fired. The bullet entered the brain from between the eyes.

Guisseny made no attempt to clean the blood from the floor or a nearby closet door. He did, however, push the body into the closet, turning the cluttered storage area into an impromptu coffin. Then he pushed the shabby heavy chair in front of the closet, hiding the patches of wet blood.

Guisseny turned off the light. He locked the door behind him as he left.

By the time the Breton boarded the métro, Anne Thatcher, the older and larger of the two sisters, was standing on top of the trunk. She was reaching up, reaching to that trap door that suggested freedom.

Her fingertips could touch. Just barely. She kept trying.

Several minutes later, the trap door opened from above. An angry booted foot shoved the little girl in the face, sending her sprawling back into the filth and darkness.

Guisseny was back. In time.

55

Françoise did not recognise the knock at her door. It was nine in the evening. She had no reason to expect a visitor.

She opened the door.

'Yes?' she asked, looking Richard Silva in the eye.

'I want to talk,' he said in French. 'May I come in?'

She hesitated for only a second, then said yes. She noticed the massive bump on the side of his head. She also noticed that his limp was more pronounced.

He looked around the main room of the small apartment. With her permission, he seated himself on a sofa.

'Where can I find your friend?' he asked.

'What friend?'

'The punk who sent me to you,' he snapped. 'I caught him ransacking my hotel room. Or did you already know?'

'If you only came here with accusations,' she replied coldly, 'you can leave now.'

He felt the side of his head throbbing with discomfort. But he calmed himself. He tried to proceed methodically. 'What's his name?' he asked.

'Yves Ramereau,' she said. 'Are you hurt?'

'Does it matter?'

'Ramereau always resorts to force,' she said. 'He makes me sick.'

Richard studied her, not knowing whether or not to believe her.

'I thought he was your friend,' he said.

'No longer,' she said. 'What is he trying to hide?'

'Guisseny, I suppose.'

'Why?'

'I haven't any idea,' he said. 'Maybe you do.'

'Me?'

'I was told you knew where he was,' Richard said. 'You still haven't convinced me that you don't.'

She crossed the room and sat down on the sofa a few feet from him.

'Listen,' she said. 'Ramereau wanted me to find out who you are. He's convinced you're not a journalist. He threatened me if I didn't find out. I tried to find out. I failed. I still don't know. But I also don't care. I don't care about him, Guisseny, or their politics.'

She looked at the side of his head. She could determine the force of the blows he'd taken. 'What are you going to do if you find Guisseny?' she asked.

'Talk to him,' he said.

She looked at him. 'I'm not sure that I believe you,' she said.

'Why would I lie?'

'What about Ramereau?' she asked. 'What will you do if I send you to him?'

'Does he know where Guisseny is?'

She shrugged. 'He must.'

'Then I'll get the information I need from him,' said Richard.

'By force, if necessary?' she asked.

He returned her gaze. 'If necessary,' he conceded.

She pondered it for a moment. With her left hand she slightly twisted a ring on a finger of the opposite hand. A slight smile crossed her face.

'He lives in a loft on the rue Pierre Levée,' she said.

'Do you know exactly where?' he asked.

She did. She told him.

He rose to leave, still not convinced that she was telling him the truth. He crossed the room towards the door, thanking her.

'Did he hurt your leg, too?' she asked.

He turned. 'What?'

'You're limping,' she said. 'Did he hurt your leg? Ramereau?'

'Yes,' he said after a moment's hesitation. 'I guess he did.'

'Now I'm convinced,' she said.

'About what?'

'You. You're not who you say you are.'

He waited for an explanation.

'A man who lies about one thing will lie about anything,' she said. 'Your leg injury isn't new. You had it the other day. It's only worse now.'

He faced her fully. 'You're perceptive,' he said. 'But what does my leg matter?'

'It doesn't. But *I* told you the truth.'

A moment passed in silence. He looked at her. He was suddenly – and for the first time in years – aware of a woman's frailties and sensibilities. A certain uneasiness was upon him, a sense of having violated a trust. Despite the pistol beneath his jacket, he felt defenceless.

'Before I leave Paris,' he said, 'I'll tell you about my leg.'

'Will you also tell me who you are?'

He wanted to say yes. 'You've seen my passport,' he shrugged. 'And my press card.'

His answer was a disappointment.

'Good-bye,' she said. 'I hope you find whatever you're looking for.'

56

When Richard Silva arrived at the address on the rue Pierre Levée it was almost midnight. The ground floor door to Ramereau's building was unlocked. Richard tried the door knob and pushed the door open.

The door led to a stairway. A light switch allowed him ninety seconds of light, enough to take him to Ramereau's door on the third floor.

Richard, conscious of the gun in his belt, stopped at the door and listened. He heard nothing. He placed his hand on Ramereau's door knob. The door was locked. He knocked. Again, nothing.

If he could enter the apartment, Richard thought, he could prowl through it. He could also wait for Ramereau. Richard found another light switch. He lit the halls again. He looked for something that would help him force Ramereau's lock.

It took twenty minutes. Eventually Richard located the caretaker's closet on the lower level. The closet was padlocked, but Richard forced the closet door upward on its aged hinges. With a long creak, the door gave way, breaking off the metal loops upon which the lock had been secured.

Within the closet Richard found tools. He returned upstairs with a hammer and screwdriver.

Before setting to work he listened again. Not a sound from within Ramereau's loft. Richard placed the blade of the screwdriver between the door and the frame just to the side of the door knob. Then he crashed the hammer against the butt end of the screwdriver. Six hard smashes pried back the lock.

The door was open.

Richard drew his pistol. He released the safety catch and pushed the door open. When nothing moved, he stepped in. He groped for a light switch, found it, and lit the room.

Richard searched through papers strewn on the floor, on a desk and on tables. He glanced at the books lining the room. Most were in French, some in German, a few in English. He was reminded of college, almost a lifetime ago. The one window in the room overlooked an alley.

Richard handled and turned over item after item in that room. Then, after several minutes, he noticed the chair position against the closet door.

Richard pushed the chair away from the closet. He looked down. Blood. On the floor. On the closet door.

The blood was dark now. It had had time to dry. Or at least most of it had. Some of it was still damp. Fresh. The freshest bloodstains had flowed from under the closet door.

Richard eased the closet door open. He felt a leap of nausea in his stomach.

'Jesus,' he muttered to himself.

Ramereau's body, with the midpoint of the skull blown in, was slumped to the left in a deathly and awkward pose. The eyes of the corpse were neither open nor closed. They were unseeing and caked with dried blood. Richard felt as he'd felt in the Montreal hotel room: as if he were about to vomit in disgust.

Richard nudged the body with a foot. The corpse slumped farther to the left. Richard reached down. He felt a wrist. No rigor mortis at all. The body was still warm. The death – the slaying – was fresh.

Richard gazed at the corpse for a few moments before reshutting the closet door.

He looked at the ruined face and the bloodied chest. This one man who could have led him to Guisseny was now dead.

It was beyond coincidence.

57

The article that was nestled onto the second or third pages of all the Parisian newspapers mystified regular readers. What did the financial status of the American Ambassador matter to them? And why was it a matter of public record, appearing in all the daily papers and occupying a reasonably prominent spot within the national affairs sections?

To one reader, André Guisseny, the mystery took a different form. Each morning he would now lock the children in that trunk and would buy the morning papers, waiting for his adversaries to correspond with him. And now this article. It was more an annoyance to Guisseny than anything else. Here Guisseny had put pressure on his own government through the Americans, enough pressure so that they may have been considering pardoning the Breton terrorists. And now they were trying to quibble about money. The cheapskates! *Les grippe-sous!*

He re-read the article. The American ambassador, Kenneth Thatcher, had been suffering reverses in his personal finances for some time back in the United States, reverses that had placed him on the brink of insolvency. Such was the situation, the story concluded, that Thatcher was anxious to return to the United States as soon as 'pressing family matters' had been resolved in Paris.

The message to Guisseny was clear. The Americans, businessmen to the end, wanted to bicker about the ransom price. Such a move amazed Guisseny. First it presupposed that the demands for eight paroles were to be met, despite a previous article hinting that only four were under consideration. And second, Guisseny had considered 500,000 francs to be a reasonable price for the two children, almost a bargain compared with what some kidnappers would charge. These Americans. No concept of the value of human life. Typical!

But as Guisseny went over the article several times, he began to draw a message from what wasn't said. There was no mention of the Bretons at all. Did the Americans simply think they could buy their way out and let the French government off the hook? Or was there a trick submerged somewhere?

Perhaps he hadn't made himself clear. The release of the Breton patriots was a prerequisite to any cash payment. Of course he'd made himself clear! What was going on? As if they had a position to bargain from!

Guisseny's anger was rising. Maybe he ought to send them the head of one of the girls and use the other head – still live – as a bargaining point. No, too many new complications.

Meanwhile, he was angry. He'd have to mail another letter, spelling out quite explicitly that there would be no bickering over money until all eight Bretons were released.

He wondered vaguely if so much correspondence was a mistake. Yet at the same time, in a different part of the city, his previous letter had been taken from a street mailbox on the rue Rémusset.

Already Dissette had drawn a second circle on the enlarged map in his office.

58

The interior minister sat in his office with his jaw set in a tense grimace. His arms were folded across his chest. The director of the DST, Jean-Claude Belfont, was concluding a summary of what he'd learned from the New York City Police Department.

'How exactly this American newsman, this Craig, is involved is something on which the New York police can only speculate. But this Frenchman – '

'Yes, this Frenchman,' interrupted de Gaubert. 'This torture specialist whom this Silva is looking for. Without doubt this is the same man we're seeking.'

'Precisely,' said Belfont. He closed the notebook in front of him. Both men looked at each other in silence for a few moments.

De Gaubert rose from the leather swivel chair behind his desk. He walked thoughtfully to the large window behind the chair and gazed towards the Seine. His arms were still folded. One hand reached up and tugged at his chin.

Belfont watched the frame of the minister, outlined by the brightness beyond the glass.

'Our alternatives are innumerable,' said the minister slowly. 'Do we know where this American is?'

'I checked with the hotel records at the main prefecture of police,' said Belfont. 'Richard Silva was registered as recently as yesterday at the Hotel Corbet.'

'Where the devil is that?'

'In the Seventh,' said Belfont. 'Better than your average flop house. Two towers, Michelin.'

'No wonder I've never heard of it,' said the minister. 'I assume he registered with that false passport. What was the name?'

'McKiernan,' said Belfont. 'We can arrest him at any time on that New York City charge. It would be easy. Then we could hold him until – '

'No,' said the minister, 'we're not going to arrest him, we're not going to send him back to America, and we're not going to let him know we're even aware of him. He's too useful just as he is.'

De Gaubert leaned pensively with his hands on the back of his chair. He looked at the head of his counter-espionage units.

'Keep Silva alive. Place him under surveillance,' said de Gaubert.

Belfont nodded.

'And have Corbeau informed of what we're doing.'

'I've already contacted him.'

'In person?'

'By phone,' said Belfont. 'I couldn't go near him without arousing suspicion.'

'Good,' said de Gaubert, seating himself again and leaning back in his chair. 'I think Mr Silva will fit into our plans perfectly. As soon as we decide how.'

59

It was a small but curious crowd that gathered around the door-step on the rue Pierre Levée. Two uniformed gendarmes stood before the door. Plainclothes police officers walked by them.

An ambulance arrived, but it would be a police vehicle that eventually took Ramereau's body away.

Upstairs in Ramereau's loft, the caretaker – a paunchy, stooped, fortyish Frenchman named Barrat – addressed a homicide detective named Faneau.

'I saw the marks on the door,' explained Barrat. 'It looked like someone had broken in.'

'And you walked in?' asked the lean, moustached inspector.

The closet door was open. A police photographer's camera flashed at Ramereau's corpse, still untouched where it reclined in the closet.

'I knocked first,' said Barrat. 'Then I tried the door. It was un-locked so I walked in.'

'What did you touch?' asked the inspector. 'Or move?'

Barrat recounted his actions. He had noticed the closet door ajar. The chair had caught his eye. Then he'd seen the blood stains beneath the chair.

'I touched the door knob on the closet,' said Barrat. He avoided looking in to where the building's only tenant had been found shot to death. 'I opened the closet and saw him.'

Barrat's hands were jittery. He was wondering if the police thought he'd killed Ramereau. The thought, in fact, had already occurred to the inspector.

'Then?' asked the inspector.

'I went to the *tabac* at rue Léonnec,' replied Barrat. 'I called immediately.'

Faneau nodded. He turned in mild boredom and watched another detective dust the apartment for fingerprints.

When the inspector broke free of the caretaker a few moments later, he glanced through the loft apartment. He noted the books, papers, and journals. About half of them were political. Marxist mostly, all with a leftist orientation.

'What was he?' asked Faneau. 'A student?'

Barrat shrugged. 'I never asked,' he said.

'What was his name?' he asked. The detective walked towards the body and looked down at it.

Barrat had to think. He shrugged. 'I never saw him much,' said the caretaker.

Faneau recognised evasiveness. 'You must have known the name,' he said.

'Yves something,' said the caretaker at length. 'Ramereau, I think.'

Faneau and the detective dusting for fingerprints glanced at each other. Faneau leaned down and tried to tilt up the head of the corpse to look at it. But already the neck was stiff. And the caked blood obscured the face.

Thoughtfully, Faneau looked at the rumpled corduroy jacket on Ramereau's body. With the index finger of his right hand, he moved the lapels on each side of the jacket.

He looked inside the jacket to examine where the first bullets had struck Ramereau.

Then he saw a packet of papers and envelopes in the inside jacket pocket.

The photographer was finished. Faneau reached for the papers.

60

It fell to Dutronc, even when he was tied up so thoroughly on the Thatcher case, to sort through other bulletins and notices as they drifted through his office at the Brigade Homicide. He would then pass on to Dissette those which merited special notice.

On May 25, something caught Dutronc's eye that sent him immediately to Dissette's office.

'I found an interesting name circulating at Homicide,' said Dutronc.

Dissette looked up. 'Yes?' he asked.

'Yves Ramereau,' said Dutronc. 'Wasn't he – ?'

'One of the forty-five hundred subversives we ran checks on in the Thatcher case,' said Dissette, finishing the sentence.

Dissette leaned back thoughtfully in his desk chair. He ran a hand across an unshaven chin.

'I can't quite place him, though,' said Dissette.

'Nineteen sixty-eight,' said Dutronc. 'Spring. Student-worker riots.'

'Ah, yes,' said Dissette. 'One of the better known punks. I was on assignment out of the country. But, of course, I remember.'

There was a pause.

'What about him?' asked Dissette. 'We never located him, did we?'

'Someone else did,' said Dutronc.

'Who?' asked Dissette. Dutronc handed him a crime report that indicated that Ramereau had been found dead that morning, evidently a victim of an unusual execution.

'Three bullets,' noted Dissette with amusement. 'Someone wasn't fooling around. Tried to turn him into a slab of gruyère.'

But beyond his amusement, Dissette grasped what Dutronc had noted. Murders with guns were not all that commonplace in Paris. It was not every day when political revolutionaries turned up in closets. What exactly *did* this indicate? And after all, Ramereau *had* been checked on during the initial investigation of the Thatcher case. Hadn't he been missing?

'What I'd be interested in doing,' began Dutronc slowly, 'is – '

'Is running a ballistics test on the bullets that killed Ramereau,' said Dissette.

'Exactly,' said Dutronc.

'Let me know what you discover.'

61

With Ramereau dead, Richard knew that his chances of finding the Imp were greatly diminished. Still, he had to keep searching. On the morning after discovering Ramereau's murder, Richard rose towards ten o'clock. Twenty minutes later he descended to a nearby café where he ate a light breakfast.

He watched the streets around him. He was particularly intrigued by a single red-haired girl who waited for a bus outside the café. She stood there for ten minutes. Richard watched her the entire time.

At times the loneliness of his mission overtook him. He could trust no one. He'd met no one to whom he could speak as a friend. He was never without his gun – even now, for coffee and croissants, he was armed.

He'd had to kill one man in a hotel room, another on the parapets of a cathedral. And he'd fired wildly to conclude an even more recent hotel stay. He was looking for one man. But now, for more than one reason, there had to be several men looking for him.

He studied the red-haired girl. Well shaped. Perfect legs beneath a short skirt. He wondered what she looked like naked. He could imagine her bare breasts.

After, he told himself. After all this was over. He could not abandon the Imp's trail. Not now.

The bus arrived. The girl was gone. His coffee was getting cold.

Richard returned to his small hotel room. He opened the map of Paris and spread it on the floor. He opened *Père Goriot* to page one. He kept a note pad by his side.

He began to read. He searched for places and names. He made notes. He had a job to do, a man to find.

Five hours later he descended the stairs. He was famished. He had almost finished the book. He had several pages of notes – all place and name references, mostly in the Fifth and Sixth Arrondissements.

The same concierge was at the battered old desk. The man looked at Richard oddly and called him aside. The man was nervous.

'Monsieur, monsieur,' said the man. 'I was on my way up to see you.'

'*Pourquoi?*'

The man looked to each side, then called Richard into a private adjoining room. His voice was hushed.

'*La police,*' said the man nervously.

Richard looked at him without speaking.

'Your name,' said the man. 'McKiernan.'

Richard felt a leap in his stomach.

'I don't know what you've done,' the man said. 'I don't want to know. But the police are looking here and everywhere else. They want you.'

'I don't know anyone named McKiernan,' Richard said.

The man nervously shook his head. His double chin palpitated slightly.

'No, monsieur,' he said. 'No stories. Just, please, leave. I saw the picture.'

'Picture?'

'They have a photograph,' he said. 'It was you.'

Now Richard felt a flash of fear in his stomach. A picture? Who could possibly have one? And how? Jesus! New York? Virginia? Montreal? Did someone know his real identity, too?

It wasn't possible. But it was happening. Richard was shaken.

'Please, monsieur,' begged the concierge, 'I don't like the police. I don't tell them anything. But they'll return. If they find you here they'll blame me. They'll ruin my hotel, drive away my customers. Please, monsieur . . . if you'd just leave quietly . . .'

Richard offered no argument. There was no point. If he stayed the concierge *could* call the police at any time. Out of fear, if for no other reason. Richard told the man to keep quiet. Richard would be gone that evening.

He was.

At five thirty Richard departed. He stuffed his belongings into his single suitcase. He walked to the car, parked two blocks away.

He threw the suitcase into the car's trunk. He got into the car, sat there, and thought.

For several minutes, he did not move. Then he made his decision.

No, he would *not* quit. He'd drawn close to the Imp. He'd committed himself. No way was he turning back.

But he was a realist. If cheap tawdry hotels like this one were being searched, so was every other public lodging in Paris. The good places and the flop houses.

There was only one safe place to spend the night.

He turned the key in the car ignition. He drove.

62

The interior minister had come from a meeting with other cabinet officials when he received the message from Belfont. The director of the DST wished to meet with the interior minister immediately. It was urgent.

De Gaubert contacted Belfont. The two men met at the Interior Ministry within the hour.

'I've come,' said Belfont, 'with good news and bad.'

'Get on with it,' replied de Gaubert.

'Corbeau thinks he has our man.'

'Our man?'

'The torturer,' reminded Belfont. The minister's mind was still in the finance meeting.

'Of course,' said de Gaubert.

'Richard Silva will provide the perfect bait,' said Belfont. 'Irresistible bait under the circumstances.'

'Exactly how?' asked de Gaubert.

Belfont explained. The interior minister listened carefully. He did not reject the plan.

'The American, of course,' said Belfont. 'may be killed in the process.'

'That's of no concern to me,' said de Gaubert. 'It will, in fact, work better that way.' He paused. 'My main concern is Corbeau,' he said.

'Monsieur?'

De Gaubert rose from his desk and, as was his habit, strolled thoughtfully behind it. He did not speak until his firm hands leaned on the back of his swivel chair.

'I don't doubt Corbeau's capabilities,' said the minister. 'Not after you tell me how far he's gone. What I'm concerned with,' he said, drawing out his words, 'is that this whole matter be accomplished neatly.'

De Gaubert looked at the man before him. He continued.

'You say that the Thatcher case and the matter of our renegade agent can be settled simultaneously?'

'Under favourable conditions, monsieur,' said Belfont.

'I'm sure,' said de Gaubert pensively. He looked at the desk in front of him.

'I'd like to see Corbeau myself,' he said. 'Here. As soon as possible.'

Belfont, surprised, did not object. He'd contact Corbeau personally and send him to the minister. 'There is one complication, too, monsieur,' added Belfont.

'And what is that?'

'We have to relocate Richard Silva,' said Belfont. 'He was involved in a shooting incident at his hotel. Afterwards he disappeared.'

63

Richard was soon stymied in traffic as he drove from the area behind St Lazare towards Montmartre to the northeast. Without any question he had picked the worst time of day to drive. But then it hadn't been his idea to leave the hotel so abruptly.

Richard managed to get to the place des Abbesses by six. He looked up the steep incline along the rue Ravignan. His eye followed the route that Françoise would have to walk from the place du Tertre to the Métro stop at Abbesses.

He parked illegally on a kerb. He stepped out of the car and considered walking up the hill towards Sacré Coeur. But his leg and hip bothered him. He opted to wait near his car.

The afternoon was dying, turning to evening. He knew that if he had any chance at all of catching her it would be within the next half hour. She followed that same path every day. She'd said so.

He waited more than twenty minutes. Then he saw her.

He stepped to the sidewalk where she would have to walk. He waited. When she was no more than ten metres away, she saw him. She stopped short. Then she almost smiled.

'*Encore vous?*' she asked.

'*Encore moi,*' he said.

She switched to English. 'You didn't find him?'

'Who?'

'Ramereau,' she said.

The question caught him off guard. He was beyond Ramereau now. The image of the body in the closet flashed before him.

'No,' he said. 'I didn't.'

'You tried where he lives?' she asked.

'No answer.'

'Then I can't help you,' she said.

He stood next to her. 'That's not why I came.'

'No?'

'I came to see you. To talk.'

She was at first on her guard, defensive. Yet he seemed sufficiently reserved and well mannered. Had he wished to harm her he would have had the chance in her apartment two nights earlier.

'I told you that I'd answer some questions,' he said. 'If you're interested. Over dinner.'

The idea did not displease her. Rather, it surprised her. 'Why not?' she said. 'But . . . ' She motioned to her paint box and easel. 'This is heavy,' she said.

'I have a car. I'll take you back to your apartment first.'

She looked at the small white Simca crammed onto the kerb. She agreed.

He drove her to her building on the rue de Pontoise. He climbed the stairs with her and followed her into her apartment. He was again conscious of the pistol under his jacket.

He sat down on a ragged sofa and looked around the small apartment. Two rooms. A large bed. Here. This would be perfect.

She stepped into the next room. He sat apprehensively. For a moment the urge was upon him to follow her, surprise her as she was changing.

But no, he decided. Patience would be more rewarding.

They dined that evening at a small old restaurant on the rue de Grenelle. He avoided the subject of his identity and spoke again, in passing, of his journalism career. If she doubted him, she said nothing.

In turn, she talked of her painting, her family in Avignon, her schooling in Nanterre, and her disillusionment with radical politics. Richard was continually surprised at her facility in English. Occasionally he tried to speak French. Inevitably, he would stumble. When he did, she would smile. He had not consumed a balanced meal for days. They ate heartily, splitting a litre of full red wine between them.

When he walked back to her building, she sensed the advance that he would inevitably make. She wondered idly whether or not to demonstrate any displeasure. Yet at the same moment she felt a flutter of excitement. A new lover. Perhaps a good one. Wouldn't

253

Yves be annoyed? And wouldn't he deserve it?

They arrived together by her door at the top of the stairs.

She turned towards him. 'You never did tell me your name,' she said.

'Howard McK –'

'Your real name,' she said. And laughed.

'It doesn't matter,' she said. 'I don't really care.'

She looked towards his eyes. He was glancing downward, over her, exploring her, and wondering. There was a certain inquisitive way that he looked at her. She liked it.

He raised his eyes. He was slightly embarrassed. She'd caught him. She slipped the key into the lock and opened her door. At the same time, she felt a strong arm around her waist.

She looked back at him.

'You never planned to leave, did you?' she asked.

He shook his head slightly. On the other side of her door was safety. No one could ever trace him there.

'*Viens*,' she said.

He followed. The door closed behind them.

64

The secret service agent known as Corbeau found himself, for the first time in his life, seated in the office of the interior minister. Corbeau had assured the minister that he was, as Belfont had promised, extremely close to resolving his assigned case.

'Your plan is excellent,' commented the interior minister. 'It will force this . . . this torturer of ours to surface.'

He looked at Corbeau.

'What about these two young girls?' the minister then asked. 'The American ambassador's daughters.'

'I think the American, Silva, will lead us to them,' Corbeau said. 'On the basis of the clues we've obtained.'

'He's involved in this, is he?' asked de Gaubert.

'It would appear so,' said Corbeau. 'Some sort of involvement is undeniable.'

De Gaubert nodded.

'I think,' said the interior minister, 'that you know what the priorities are. And you understand what will be necessary.'

'I do, monsieur,' said Corbeau.

'There is no way that anyone can ever learn the identity of the French agent in Indo-China. The international repercussions would be immeasurable.'

Again Corbeau nodded.

'This renegade agent, this man who tortured the American prisoners,' said de Gaubert slowly and thoughtfully, 'was in the employ of my ministry. Granted, this agent clearly overstepped his authority. He was never *ever* to involve himself in the interrogation of Americans.'

De Gaubert paced thoughtfully behind the chair to his desk. He looked out of the tall window of his office. 'It would reflect very poorly on this nation, this government, and this ministry,' he said softly, 'if the truth were ever to become known.'

'It won't, monsieur,' said Corbeau. 'As soon as the time is right, this torturer and the one man who can identify him will be destroyed.'

'And when will that be?'

'Within days. If not hours.'

De Gaubert nodded, 'Proceed. Contact me again when this matter is settled.'

65

'We may open on two optimistic notes,' said Dissette.

The small conference room in the Justice Ministry was warm and humid. The map remained on the wall behind Dissette. Dutronc sat nearby. De Gaubert and Latour sat a few chairs away.

'First,' continued Dissette, 'Madame Thatcher is apparently out of physical danger. I have been kept informed by the hospital staff. Unfortunately, she has undergone an understandably traumatic experience. She remembers little of what happened. Her description of the assailants is no better than the one received from the vagrant in the SNCF warehouse. It gives us nothing new.'

Dissette looked to Dutronc and motioned to a folder.

'Yet second, we have received another letter,' Dissette said. Dutronc handed him the folder. 'As usual, the letter consists of newsprint. Free of fingerprints. The stationery common and untraceable.' Dissette circulated a photocopy. 'Monsieur Dutronc and I pulled this out of the mail this morning. Again the mailing was from the Fifth Arrondissement. And again, we know what box was used.'

Dissette then took out his felt-tipped pen on the string. He turned towards the map upon which he'd already drawn two intersecting circles.

'The mailbox used was here,' he said, placing his right forefinger on the map with his back to the conference table. He marked a spot on the rue de l'Arbalète. Then Dissette stretched the string to its scale of one thousand metres. 'Watch carefully,' he said.

Dissette drew another circle. The six other eyes in the room followed the route of his pen. The circle intersected the previously drawn two circles. Part of each circle overlapped the others. Yet part of each had also been eliminated. Dissette eyed the area within all three.

'An area of about seven hundred and fifty metres square, messieurs,' said Dissette. 'Not a large area if my calculations are correct,' He paused.

'I only wish this were the simple matter of tracking down a killer,' he said. 'Then we could cordon off the area at this moment and search everything and everybody. But as you've all observed, it is not that simple. We must locate this man to within a few metres. Then we must strike with devastating swiftness and accuracy.'

Dissette turned towards the postal minister.

'Monsieur Latour,' he said, 'you are asked here again today for a reason. Have you noticed any pattern with which these letters are dropped in PTT boxes?'

'Aside from the location?'

'Aside from the location.'

Latour thought. 'They've all been mailed after dark,' he said. 'After the last pickup of one day and before the first pickup of of the next.'

'Exactly,' said Dissette. 'The mailings take place at night. How many people in Paris go out in the middle of the night to post their mail?'

'Not many,' shrugged Latour.

'And how many in this particular area?' pressed Dissette.

'Fewer still,' offered the postal minister. 'A handful.'

Dissette shifted his gaze to de Gaubert. 'Monsieur, we are dealing with approximately one hundred and forty mailboxes. If we should need a stake-out of some sort, it could be managed,' said Dissette. 'But we have one other tactic first. Do I need to remind anyone here who Jean Le Barazer is?'

Latour did not know. Dissette explained.

Le Barazer was the youngest of the eight Bretons jailed in the 1969 Brest bombing. He had also drawn the shortest sentence. But now, Dissette explained to the postal minister, Le Barazer's sentence had been cut short in its final months.

'I've arranged with the interior minister,' said Dissette, 'to have Le Barazer freed today. Very quietly. No press coverage at all. This is a test.'

'Of what?' asked Latour.

'Of the man holding the hostages,' said Dissette. 'I want to know whether he is contacted or has any way of knowing whether the jailed Bretons are in or out of prison.'

'And how will you know?' asked the postal minister.

'From his correspondence,' said Dissette. 'And by elaborate surveillance that will be placed on Le Barazer. And yet that brings us to the specific reason why I have asked you here today.'

'Monsieur?' asked Latour.

'I wish to have personal immediate access to every mailbox in this area of the Fifth Arrondissement. How quickly can that be arranged?'

Latour thought a moment. 'Almost immediately,' he replied. 'I can provide you with a series of master keys.'

'Excellent,' said Dissette. 'That's exactly what I will need.'

66

On the evening of the twenty-seventh, Françoise Durand and Richard Silva dined leisurely and enjoyably at her apartment.

At the same time, Jean Le Barazer had checked into a modest hotel in the south central part of France not far from where he'd been serving the final days of his prison sentence. Incredibly, that same morning he'd been plucked from his cell, given a small amount of cash, and checked into that hotel, courtesy of the French Republic. No one was more confused than he, unless, of course, it was the men who'd been assigned to watch him.

The story of Le Barazer's release was kept from the media. The value of releasing Le Barazer would have to be in where he led the police, if anywhere. Le Barazer led them, but not to any spot of value.

On his first night of freedom, Le Barazer simply bought a pulp paperback and two Danish 'sun worship' magazines, and returned to the privacy of his hotel room. He had made one telephone call, that to his mother. A Breton-speaking CRS agent, assigned to the tapped phone in Le Barazer's hotel room, heard nothing of substance discussed in the call. Similarly, those police agents who watched the Le Barazer house in Brittany saw no one come or go from that house all evening. Nor were any other calls made out.

The vigil maintained on Jean Le Barazer therefore was both peaceful and unproductive. And, for the moment at least, it was viewed as a failure by the time Le Barazer turned out his room lights. The next day he would return home. Again, he would be both followed and watched. And again, the surveillance would be in vain.

67

Dissette was studying a postal map of Paris when he heard the knock on his office door. Seconds later Dutronc entered, carrying several papers and a file envelope.

'You're going to like this,' said Dutronc. Dissette watched as Dutronc seated himself.

'Let's hear it,' said Dissette.

'They ran a ballistics test on the bullets that killed Ramereau.'

'And?'

'The same gun killed the American soldier and the same gun wounded Barbara Thatcher.'

Dissette, who had been leaning back in his chair, returned to earth slowly, leaning forward pensively at his desk.

'You're sure?' he asked.

'Certain,' said Dutronc. 'But it's even better than that.'

'How?'

'Whoever shot Ramereau didn't even think of stripping the body of any papers or identification. Maybe the killer was in a hurry. Maybe he was just careless.'

'And?' pressed Dissette.

'When Ramereau was found there was an envelope in his inside jacket pocket. There was a name with a hotel address on it. Howard McKiernan. Hotel Corbet. Rue des Chèvres. Septième.'

Dissette's expression was unchanging. 'Should the name mean something?' he asked.

'Homicide got a bulletin on someone by that name two days ago. There's an American using that name who's wanted for an attempted murder in New York. This may be the key to the Thatcher case.'

'Why?' asked Dissette, folding his arms before him.

'Some of the pieces are missing,' said Dutronc, 'but here's what we have.'

Dissette studied his assistant carefully.

'Madame Thatcher, the American guard, and Yves Ramereau were all shot with the same gun. A link would appear obvious.'

Dissette nodded.

'In Ramereau's pocket was McKiernan's name and address. "McKiernan" is the pseudonym of a man travelling in France under a false Canadian passport. The same man attempted a murder in New York. He shot some sort of television performer. Brigade Homicide received an extradition request for McKiernan two days ago for the New York shooting. Fingerprints were included. The same fingerprints were found in Ramereau's apartment.'

'Further implicating this man in the Ramereau shooting,' noted Dissette.

'Exactly. But the McKiernan name is assumed. The man's real name is Richard Silva. An American.'

Dutronc paused for a moment, pulling certain classified documents from a filing envelope. Dissette, while attentive, was silent.

'The New York police think Silva's some sort of deranged nut. He's in France pursuing some man who he claims tortured him in Vietnam.' Dutronc handed a translated New York City police file to Dissette. 'Here,' he said. 'Read it for yourself.'

'I have,' said Dissette.

Dutronc stopped cold.

'You're not the only one who's done his homework,' said Dissette. 'I know everything you told me about this Richard Silva. Everything you told me. And more.'

Dutronc was stunned.

'As you know,' Dissette continued slowly, 'I have a security pass for DST files. I used it this morning when I checked Ramereau for myself. I came across the New York City police request for Silva, filed through the U.S. State Department. But then I found a new file on Mr Silva. A United States *Intelligence* file. His own government has requested his execution.'

'And?'

'An agent has been assigned to the job.'

'What agent?' snapped Dutronc impetuously.

Dissette grinned broadly. 'Recovering the Thatcher children

and executing Richard Silva are inextricably intertwined. Both assignments will flow together very neatly.'

Dissette leaned forward, his elbows on his desk, and allowed a sparkle of enthusiasm to flash in his dark eyes. 'And you know, Marius,' he said, 'I think I'm going to enjoy this.'

Part Three

68

Dissette convened the morning meeting at the PJ building. De Gaubert, Latour, and Dutronc were present by the time Dissette had entered the small conference room.

'I have two items of interest this morning,' said Dissette. 'I have a letter and I have a suspect.'

The three men around the conference table watched Dissette attentively. 'It might be more accurate to say,' Dissette went on, 'that I want a certain man for questioning. A certain American man. I will explain presently.'

Dissette displayed the most recently received letter, plucked from the mails that morning. 'Our friend has chosen to contact us again,' he said. 'He says that he is sorry to hear of the financial difficulties of the American ambassador and his family, but his price will not decrease. He also adds,' said Dissette as he circulated photocopies of the letter and its envelope, 'that the Breton nationalists must be released before any discussion of ransom money can be made.'

Dissette looked around the room and added, 'More important, we again know what mailbox this letter came from. Please observe.'

The letter had been placed in a mailbox just a few city blocks from the last one to be used. Dissette strung his finger and marking pen to the map again and drew another circle. The circle dissected the other circles and left a still smaller area within. The area was in the southwest corner in the Fifth Arrondissement. It included the rue Rastignac.

'I think,' said Dissette thoughtfully, 'that we begin to see what type of area our friend has selected. A low key, quiet, informed section of the Latin Quarter. An area made up of students, intellectuals, writers, musicians, transvestites, homosexuals, and petty crooks.'

All the people, thought de Gaubert silently, contributing so generously to the decline of the republic. There was nothing in that area of the Left Bank that an ample dose of tear gas couldn't improve.

Dissette drew a red line around that area enclosed by the intersection of the circles. Then he circulated another paper. This paper was a picture of a man, a picture forwarded by the police in New York City.

'This, messieurs,' said Dissette, 'is the man we must find. His name is Richard Silva. He is in France, presumably Paris. He travels with a false passport and a false name. Gentlemen,' added Dissette, 'I intend to apprehend this man personally. I neither need nor want any police back-up of any sort.'

Dissette explained the link between the gun in the Thatcher abduction, the gun in the Ramereau slaying, and the notation on an envelope in the dead Ramereau's pocket.

De Gaubert spoke.

'Monsieur Dissette,' he asked, 'aren't there some very evident loose ends here?'

'There are,' conceded Dissette.

'Could you explain them?'

Dutronc watched Dissette carefully as the head of the investigation handled the key questions.

'The involvement of Silva,' said Dissette, 'answers some questions and poses others.' He glanced at the intersecting circles on his map. 'For example,' he continued, 'we've been looking for a man who has shown every indication of being hidden with his captives in this area of the Fifth Arrondissement.'

Dissette jabbed at the map with a finger. His fingertip moved within an inch of the rue Rastignac.

'Yet today,' he continued, 'I tell you that a key figure in the case is a man who has been, at least part of the time, in a hotel under an assumed name.'

'And there's no contradiction there?' inquired de Gaubert.

'None. Three men were involved in the abduction. Two grabbed the children. One fired a gun. One man, probably the mastermind, has been with the children all along. A second man,

268

probably the trigger man, has been at large in Paris. He may be – or may have been – Silva.'

'And the third man?' interjected de Gaubert.

'Ramereau, I suspect,' Dissette proclaimed. 'We know that Silva took two shots at him in the Corbet. A different gun was used, but Monsieur Lechêne at the Corbet did identify Ramereau as one of Silva's visitors. Similarly, Silva's fingerprints were all over Ramereau's apartment as well as the tools used to break in. Further, Ramereau's location at the time of the Thatcher abduction is still unaccounted for.'

'What about witnesses to the abduction?' asked Latour. 'Have they identified either Ramereau or the American?'

'Not conclusively one way or the other. That includes Mrs Thatcher and the vagrant I questioned.'

Dissette thought he sensed an unsettled feeling in the room. 'Yet, messieurs,' he continued forcefully, 'the link of the pistol is irrefutable. We have no alternative than to assume that Silva will lead us closer to both the kidnappers and the Thatcher children.'

'What about the issue of Breton nationalism?' asked the interior minister.'

'A clever smokescreen,' replied Dissette immediately. 'The real issue is the ransom.'

There was silence in the room.

'That, messieurs,' said Dissette, 'is why all of our leads in Brittany revealed nothing. That is why Le Barazer was surprised to be released and it's why he led us nowhere. The three abductors tried cleverly to send us in the wrong direction. Up until now, gentlemen, they have succeeded.'

Dissette turned to his map.

'Silva has disappeared from all hotels, rooming houses, or flop houses in Paris,' he continued. 'I have a strong suspicion that he has withdrawn into hiding. There is only one logical place.'

Dissette again pointed to the area within the circles in the Fifth Arrondissement. 'Here,' he said.

'With the other man?' asked Latour.

'I suspect so,' said Dissette. 'He would be remaining close in anticipation of a ransom delivery.' Dissette paused thoughtfully. 'The temptation would be to saturate the area with CRS agents and search door to door. But the area is too large, the risk of failure too great. This area must be at least halved again with further correspondence.'

'But isn't your basic premise concerning the letters no longer valid?' interrupted the interior minister.

'How?'

'You theorised that this kidnapper couldn't move far from his hiding place to mail a letter. But now you theorise that there are two of them hiding together. Couldn't one correspond with us while the other stays with the hostages?'

'Perhaps,' conceded Dissette. 'But we don't *know* that Silva has joined with this man. And even if he has, I doubt that he would stray too far from a proven hiding place.'

'Why?'

'By now, he knows we're looking for him,' said Dissette.

The man who headed the investigation paused, then glanced around the table.

'Accordingly, messieurs,' Dissette continued, 'I'm moving the case to the point where only the ransom remains to be discussed. I released to the newspapers today a false story stating that the remaining seven Bretons have been released. Our enemy will have no way of knowing that the story is a hoax.'

De Gaubert and Dutronc exchanged glances.

'But,' concluded Dissette, 'the story will provide us with just what we need to conclude this case and recover the children. One more letter.'

Dissette turned and looked at the intersecting circles on his map. His hands, though calm, fidgeted with the string and pen used to draw those circles.

'One more letter,' he repeated, 'and we can draw one more circle. The area in question should be greatly narrowed down. We can then close in. And we'll know who we're looking for.'

Dissette smiled slightly.

'An American with a limp. Richard Silva.'

69

At the same time as Dissette and Dutronc were agonising through
another of those briefings, Richard Silva was waking slowly, com-
fortably, and more relaxed than he had been in years. Beside him,
in her apartment, was Françoise.

He lay awake for several minutes, thinking to himself, as she lay
naked beside him. How had he survived these last years, he wondered, without the tenderness that only a woman could provide?
How had he preserved his sanity all that time? How had he been
able to abstain, not just from sex, but from the warmth and com-
panionship of a woman? Was that what had been missing in his
life that had driven him to accept a contract to kill and then to
set out to find and kill this European torture specialist?

He thought of the pistol that he'd successfully hidden in that
apartment. Now that he considered it, he would have been quite
happy never to hear a gun fired again in his life.

And yet, he had come this far. He'd made sacrifices. Committed
crimes. Risked his own life. Didn't he owe it to himself to continue? Didn't he owe it to the men who'd been slain by the Imp?

Sunlight was in the room now. The sheets had fallen away from
their bed. He looked at her naked body and, as he had the night
before, felt desire stir within him.

Then he saw that her eyes were open.

He leaned down and kissed her, placing an arm around her
waist. Her own arms wrapped around his strong shoulders.

'*Encore?*' she asked with a smile.

'*Encore*,' he said, confirming that although they were both awake, it was not yet time to get up for the day.

Later, he showered immediately after she did. When he stepped from the shower she flung him a towel. He wiped the water from his face as she looked at his strong young body. She was still undressed.

'I've figured it out,' she said in English.

'Figured what out?' he asked, drying his back.

'Your limp,' she said. 'The result of an accident.'

'How do you figure that?'

'The scars on your hip,' she said. 'A bad accident.'

He looked at her thoughtfully, intrigued by her perception. He almost wanted to tell her more than he should.

'You really want to know about it?' he asked.

'You have me curious,' she said. 'About many things.'

'I was in a plane crash,' he said.

'A bad one?'

'There's no such thing as a good one. Half the people were killed.'

'I'm sorry,' she said. 'It was none of my business. If you don't want to talk about it, I – '

'It's nothing now,' he said. 'But now you owe me one.'

'One what?'

'An answer,' he said. 'I'm still trying to find André Guisseny.'

'I've told you everything I know.'

'Sure,' he said. 'But I've got a list of name and place references from a book. I want you to look at them. I want to know if they remind you of any particular place or part of Paris.'

'Are there a lot?'

'Enough.'

'Tonight,' she said. 'This evening. Meet me when I'm through painting and I'll help you.'

He rubbed the towel briskly across the front of his body, drying himself completely and, for a moment, obscuring the scars on his left hip.

He nodded. 'It's a deal,' he said.

Richard sat back on the bed. His attention was divided between the bright spring day outside the open window and the attractive young woman dressing before him. Françoise proved the more interesting until she was completely dressed. Then Richard walked to the window, leaned on the sill, and inhaled deeply.

A new feeling filled him. He was happy to be alive in this apartment with this woman. No one else knew where he was. No one could harm him here. He was, for the first time in memory, safe, comfortable, and happy. He could stay here forever. He savoured the feeling.

Françoise kissed him good-bye and departed for the day.

Richard looked out over the city for several minutes. Suddenly an uncontrollable anger was upon him. He had flirted with the idea of giving up, of letting the Imp go. How *dare* he?

He saw Howard McKiernan. He saw William DeMeo. One by one he envisioned all the others who'd been deprived of ever again enjoying a spring day. He clenched a fist and nearly cried out in anguish. And the Imp was very possibly right there in Paris with him.

He dressed quickly and stuffed his pistol in his belt beneath a jacket. He seized the list of places that he'd found in *Père Goriot*. Fifteen minutes later he was in his car. He would spend the day exploring everything on that list.

He spent the morning in the Latin Quarter. The word of Ramereau kept returning. An abandoned street. And Père Goriot would recognise the name. What had Ramereau meant? Or had he meant anything at all? The search was leading Richard to a dead end.

Richard thought about many things. Maybe the forces that control the universe hadn't meant him to kill any more. He began to hope that they didn't. He was tired of being part of the insanity. But he continued.

During the afternoon, Richard walked from the old Val-de-Grace church to the Jardin des Plantes, through the southeastern part of the Fifth Arrondissement. He passed within two hundred metres of André Guisseny. But again, he saw nothing.

Then in the evening he drove to Montmartre. From the steps of the Sacré Coeur he looked down upon Paris.

The skyline of the city was now blemished with skyscrapers. But enough of the old pastel roofs and shaded buildings remained in the light of a May evening. There was still a magic in the air. Paris was, well, it was still Paris. It remained one of the few magic cities in the world.

In the face of a city so beautiful, the ugly idea of a hidden gun on his hip embarrassed him. The gun would have to go. Soon. The hate was leaving him.

A few minutes later he walked around the corner from the Sacré Coeur and met Françoise. She embraced him and, his arm around her waist, they walked slowly back to his car. They each savoured

273

the early evening. They ate dinner at a small dark bistro not far from where she lived.

It was back up at her apartment that Richard took out the city map and again opened it, looking to see exactly where he had been that day. His eyes roamed over the student area of the Fifth and through areas where he had walked. He was about to have her help him with his list of names.

And suddenly his gaze froze. He felt excitement leap inside of him. There it was. In the old quarter of the Fifth, in a spot that he'd passed so painfully near. The street named for a central character in *Père Goriot*.

Rue Rastignac.

He had found it.

He would go there tomorrow. He had to.

70

The late newspapers and the radio news had stated the improbable. The French government, the media said, was paroling unconditionally all seven remaining Bretons held in the 1969 bombings. La Barazer had already been freed the previous day. Guisseny, when he heard that, allowed a long smile to crease his face. If it were true, and he'd wait to see if it were, he had done the virtually impossible. It showed how much the French government courted the Americans. They'd knuckled under to the Breton terrorism on one side and what had obviously been U.S. pressure on the other.

His supplies of food were low. He'd given bread, milk, and a few slices of processed meat to the girls, but they had continued to lose weight. Not that it mattered to him. They'd been down in that dungeon-like hole for seven days now.

They had spent most of their time tied with rope. Their limbs were stiff and their faces dirty. Their hands and feet were black from the dirt. And they smelled almost as bad as that reeking cellar.

At one point in the middle of a night, Anne had started to scream uncontrollably. The crying had been so maniacal and so intense that Guisseny angrily had thrown open the trap door and had jumped down to the girls, dressed only in a pair of underpants. He did, however, bring his gun and lantern.

He saw the older girl hysterical, her right hand covering part of her left arm. Beneath the palm there was blood. The girl screamed almost incoherently, but Guisseny understood the word 'bitten'.

Then he saw what is was about. He shone the lantern into the darkness by the wall. Two red, radiant eyes glared back at him.

A rat. The girl had been bitten by a rat, probably as she slept. Guisseny pointed the pistol at that ugly creature and fired. The shot tore the animal's head off. It tumbled until it was still.

Then he walked back to Anne. He looked at the arm. The girl was terrified.

'You want I shoot you?' Guisseny asked.

The frantic little girls shook their heads. He pointed the gun at them.

'Then quiet,' he said. And still sobbing, they stopped screaming.

Guisseny wiped away the blood from the wound and tied a cloth around it, stopping the bleeding. Possible infection was beyond his concern.

And now it didn't matter anyway. The Bretons were freed, or so the radio said. He constructed a final letter out of newsprint, one that he hoped would allow him a few days to leave France safely, following the execution of his small captives. That night, at about 2.00 a.m., he woke the children and locked them again in the trunk, noticing the swelling on Anne's arm. Blood poisoning? He didn't give it much of a thought. In twenty-four hours she'd probably be dead.

He exited from the trap door and then moved through that cavernous, underground passage through the other basements. He exited from under that building at the rue Rastignac. He was on his way to mail the final letter.

This letter stated that he'd be in touch concerning the ransom money within another day or so. He would also offer false proof that the girls were still alive.

He crossed rue Rastignac, walked two blocks, and found himself on a very quiet street. It was a Sunday night. The neighbourhood was almost dead. Few cars. No one on foot. What did it matter now? He'd use the first mailbox he saw. He saw one across the square, went to it, and was about to post his letter when he realised that about seventy metres away, down the square, there was a man. The man was standing completely still and watching him.

The man, Charles Dissette, was intrigued. He was there to look for anyone who couldn't wait for morning to mail a letter. What he really wanted was a man with a limp. But since this was the first man whose impatience to use a mailbox had brought him out after dark, Dissette turned and walked slowly towards him.

Guisseny abruptly turned and walked instinctively back the way he came. He clutched the letter in his hand. He had moved perhaps thirty metres when he looked back over his shoulder and saw that the man was still coming. He was closer. Much closer The brisk walk was now a jog.

That was enough for Guisseny. He began to run.

So did the other man.

Madly, Guisseny turned a corner and darted down an alley. Panicked, he was not looking back now. He could hear the steps, even at a distance of thirty metres.

Guisseny rounded a corner and saw a clear street leading back to rue Rastignac and the abandoned buildings that formed his cavern. On the sidewalk there was a wire sanitation basket.

The letter. He *had* to get rid of that letter.

As Dissette rounded the corner on a full run he saw Guisseny's hand dip into, and then leave, the wire trash basket. Then the running figure made another turn and dipped into the shadows leading to rue Rastignac. Guisseny plunged through the door to the abandoned building, slipped into that hole between the wall and the concrete floor, and slid down into the passage that led down to what had, until then, been safety. He stayed there with his gun drawn. In the dark he watched and waited. If any man followed him through that door he would have to shoot.

He thought of the children then. He might have to let them suffocate now. It might be his life or theirs.

Dissette, however, had lost his man. Guisseny had evaded him through the shadows. And although Dissette was sure he disappeared somewhere down the rue Rastignac, he could not know where. Nor was Dissette going to allow himself to take a bullet in the dark.

Dissette retreated to the safety of a car from which he could survey the area. He would return the next morning. With daylight, he would end this affair.

Then, almost as an afterthought, he carefully retraced the path of his chase, starting at the post box and continuing down those winding streets. When he passed the wire litter basket he stopped.

He reached in.

Right on top, slightly crumpled but still in perfect condition, was an addressed, stamped letter. It was addressed to the Thatcher family at the U.S. Embassy.

71

It wasn't until eight fifteen that Richard arrived in that quarter of Paris. He'd already walked through the area twice and both times failed to observe the rue Rastignac. But now he easily found the old street of abandoned houses. The street was completely vacant despite the fact there was activity in the nearby public square.

Richard wondered if Ramereau had made a fool of him by sending him to one of the few dead streets in the city. Or had Ramereau led Richard too close already, hence the execution. Richard wondered who'd made a fool of whom.

Richard, carrying the pistol in his belt and a morning paper under his arm, walked up and down that old street twice. He saw nothing, but, separated by walls and earth, passed within a few metres of André Guisseny. Now, in the absence of an enemy, the gun on his hip was useless.

Richard retreated to a public square. He sat on a long green bench. An old man gave him a toothless smile and a nod. Richard thought for a few moments and enjoyed the morning. He wondered what it would be like to grow old.

Several minutes passed. Then at one point Richard suddenly discovered that he was staring at a man who was walking up the rue Rastignac, coming the other way and approaching him. The man had a familiar walk and, Richard realised, an all too familiar face, even after the passage of nineteen months.

The man wore a trench coat now, not jungle fatigues. But there was no question about it. It was he. His torturer. The executioner of William DeMeo, the real Howard McKiernan, and innumerable others. The Imp.

Richard bitterly eyed Charles Dissette, the renegade French agent who had so enthusiastically exceeded his authority in Indo-China. Now it was simply a matter of closing in for the kill.

Richard quickly raised the newspaper in front of his face. He felt his hands suddenly wet with sweat. He held the paper so that he could see just over the top of it. It appeared that Richard was reading. But he wasn't. He was watching. And he felt all the old hatred returning, the anguish, the vehemence, the soul-wrenching urge to kill.

He moved one hand beneath his jacket and unclicked the safety catch on the pistol. The gun was loaded. He had his target. This was it, the moment he'd waited for, worked for, lied for, travelled for, almost killed an innocent Clifford Craig for. Now the man he hunted was closer, just twenty metres away. The man was examining the structures of those old buildings, as if he were looking for something.

All Richard had to do was walk close to the man. Surely he'd not be recognised. Not immediately. He'd simply empty his two shots into the man and flee. Richard couldn't miss. The shot was that good.

But he couldn't do it. Not there. Not yet.

There were occasional people around. Witnesses.

At one point not too long ago he wouldn't have cared. He would have fired on sight and have taken his chances at escape. But now. Richard now had other things to live for besides this . . . execution. Richard would follow this man and corner him unobserved, blast him, and be gone. To where? To freedom and to an end to this whole bloody ordeal.

Dissette, the Imp, made it easy. He stopped by number 11 on rue Rastignac and pushed firmly at the door.

The door gave way, despite the fact that it had appeared to be boarded shut. Then Dissette disappeared through that same door.

What in the name of God, pondered Richard, was a decently dressed man in an overcoat doing in an abandoned building?

Richard had an answer. The man was providing a perfect place for an execution. Sometimes, Richard thought, life provided flashes of circumstantial justice. This killing, he thought, might be pathetically easy.

Richard stood and folded his newspaper under his arm. He walked to the head of rue Rastignac and waited a few moments. He turned once and made certain that he was the object of no one's attention. He continued. He followed through that same doorway.

He stepped into the rubble of an abandoned building.

He drew the gun, looking in every direction and almost waiting to hear a shot.

There was no one.

Then he saw that slim passage through the wall, that passage which led downward and to the subterranean levels beneath the other buildings.

It made no sense. But the Imp wasn't getting away. Not this time. Richard, gun drawn, followed.

72

At an early hour that morning, the telephone rang on the desk of the interior minister. De Gaubert answered.

'*Ici Corbeau*,' said the voice on the other end.

'*Oui?*'

'I think this is it,' said Corbeau. 'Dissette tried to slip away from me this morning. He's going somewhere important.'

'Where?'

'Just about where we thought,' said Corbeau. 'I followed.'

'Do you want extra police support?' asked the interior minister.

'I want the police out of the area,' said the man calling from a pay telephone. 'If they get in the way, they'll ruin everything.'

The interior minister agreed. 'I'm counting on you,' he said.

'Stay by the telephone,' said Corbeau. 'I'll advise you as soon as I can.'

Both men hung up. De Gaubert, chewing two aspirin tablets at his desk prepared to wait it out. Yet in sitting and waiting that morning, de Gaubert was not alone.

In an unlit subterranean corridor on the other side of the Seine, André Guisseny also sat and waited. He had been awake all night, on guard in his underground chamber. He knew that the man who'd chased him had been pursuing him in particular. But how could he have been found? There weren't enough police to have monitored every mailbox in Paris. Yet some way someone was on to him. His mission of abduction and extortion was over.

He'd stayed awake that entire night, holding his weapon in his hand, often trembling, and afraid to move. But during that long tense night he'd made his decision. The eight Bretons were being freed according to both radio and the newspapers. Guisseny was the victor. Now the children could be executed that evening and quickly thereafter Guisseny could leave France. If only he could now stay awake on guard through this final day, he could escape through darkness the next night.

Guisseny suddenly clicked off the radio that had been playing softly. He heard the sound that he'd grown to fear most. Footsteps. Slowly and quietly, almost imperceptibly, someone was in that narrow dark corridor that led to his cellar. Damn. Damn it all. He held his pistol in his hand and took cover behind a turned-over table.

He waited. And he thought.

Was this the end? Was this the police, closing in after all these days? And the children? Now? Was now the time to execute them?

It had been close enough just hours earlier. Last night he'd thrown open the trunk with no more than a minute or two to spare. The children had been hysterical. He'd been forced to keep them gagged. He'd given them some water that morning, but nothing else. Why bother? Maybe he'd erred by not having killed them yet. Yes, perhaps he should have. If this threat passed, he'd do it immediately. No reason to postpone what was now inevitable.

Then the door to that underground room flew open. The exhausted, over anxious Guisseny fired immediately, betraying his position.

Dissette, crouched low, returned a withering volley of bullets from an automatic pistol.

In the dim light, Dissette was only a blur with a lethal flashing hand. But Guisseny, pinned defensively behind the overturned table, blasted blindly at the intruder whom he couldn't clearly see.

The gunfire rattled deafeningly in the small room. It echoed up into the corridor where Richard Silva did not move.

Then, in the amount of time it would take to execute a captive prisoner, Richard heard two more shots.

He waited again for several seconds. Then he cautiously advanced.

He eventually saw the open door. He heard a movement beyond.

He moved closer until he was within a few feet of the doorway.

73

Richard glanced from the doorway into the rubble-strewn room. He saw a man's body lying on the ground. Another man stood examining the corpse, looking down at the dead face without recognition.

Dissette didn't understand. The man at his feet was not Richard Silva. The face was wrong. The man he'd killed, it appeared, was a Frenchman. But why had this man opened fire on Dissette? And was this the man he'd chased the previous night?

Dissette's second and third shots had crashed through the wooden table top and into Guisseny's upper chest. The bullets had picked up the Breton and had spun him backward to where he died.

Then, approaching cautiously through the dim light, Dissette had fired twice again. He'd walked to the man he'd killed and had turned over the body with a condescending flick of his foot.

And he'd looked down, fully expecting to see a different face. Dissette looked into those stunned empty eyes and then he knew. He'd never seen this man before. Hadn't it been Silva that previous night?

Dissette tucked his gun into a hip holster in preparation for searching this strange place. And in doing so, he erred.

He turned and realised that the man standing in the doorway *was* a man he'd seen before. The face was familiar but the circumstances were not. The last time Dissette had seen this man it had been Dissette who'd held the gun. Now it was the other way around.

Richard stepped forward as Dissette held his hand away from his weapon. Dissette could not help noticing that limp. The hip, in fact was suddenly paining Richard.

The Imp was silent. Dissette knew why Richard was there. The gun was almost shaking in Richard's hand. Faced with the Imp at last Richard found words momentarily impossible.

Dissette spat. *'Va te faire enculer!'*

The expletive jarred Richard.

'My name is Richard Silva. My rank is lieutenant in the United States Air Force.

Dissette's eyes were fiery and angry.

'Five one three nine four nine one two,' Richard uttered.

There was a pause.

'All right, you bastard,' said Richard. 'Kneel. . .'

Suddenly Dissette's hands were in motion. He grabbed for the gun in his hip holster. But as Dissette's hands lunged for a weapon Richard fired. Richard's pistol blasted at point-blank range. Dissette tumbled backward in agony.

The bullet had crashed into his left hip-bone, shattering it. Dissette was convulsed with pain. Blood flooded and spasmed from his left side. He writhed on the floor, choking in anguish.

Richard let Dissette's torment continue for several seconds. Then he stepped closer. Carefully and methodically he held the nose of his pistol a few inches from the fallen man's brain.

He fired.

Again the shot echoed on the dim chamber and empty corridor. For a few moments Dissette's body lurched and kicked. Then it was still.

The hunt was over.

And instantly thereafter the door to that chamber creaked. Another man entered.

The command to halt was shouted in French. But Richard did not understand. He whirled instinctively and aimed his empty gun towards the door. A volley of shots came at him. One bullet crashed into his mouth. A second and third hit him in the midpoint of his chest.

He was spun around, his empty gun flying from his hand.

Moments later both Richard and the underground chamber were still.

Dutronc, service revolver in his hand, walked slowly from the doorway into the room. He'd followed Dissette to this incredible place. Now he inspected the carnage.

Beyond the three bodies, Dutronc made another discovery.

A trap door.

Dutronc opened it and shone a light downwards. He saw them. Anne and Cynthia Thatcher. Motionless.

Bound, gagged, gaunt, and terrified.

But alive.

He freed them and led them to the first daylight they'd seen in days. Then to his car.

Dutronc drove three blocks, then stopped.

He parked the car immediately in front of a *tabac*. He told the children to wait. He never took his eyes off them as he entered the *tabac* and dropped a *jeton* into a pay telephone.

He dialled.

A private number rang on the desk of the interior minister.

Dutronc spoke.

'*Ici Corbeau*,' he said.

'*Et alors?*' asked de Gaubert anxiously.

'I have the two children,' said Corbeau. 'Alive. Unharmed.'

'And the other matters?' asked de Gaubert.

'Completed,' said Corbeau. 'Both of them.'

Dutronc could hear the sigh of relief on the other end. He hung up and walked calmly back to his car. The Thatcher children watched him curiously.

THE DOMINO PRINCIPLE

by Adam Kennedy

Roy Tucker, a convicted murderer, was in the slam for twenty years. Twenty years, and he'd only done five.

So when 'they' proposed a deal that included freedom and $200,000, it was an offer he couldn't refuse.

But freedom was just the first domino of the deal to fall. And as the other dominoes toppled, Tucker realised the gravity, the danger, the horror of his mission – and by then it was too late.

Now a major film, released by ITC Entertainment

NEW ENGLISH LIBRARY

NEL BESTSELLERS

Crime

T026 663	THE DOCUMENTS IN THE CASE	Dorothy L. Sayers	50p
T031 306	THE UNPLEASANTNESS AT THE BELLONA CLUB		
		Dorothy L. Sayers	85p
T031 373	STRONG POISON	Dorothy L. Sayers	80p
T032 884	FIVE RED HERRINGS	Dorothy L. Sayers	75p
T025 462	MURDER MUST ADVERTISE	Dorothy L. Sayers	50p

Fiction

T030 199	CRUSADER'S TOMB	A. J. Cronin	£1.25
T029 522	HATTER'S CASTLE	A. J. Cronin	£1.00
T027 228	THE SPANISH GARDNER	A. J. Cronin	45p
T013 936	THE JUDAS TREE	A. J. Cronin	50p
T015 386	THE NORTHERN LIGHT	A. J. Cronin	50p
T031 276	THE CITADEL	A. J. Cronin	95p
T027 112	BEYOND THIS PLACE	A. J. Cronin	60p
T016 609	KEYS OF THE KINGDOM	A. J. Cronin	60p
T029 158	THE STARS LOOK DOWN	A. J. Cronin	£1.00
T022 021	THREE LOVES	A. J. Cronin	90p
T031 594	THE LONELY LADY	Harold Robbins	£1.25
T032 523	THE DREAM MERCHANTS	Harold Robbins	£1.10
T031 705	THE PIRATE	Harold Robbins	£1.00
T033 791	THE CARPETBAGGERS	Harold Robbins	£1.25
T031 667	WHERE LOVE HAS GONE	Harold Robbins	£1.00
T032 647	THE ADVENTURERS	Harold Robbins	£1.25
T031 659	THE INHERITORS	Harold Robbins	95p
T031 586	STILETTO	Harold Robbins	60p
T033 805	NEVER LEAVE ME	Harold Robbins	70p
T032 698	NEVER LOVE A STRANGER	Harold Robbins	95p
T032 531	A STONE FOR DANNY FISHER	Harold Robbins	90p
T031 659	79 PARK AVENUE	Harold Robbins	80p
T032 655	THE BETSY	Harold Robbins	95p
T033 732	RICH MAN, POOR MAN	Irwin Shaw	£1.35
T032 639	EVENING IN BYZANTIUM	Irwin Shaw	80p
T031 330	THE MAN	Irving Wallace	£1.50
T034 283	THE PRIZE	Irving Wallace	£1.50
T033 376	THE PLOT	Irving Wallace	£1.25
T030 253	THE THREE SIRENS	Irving Wallace	£1.25
T020 916	SEVEN MINUTES	Irving Wallace	90p

Historical

T022 196	KNIGHT WITH ARMOUR	Alfred Duggan	50p
T022 250	THE LADY FOR A RANSOM	Alfred Duggan	50p
T017 958	FOUNDING FATHERS	Alfred Duggan	50p
T022 625	LEOPARDS AND LILIES	Alfred Duggan	60p
T029 492	LORD GEOFFREY'S FANCY	Alfred Duggan	60p
T024 903	THE KING OF ATHELNEY	Alfred Duggan	60p
T032 817	FOX 1: PRESS GANG	Adam Hardy	50p
T032 825	FOX 2: PRIZE MONEY	Adam Hardy	50p
T032 833	FOX 3: SIEGE	Adam Hardy	50p
T032 841	FOX 4: TREASURE	Adam Hardy	50p
T028 092	FOX 14: CLOSE QUARTERS	Adam Hardy	50p

Science Fiction

T027 724	SCIENCE FICTION ART	Brian Aldiss	£2.95
T030 245	TIME ENOUGH FOR LOVE	Robert Heinlein	£1.25
T029 492	STRANGER IN A STRANGE LAND	Robert Heinlein	80p
T029 484	I WILL FEAR NO EVIL	Robert Heinlein	95p

T030 467	STARMAN JONES	*Robert Heinlein*	75p
T026 817	THE HEAVEN MAKERS	*Frank Herbert*	35p
T031 462	DUNE	*Frank Herbert*	£1.25
T022 854	DUNE MESSIAH	*Frank Herbert*	75p
T023 974	THE GREEN BRAIN	*Frank Herbert*	35p
T023 265	EMPIRE OF THE ATOM	*A. E. Van Vogt*	40p
T027 473	THE FAR OUT WORLD OF A. E. VAN VOGT	*A. E. Van Vogt*	50p

War

T027 066	COLDITZ: THE GERMAN STORY	*Reinhold Eggers*	50p
T020 827	COLDITZ RECAPTURED	*Reinhold Eggers*	50p
T012 999	PQ 17 – CONVOY TO HELL	*Lund & Ludlam*	30p
T026 299	TRAWLERS GO TO WAR	*Lund & Ludlam*	50p
T025 438	LILIPUT FLEET	*A. Cecil Hampshire*	50p

Western

T017 892	EDGE 12: THE BIGGEST BOUNTY	*George Gilman*	30p
T023 931	EDGE 13: A TOWN CALLED HATE	*George Gilman*	35p
T020 002	EDGE 14: THE BIG GOLD	*George Gilman*	30p
T020 754	EDGE 15: BLOOD RUN	*George Gilman*	35p
T022 706	EDGE 16: THE FINAL SHOT	*George Gilman*	35p
T024 881	EDGE 17: VENGEANCE VALLEY	*George Gilman*	40p
T026 604	EDGE 18: TEN TOMBSTONES TO TEXAS	*George Gilman*	40p
T028 135	EDGE 19: ASHES AND DUST	*George Gilman*	40p
T029 042	EDGE 20: SULLIVAN'S LAW	*George Gilman*	45p
T029 387	EDGE 21: RHAPSODY IN RED	*George Gilman*	50p
T030 350	EDGE 22: SLAUGHTER ROAD	*George Gilman*	50p

General

T034 666	BLACK ROOTS	*Robert Tralins*	95p
T020 592	SLAVE REBELLION	*Norman Davids*	35p
T033 155	SEX MANNERS FOR MEN	*Robert Chartham*	60p
T023 206	THE BOOK OF LOVE	*Dr David Delvin*	90p
T028 828	THE LONG BANANA SKIN	*Michael Bentine*	90p

Mad

N862 185	DAVE BERG LOOKS AT LIVING		70p
N861 812	MAD BOOK OF WORD POWER		70p
N766 895	MORE MAD ABOUT SPORTS		70p

NEL P.O. BOX 11, FALMOUTH TR10 9EN, CORNWALL:

For U.K.: Customers should include to cover postage, 19p for the first book plus 9p per copy for each additional book ordered up to a maximum charge of 73p.

For B.F.P.O. and Eire: Customers should include to cover postage, 19p for the first book plus 9p per copy for the next 6 and thereafter 3p per book.

For Overseas: Customers should include to cover postage, 20p for the first book plus 10p per copy for each additional book.

Name ....

Address..

....

Title ....
(MAY)

Whilst every effort is made to maintain prices, new editions or printings may carry an increased price and the actual price of the edition supplied will apply.